PERSEPHONE

A PREQUEL TO THE UNDERWORLD SAGA

Eva Pohler

Eva Pohler Books
20011 Park Ranch
San Antonio, Texas 78259
www.evapohler.com

Publisher's Note: This is a work of fiction. Names, characters, places, and incidents are a product of the author's imagination. Locales and public names are sometimes used for atmospheric purposes. Any resemblance to actual people, living or dead, or to businesses, companies, events, institutions, or locales is completely coincidental.

Book Layout ©2017 BookDesignTemplates.com

Book Cover Design by B Rose Designz

Persephone/ Eva Pohler. -- 1st ed.
Paperback ISBN: 978-1-958390-44-3

For my children.

Contents

"Life isn't fair, but death is."

--HADES

CHAPTER ONE

The Meeting in the Asphodel

Hades sat on his throne alone in his underground palace. What did it matter that he had more subjects in his kingdom than either of his brothers? What did it matter that he had the world's most precious and beautiful jewels displayed on shelves in his chambers? His life couldn't be more boring. He stood up and kicked a golden turtle that was a part of the altar leading to his throne. The golden image flew through the air until it crashed against the wall opposite him. Even tormenting the evildoers of the world no longer brought him any satisfaction. He hated his life. He might as well still be a prisoner in his father's belly.

It still hurt him to think about how his mother hadn't tried to save him. She'd saved her youngest son, but she'd allowed her husband—Hades's father, Kronos—to swallow the rest of them. And once her children had finally been set free, they fought their father and his supporters for ten years. During that time, Hades's mother, Rhea, had disappeared. He'd never had a chance to know her love. Had she cared about him at all? Had she wondered about the person he'd become? If not, was there a person anywhere in this whole world who loved him?

He flew from his realm to spy on the people in the upperworld. As he hovered in the sky above them, he hoped for entertainment, but since he didn't care about any of the players below him, he found no joy in their pleasure or sorrow in their pain. He felt numb to everything around him and went home.

Weeks, months, and years went by. The only break he had from this growing despair were the few minutes each day when he wrestled with Cerberus. The three-headed guard dog was his only friend, but the beast could never leave his post at the gate. As it was, Hades took a huge risk in distracting him for even a few minutes.

Was there no way a god could end his existence?

Hades decided to pray to the Fates. He prayed to them every day. His request?

Bring me change. Anything is better than this.

"Enter," Hades said in the language of the ancient Greeks when, months later, he sensed the Fates outside his door.

He wondered if their arrival had something to do with his prayer. He could only hope.

Clotho, the oldest of the three and the spinner, lifted a bony finger and said, "We already know you will agree."

Hades narrowed his eyes. "I thought you couldn't see your own futures."

"No," Lachesis, the measurer, said. "But we can see yours."

"And you agree," Atropos's hoarse voice snapped, like the shears she used to cut the thread of life. "So, here's the deal."

Hades hung back in the shadows at the edge of the clearing watching his future bride. Although she was alone in a field of flowers with nothing but blue sky above her, she walked with a sense of purpose, as if she were looking for something.

He'd seen Demeter's daughter many times when he had dealings on Mount Olympus, but he'd never looked at her with the knowledge he possessed today. The Fates were never wrong. In exchange for refuge in his kingdom, they had told him to choose wisely, and when he had given them a blank look, they had pointed him in the direction of Persephone. This was the woman who would spend eternity married to him.

So why was he hiding from her? He'd had no problems attracting women into his arms, but as soon as he'd invited them home to the dreary depths of his underground palace, the delight in their eyes dimmed as quickly as the souls ferried through the gates by his boatman, Charon. Yet this beautiful, shining young goddess, as bright as springtime, was destined to be his. Why should he hide?

This was the change he'd been longing for.

He removed his helm of invisibility and stepped into the light. The goddess, Persephone, noticed him at once.

She had no smile for him. Lifting a delicate wrist into the air, she used a golden bracelet to deflect the sun's rays into his eyes. He blinked against the reflection of Helios, the sun god, and when Hades looked once more for Persephone, the goddess was gone.

CHAPTER TWO

Persephone's Request

Since their meeting in the asphodel, Hades sought every opportunity to see Persephone again. So what if the Fates were right (and they always were)? It could be centuries before Persephone ever noticed him, and he was beginning to feel impatient.

He saw her at court on Mount Olympus when Zeus laid out a plan to prevent a Titan uprising. Persephone sat stiffly and quietly on the double throne beside her mother. Hades stared at her, willing her to look at him, but she ignored him. Suspecting that Demeter had blocked others from communicating with her daughter, he left Mount Olympus that day feeling frustrated.

Hades saw Persephone again at court when the gods banded together to think of ways that they could help Perseus defeat the Gorgons. Persephone sat beside Demeter again, but this time seemed restless. Hades sensed that she wanted to be anywhere else but among the gods at court. But no matter how often he looked her way, she never returned his gaze. How long was he supposed to wait before his future bride became aware of his existence?

He saw her a third time on Mount Olympus during the discussion of the impending war between the Greeks and the Trojans, after Eris's apple was awarded by Paris to Aphrodite—not because she was necessarily the more beautiful, but because she had the best bribe.

Again, he tried to get Persephone's attention, and again she ignored him.

So Hades resigned himself to the Fates. He would stop trying. He would stop allowing himself to get so worked up in her presence. He would be patient if not indifferent. Their meeting was bound to happen one day—the Fates were never wrong.

One day, he was walking among the asphodel in the same location he had first seen Persephone—after the Fates had revealed her as his future wife. He found it interesting that she, too, often walked near the chasm with the flowers at her feet and the sound of the rushing falls behind her. This was one of his favorite spots in the world, for it was near one of the entries to the Underworld; but it was also bright, fresh, and full of sweet songbirds and scent. He came here to refresh his mind before returning to his duties and to the dead.

This time, he didn't try to speak with her. He didn't want a repeat of their first encounter. Instead, he turned his back to her and continued his walk. If the Fates were right—and they always were—then there was no need for him to force a union.

Today he had come directly from an argument with Poseidon about the Hydra's sinkhole. Hades was frustrated and needed to breathe in the song and the scent before descending back down, down into the loneliness of his chambers. He was taken by surprise with her approach.

"Why do you come here?" she asked, half hidden behind an evergreen.

Although he was startled, he didn't turn to look at her, afraid he would scare her off. "For the same reason as you, I suppose." He tried to keep the desperation from his voice. He'd been longing for this chance, and he didn't want to screw it up.

"I doubt that," came her frank reply.

Hades grinned, but she wouldn't have seen it, since he continued to keep his back to her. "Then why do you come?"

"You must swear an oath on the River Styx to tell no one."

This time he turned and met her steady gaze. If he had ever believed she was frightened of him, her wry smile and cool demeanor proved him wrong. He himself was trembling, and she was as firm as rock. "An oath? This must be serious."

"Do you swear?"

"Yes."

She moved closer to him. "I come here to hide."

"From what?"

"My mother."

He bent his brows, wondering why such a beautiful goddess would have a need to hide from an equally beautiful mother. She shared Persephone's corn-colored hair and golden-brown eyes. Perhaps Demeter was harsh, or demanding, or belittling. Hades had no relationship with his own mother, and, since becoming adults, his sisters had always been distant—he ruled what they considered to be the most repugnant realm on earth. Consequently, he knew very little about women. He'd gone from living the first part of his life in his father's belly to the second part in the depths of the Underworld. "Does she mistreat you?"

Persephone shook her head. "Never. It's nothing like that. In fact, it's the opposite. She smothers me."

"I don't understand." He picked at his curly black beard—an old habit that was hard to break. While he'd been inside the belly of his father, touching his beard had been Hades's way of figuring out how old he was.

Persephone stepped from the edge of the woods into the clearing and sat on a stump at his feet, sending a rush of excitement up his limbs and to his chest. "I love my mother. I truly do. But sometimes I can't breathe around her. Honestly, I just want some time to myself."

Hades frowned, worried he had infringed upon her solitude. He shifted his weight, ready to leave her company, when she grabbed his boot.

"Wait," she said. She gave him a nervous laugh as she let go of his boot. "I meant I want time away from her, in the company of others."

"I see," he said, hiding his relief.

She climbed to her feet and looked up at him. "I want to go on an adventure. Can you take me someplace different?"

He narrowed his eyes, unsure if he could trust what was happening. Was this the same goddess who'd ignored him for so many months? "You do know who I am?"

"Of course, Lord Hades." Her face turned bright red, and she took a step back. "I'm sorry. Am I bothering you?"

"Not at all. I just wonder what kind of adventure you hope to have with the lord of darkness."

At that moment, Hades sensed Demeter calling out to Persephone from the sky above them.

"It's my mother!" Persephone said, rushing into Hades's arms. "Hide me!"

He conjured up his helm and slipped it on, and, as long as she was in his arms, she remained invisible to all but him.

Don't speak, he warned her telepathically. *The helm offers invisibility, but we can still be heard.*

She looked into his eyes with a mischievous grin, and he was at once exhilarated.

Take me for a ride in your chariot, she pleaded. *I want to see the Underworld.*

CHAPTER THREE

Persephone's First Descent

Hades was relieved that Persephone seemed happy beside him as he took her in his chariot across the evening sky, above clouds of pink and purple. Just because she was fated to be his bride didn't mean she would be happy. He was really hoping for happiness, though.

"Are you sure my mother won't see us?" Persephone twisted her beautiful mouth into a playful grin.

"So long as I wear the helm, everything I touch is undetectable, even to the gods."

"Is that true for anyone who wears it?" she asked.

"Yes, but none but I do."

"Won't you let me try it on?" Her golden-brown eyes gazed at him expectantly, and for a moment, he almost said yes.

What power was this? She was capable of spellbinding him with a look? Maybe he needed to be more guarded around her. "Would Zeus let you hold his lightning bolt, or Poseidon his trident?"

She frowned and turned her head to gaze at the pink clouds below.

He wanted to please her, but his helm was off limits. It was one of the three most powerful objects in existence. Surely she would under-stand. "It was a gift from the Fates, meant for me alone."

"I thought it came from the Cyclopes, after the war with the Titans."

"Yes, but the Fates decreed it."

"Oh."

He changed the subject. "Would you like to see my palace?"

She turned her lovely face to him once more. Her corn-colored hair streamed like a wedding veil in the wind behind her. He wanted to reach out and touch it. "If it's not an imposition."

"Not at all, if you're sure you want to go."

"Why wouldn't I be?" She frowned.

"You must not be familiar with the general attitude of the Olympians toward my domain."

"I'm familiar. I just find that attitude a bit obtuse."

He suppressed a grin as he guided his black stallions—Swift and Sure—down into the nearest chasm leading to the Underworld.

He gave a subtle wave to his boatman, Charon, and then to his guard dog, Cerberus, as he flew the chariot over the Acheron River where it met the Styx. His heart skipped a beat as the gates closed behind them. This was his very first willing guest to come with him this far into his domain in all the years he'd been lord of it, and he was especially delighted that she would one day live with him here forever.

She just didn't know it yet.

He parked the chariot in the garage and left the horses bridled for their return trip. He doubted she would want to remain with him in the Underworld for long.

When she stepped from his chariot, she cried, "Where have you gone?"

He removed the helm. "If I wear this, you can only see me when we're touching, and even then, only if I tell it to."

"You *speak* to it?"

"As a matter of fact, I do. It does get lonely down here." He laughed, to make sure she knew he was joking.

She laughed, too. "I can imagine. What do you do down here?"

"The dead keep me busy." After saying so, he realized he needed to be less morbid if he was to woo her. Why did this have to be so difficult?

He led her from the garage and into his enormous chambers, which were full of brilliant stones—one of the advantages of being the lord of the Underworld.

"You have every precious stone imaginable," she said, gazing around at his collection.

"Take anything you like," he said.

"You can't be serious!"

"I'm rarely anything else."

She laughed. "Well, that's no fun. Maybe you need someone to help you be less so."

He watched as she picked up an emerald here, a diamond there, studying them before putting them back.

"These are exquisite." She looked up at him. "But I just want to admire them, not keep any of them for myself."

He was hurt.

She seemed to notice his frown, because she quickly added, "Except maybe this one."

She chose a small opal he had polished to a radiant sheen. It was his favorite of the specimens, and he was glad that she would keep it.

"To remember you by," she added.

"Will we never meet again?" He sounded more arrogant than he had intended. He couldn't help but appreciate the irony, considering what he knew.

"I don't know," she said, coyly. "Will we?"

She was a crafty one, turning it around on him. He liked it.

"I believe we will," he said.

She smiled. "Can you show me more of your kingdom?"

He wasn't sure how much to show her—he didn't want to bore her—but he decided to start at the beginning. He took her hand and led her to the chamber of judgment, which a soul entered as soon as it passed Cerberus.

Hades told her about the three places to which the souls were sent by his judges—The Fields of Elysium for the good, Tartarus for the wicked, and Erebus for those who needed more time to forget their pain. He also showed her the five rivers that flowed through his realm and told of their purpose. She was already familiar with the Styx, on which the gods swore their oaths, but she had not seen the beautiful river of fire, known as the Phlegethon.

"I love the way it reflects on the cavern walls," she said, much to his pleasure. "Sometimes a crystal catches the light just right."

"I put the crystals in the walls for that purpose," he said, pleased that she had noticed it.

"It's breathtaking."

He took her hand. It was a soft and dainty thing, but he knew it was also powerful, and he shouldn't forget that.

He led her along the Phlegethon and showed her the various realms. He first took her to the Elysian Fields, which were cast in the purple glow of embers washed up on its shore. Elysium was an island surrounded by the Lethe, with streams marbled all through it.

"The Lethe is the river of forgetfulness," he explained. "It helps the souls forget so they can spend eternity in bliss."

The island stretched further than any eye could see, and it was populated with thousands—hundreds of thousands—millions—of souls frolicking in the fields, lounging beneath trees, and playing in the streams.

"They do look happy," she said.

He then showed her Erebus, where the pained souls lay at the bottom of a pit full of the Lethe waters.

"Those souls need more time," he explained. "They're not yet ready for the fields. Some of them are victims of terrible crimes."

"You're more compassionate than I expected," she said.

"Not compassionate," he corrected. "*Just*. Life isn't fair, but *death* is."

"I like that," she said.

Then he took her to Tartarus and showed her the three main areas—the main hall of torture, the seers' pit, and the Titan pit, which was the deepest of all.

"That's where we keep the Titan prisoners, the ones we fought during Zeus's uprising," he explained.

Her eyes widened. "How exciting! Do you ever worry they might escape?"

"Never. That iron door is impenetrable."

He showed her the fields of poppies and asphodel near the dream world. Then he led her back to his rooms.

"Where do you sleep?" she asked.

He found it curious that a maiden would wish to see his bed chamber. He was more amused than offended.

"Right this way," he said.

He walked through the main room of the palace to the corridor which led to his bed, explaining the reason for the inlaid Mother of Pearl in the door—the shell was the best at maintaining the most powerful wards. When he turned back to her to get her reaction, she wasn't there.

He flew back to the main hall of the palace. She wasn't in sight.

He balled his fists as he looked over to where he had carelessly laid his helm.

It was gone.

CHAPTER FOUR

Hide and Seek

Persephone lifted the helm and placed it on her head. She'd only planned to wear it for a moment before putting it back, but the lord of the Underworld noticed her absence immediately.

Within an instant, he was standing right in front of her. She froze, terrified, expecting him to scold her, to threaten her, to throw her out, but he pounded his fist on the table from where she had taken the helm and roared. He couldn't sense her. Tremendous relief swept over her. She covered her mouth to stifle a giggle.

This could be fun.

For many minutes he just stood there, thinking, and this gave her the chance to study him. Now that she could freely stare without his knowing, she was able to more fully appreciate his beauty. Dark curly hair and a dark curly beard starkly contrasted his deep blue eyes and pale skin. His nose and forehead were classically prominent, his neck thick, his lips full and moist. She leaned in and took in his musky scent. His massive chest rose and fell quickly with his agitation. The muscles in his jaw flexed.

Then he god-traveled out of the room, and she was left alone.

She wandered down a winding cavern toward the garage, where she heard his voice.

"On my orders only, boys. On my orders only." He was talking to his black horses.

He thought she would dare to take his chariot?

Suddenly he turned and glanced in her direction. She froze and held her breath. He stared her way for several minutes, sniffing the air. She broke into a sweat.

Then he walked right past her down the winding tunnel. She followed him, realizing now that she should have given back the helm as soon as he had noticed it missing. She could have apologized, and he might have accepted it. Now, she'd gone too far.

She hadn't meant for him to notice! She was going to slip it right back off. She'd just wanted to see what it was like to wear it for only a moment, but his senses were too sharp for that. She should have known!

Now what was she going to do? He might eat her alive and she'd be stuck in his belly forever. Her mother had told her stories of angry gods swallowing their enemies. Demeter had spent countless years, along with Hades, in the belly of their father. Later, Zeus, now lord of them all, had swallowed Athena's mother, Metis. As far as anyone knew, Metis was still in his belly.

Persephone wondered if she should run away and hide.

Hades passed his chambers and continued along the Phlegethon.

It occurred to her that he knew she was there and that he wanted her to follow. Why else would he walk rather than god travel?

They walked for what seemed like miles before the lord of darkness stopped and pounded on a wooden door. The door opened and he went inside. She barely made it in behind him before the door slammed closed.

In the center of the room was a table, and around it sat the Fates.

Lachesis, the measurer and the plumpest of the three, said, "We see you."

"I came to ask about our deal," Hades said.

Clotho, the spinner, looked directly at Persephone.

Please don't tell, Persephone prayed to them.

"What about it?" Atropos, the cutter asked.

Lachesis rolled a set of clay dice. Then she cried, "Double six! The throw of Aphrodite! I win!"

"We knew it would happen," Clotho said. "The minute we saw Hades, we knew it was time."

"I have been waiting for this moment!" Lachesis said. "I already know what I will make the two of you do." She said this to her sisters.

Hades took a step closer to the table. "When I agreed to provide you a safe haven here in my kingdom, in exchange for the name of the goddess I was destined to marry, was that name based on my own choice?"

"You will choose," Clotho said. "We just know the choice ahead of time."

Hades put a fist on his hip and shifted his weight. "So it is possible for me to choose differently?"

The three Fates glanced at Persephone. Surely they weren't discussing *her*.

"Why would you wish to choose differently?" Atropos asked. "Demeter's daughter is lovely, is she not?"

Persephone flinched. They *were* discussing her!

"She's a thief," Hades said angrily.

"What makes you say that?" Lachesis asked, glancing from Hades to Persephone.

Please stop looking at me, Persephone prayed to them. *You'll give me away!*

"She's taken the helm," he replied. "She could be anywhere."

"Indeed," Clotho sang. "Now roll the dice, Atropos. It's your turn."

"Can you at least tell me how long I must wait before the helm is returned?" he asked.

"That wasn't part of the deal," Atropos complained as she shook the dice in her cupped hand.

"But I will tell you this," Clotho said. "One of your descendants will have a set of twins who will one day restore faith in the gods and in humanity after both have been all but lost."

"Clotho!" Atropos chastised. "Why can't you contain yourself?"

"You knew I was going to say it," Clotho said dismissively.

"Nothing good ever comes from knowing the future," Lachesis insisted.

"Don't worry about the helm," Clotho said. "You know it comes back. Just wait for it."

"It might not be as far away as you think," Lachesis added.

The other two Fates chuckled, and Persephone knew her goose was cooked, but she was still reeling with the knowledge that one day, she was to be the Gatekeeper's bride.

Hades stomped out, and Persephone followed, flying rather than walking to keep up with his fast pace, so as to make no noise. As they entered his chambers, she nearly gasped when he removed his shirt and tossed it on the table. His muscular back rippled with his movements. When he turned, his hard stomach drew her eyes. He kicked off his boots, leaving them in the middle of the floor. Before she could look away, he'd pulled down his trousers and stepped out of them, adding them to the pile on the table.

He stood before her completely bare.

CHAPTER FIVE

A Spy Is Shocked

Persephone turned away from the bare god standing before her, but then, remembering that she was invisible, she slowly turned back around to stare. She observed every muscle on his body as he stepped into a pair of lounging pants. Without thinking, she gasped. Then she covered her mouth and hoped he hadn't heard. If he had, he didn't show it.

She followed the shirtless, bare-footed god from his bed chamber into a pantry, where he loaded a bag with apples, pomegranates, and cake. He slung the bag over his shoulder and strolled, on foot and without god-travel, along the Phlegethon toward the River Styx, turning left at the Acheron, past the room of Judgment, to the main gate.

Hanging back some distance, she watched the god set down his bag and give the cake to his three-headed guard dog. As she studied Hades, she thought on what she had overheard him say to the Fates. Was she really to be his bride?

She was delighted when, after the cake was eaten, Hades took a stick and played a game of fetch with Cerberus. The two of them made an adorable picture, until things seemed to get out of hand, and she thought for sure one of them would get hurt. She almost intervened when the game ended with Hades pinned to the ground. All three heads bared their teeth and growled. Persephone took a step toward them, on the brink of giving herself up. One of Cerberus's three heads turned in her direction. She held her breath.

Hades seemed unconcerned and only laughed. "Okay, Cerberus. As you wish."

The god and beast wrestled, flailing and rolling all over the rocky embankment of the river. At one point, Hades slammed Cerberus against the iron bars of the gate, and then Hades was flung into the river. Cerberus panted on the shore as Hades flew from the water, soaked. Persephone had expected him to be angry, but he wore a playful smile.

At the sight of him, she began to feel rather warm beneath the helm.

"Well, done, boy. You've earned yourself another treat."

Hades reached for his bag and tossed three apples up into the air, and each was aptly caught by a different head. Then Hades did something she did not expect. He carefully approached the beast and wrapped his arms around the center neck.

"You're a good boy," Hades said.

The beast licked its master with, not one, but three, tongues.

Persephone giggled, and then cupped her hand to her mouth.

"I had a feeling you were there," Hades said. "Remove my helm and give it back."

Her face burned with mortification as she lifted the helm from her head. "I'm sorry, I…"

He took his helm and glared at her. "Never do that again."

"I swear. I only meant to try it on, but then you noticed right away, and…"

He stepped closer, the rise and fall of his chest nearly touching hers. "Swear on the River Styx that what you say is true."

She looked up at him, frightened and breathless. His black curly hair and beard glistened with moisture, and beads of water dripped down his bare skin. Even his lips were wet. "I swear on the River Styx."

Then he circled an arm around her waist, pressed her against him, and kissed her.

C H A P T E R   S I X

Persephone's Plea

Hades looked down at his wife-to-be, who gazed up at him in shock. He relished the sight of her trembling form, her expectant eyes, and her opened mouth. He had punished her long enough. He knew she'd been spying on him, so he'd decided to shock her. He'd meant to embarrass her when he'd stripped down and then to frighten her with his rough play, but she'd managed not to give herself up until now.

"It's time to get you home." He turned away from her and headed toward the stables.

"Wait."

He glanced back.

She put her hands on her hips, like a petulant child. "I don't want to go home."

He arched a brow. "What about your mother?"

"What about her? I'm a grown woman."

Hades frowned. She wasn't a child, and she was certainly feisty, but she was also innocent—a deadly combination.

"I don't want to get on Demeter's bad side," he said as he continued down the path. *Especially if she was to be his future mother-in-law,* he thought.

She ran to catch up to him. "Please, Lord Hades. I beg you."

"What do you suggest, then?"

"Hide me here for a little while longer. That way we can…" she stopped.

He cocked his chin up and looked down his nose at her. "We can what?"

"Well, I heard what the Fates said about you and me."

"And?" Just exactly what was this goddess getting at?

"And we could get to know each other." Her smile was a mixture of coy and meek, if that was even possible.

He stared back at her blankly.

"Well?" she asked.

Cerberus whined for attention.

"Stand guard, boy," Hades said. "I'll be back again later."

Persephone paled. "Unless you *want* to take me home."

Hades took Persephone's hand. "Come on, then."

He led her via god travel to the stables, where his stallions stood bridled and waiting.

"We're leaving?" Persephone whispered. She covered her face. "I stole your helm. You'll never forgive me."

"You've seen most of my kingdom," Hades explained. "What else would you like to see?"

Persephone's face brightened, delighting him. "Really?"

He gave her a nod.

"Um, the entire upper world? My mother never lets me go anywhere or do anything."

"My chariot awaits you." He waved his hand, inviting her to climb aboard.

"But Demeter…"

"I'll wear the helm and keep you under its protection. She won't be able to find you. Where shall we start?"

Persephone brightened again. "I've always wanted to go watch the Northern Lights from Mount Thor."

"You're the goddess of spring, and you want me to take you to the coldest place on earth?"

"Exactly."

"Your wish is my command."

As he flew the chariot high above Greece, Persephone shrieked with pleasure. They flew over Athens, Thebes, Delphi, and Corinth, following the ships that sailed toward the island of Ithaca.

"They're looking for Odysseus," Hades said of the ships, to make small talk. "He was expected to join the army, but instead, he's pretending to be insane, to avoid leaving his wife and son."

"I don't blame him," Persephone said. "I hope my future husband will choose in kind—to stay by my side rather than fight in someone else's war."

Hades grinned. "I can't imagine he'd ever choose otherwise."

She blushed and averted her eyes, but she was soon smiling again when he turned the chariot north and flew at his stallions' top speed toward the North Pole and the shimmering northern lights.

CHAPTER SEVEN

Demeter's Search

Demeter stormed across the fields at the base of Mount Olympus, where Persephone liked to hike in the sunshine. Any number of gods and primordial beings could snatch up a young and naïve goddess roaming around alone. Why didn't Persephone do as Demeter wished and stay by her mother's side?

It wasn't enough to be immortal. That had been Demeter's mantra to her daughter over and over, whenever Persephone would complain about Demeter's careful supervision. It wasn't enough to be immortal.

How could Demeter get it through her daughter's thick skull that the world was skewed against her and all the female deities? After Demeter and her brothers and sisters overthrew their tyrannical father and the other Titans, who was it that drew lots for dominion over the Sky, the Sea, and the Underworld? It wasn't the *sisters*. Demeter had tried to remind Persephone as often as she could that only the brothers drew lots because they did not recognize their sisters as having equal authority and power.

So it wasn't enough to be immortal. Goddesses and nymphs were subject to the whims of their fathers, uncles, and brothers, and no goddess was exempt. Look how the unfaithful Zeus treated Hera. And how many nymphs and princesses had had their lives ruined by the lord of the sky? Poor Callisto was one example. She hung from the sky as Big Bear for all eternity, never again to hunt with her favorite friend, Artemis. And then there was Io, who'd once been a princess but was changed into a raving beast by jealous Hera because Zeus had fallen in love with the hapless princess. Europa was another princess deceived by Zeus when he appeared to her as a gentle and luminescent bull. She rode on his back, and he stole her away to Crete to have his way with her.

That's what happened to female mortals and deities. Not long ago, Hephaestus tried to abduct Athena. Thank goodness the goddess of wisdom got away.

After hours of looking, Demeter wondered which male deity had taken her daughter. Demeter could think of no other explanation for her daughter's disappearance.

Unless Persephone ran away of her own accord, hoping to liberate herself from what she perceived as a tyrannical mother. Demeter burst into tears. Yes. Persephone may have run away. Demeter flew up to her rooms at Mount Olympus, found her favorite traveling cloak, and then returned to the earth to hunt the lands for her daughter. Before angering the gods with false accusations, she would conduct a thorough search.

CHAPTER EIGHT

The Conspiracy Begins

Hades held the reins beside Persephone as Swift and Sure pulled the chariot away from the white-covered lands of Canada. The scenery had been almost as breathtaking as the goddess standing beside him.

"This has been the best day of my life." Persephone gazed up at him.

"I wonder if I can make it any better." Hades put a hand on each of her shoulders and leaned his face down toward hers. When she didn't move away, he pressed his mouth to hers and gave her the kiss he'd been dying to give since that first kiss in the Underworld. Her lips tasted sweet, like cinnamon and sugar.

A soft moan hummed in her throat, and he rejoiced.

He looked down at her beautiful face, happy to see another smile for him.

Won't you kiss me again? she said to him telepathically.

He leaned in, without closing his eyes. He grinned when she did the same. Her eyes held his until their lips touched, and then both of them dropped their lids, and, this time, the moan came from him. As their mouths pressed more urgently together, joy surged through Hades, and he blessed the Fates for revealing the identity of his bride. All of the gloom and despair he'd been carrying in his heart for so long, since the day he drew his lot and was made lord of the darkest place on earth, fled from him. The realization that he would spend eternity with this beautiful and adventurous goddess made even the dreariest thoughts disappear.

Then he noticed they were riding too close to a mountain below. He grabbed the reins and pulled up to avoid grazing the mountaintop with the bottom of the chariot.

"That was close!" Persephone cried.

"I guess I should pay better attention," he said with a laugh.

As they neared Greece, Persephone pointed to the Greek ships, anchored near Ithaca and said, "I wonder if the army succeeded in recruiting Odysseus."

Hades spotted the king in the marketplace. "That's him there."

"Is he running away?"

"No. It seems he's found Achilles, who was also in hiding."

"It's no wonder," Persephone said. "I heard he's fated to die in The Trojan War. Why *shouldn't* he avoid it?"

"It's impossible to avoid one's fate," Hades said, which brought another blush to Persephone's cheeks.

"They say it will be a long war," Persephone said. "That the gods will be divided, and all hope will seem lost."

Hades took her hand. "But you and I play no part in it. Let's not let the evil deeds of men and gods ruin our own chances of happiness." He kissed her hand.

Then she surprised him by taking *his* hand and kissing it in turn.

He couldn't recall being happier. The way she responded to him was utterly surprising to him. Was it possible that there was someone in the world who would love him? She wouldn't just be his bride? But she would also love him? "Where now, my lady?" he asked.

She gazed around the lands below.

"Oh, no," she said with a frown.

He followed the line of her sight to Mount Olympus, where Demeter was leaving the gates with Hermes and Hecate.

"So to Helios, then, as your father commanded you," Demeter was saying to Hermes. "I don't know why I didn't think to ask him first. Thank you, Hecate, for suggesting it."

"It's always a pleasure to help you," Hecate said, her long black hair, streaked with white, flowing loose in the wind.

"You've been away from me for too long," Demeter, whose golden hair was braided, said. "Once I've found my daughter, I hope you'll visit me as you used to do, before Persephone was born."

Hecate's face brightened. "I didn't think you wanted anyone but your daughter at your side."

"I have two sides," Demeter said. "And I wish you were on one of them."

Hermes cleared his throat and raked his hand through the brown curls on his head. "Let's get on with it, shall we? The sun god doesn't always see all. But we can start with him."

Hades turned to Persephone, where they hovered above Mount Olympus in his chariot. "It hasn't been two full days since we've been together, and your mother has already enlisted the help of Zeus?"

"That's my mother for you."

And everything had been going so perfectly. He should have known it wouldn't last.

Hades cupped her cheeks. "You have to tell her where you are. We can't afford to start a war among the gods, especially with the one brewing below between the mortals."

"But if she finds out I ran away, who knows who will pay for her broken heart? I wish I could say it would be me, but I know my mother too well."

"You think she'll take out her pain on an innocent?" Hades asked.

Persephone closed her eyes and nodded. Then she looked at Hades and asked, "Wait. What if we tell her that you abducted me?"

Hades furled his brows and frowned. "You can't be serious." He couldn't imagine anything good could come from such a lie.

"It would kill her spirit to know I wanted to go away from her. Please?"

"Not the best way to start off with my future mother-in-law."

Blood rushed to Persephone's cheeks, making her even more beautiful to him. "If we tell her the truth—that I wanted to leave her for *you*—then she'll always be jealous of you, and she'll despise you, and she will suffer a broken heart forever. But if we tell her that you found me too beautiful and delightful to resist, she'll take it as a compliment and eventually forgive you."

Hades crossed his arms. "But in reality, your wanting to leave her had nothing to do with *me*. You just wanted to get away from her."

Persephone arched a brow. "Are you certain?"

"Don't lie to me."

More blood flooded the goddess's cheeks. "You don't believe me?"

"I don't have the sight of Apollo, and I haven't known you long."

"The first time I saw you near the chasm beneath Mount Olympus, I admit, I was frightened," she said. "My mother has told me so many stories of what horrible things gods have done to the female deities. But after that day, I studied you."

"*You* studied *me*? My dear Persephone, I'm sorry to contradict you, but *I* studied *you*, and during that time, you ignored me."

He remembered it all too well.

"I pretended to ignore you," she said, turning away.

"Pretended?"

"Oh, this is hopeless. You'll never believe me, anyway."

Why shouldn't he believe her? Was it so surprising that a beautiful young maiden would desire the lord of the Underworld?

Hades sent a prayer to Helios, just as Hermes approached the sun god. *Tell Hermes I, Lord Hades, have abducted Demeter's daughter. She is safe in my care.*

I will do it, Helios replied.

CHAPTER NINE

Persephone's Second Descent

Persephone tipped back her head and guffawed as Hades flew her in his chariot across the bright sky. She lifted her arms above her head to enjoy the feel of the wind. "Chariot rides are so much more fun than regular flight."

"And safer, too," Hades said. "That's why the mightiest gods have them."

Persephone lowered her arms and frowned.

"What? You don't believe me?" he asked.

"My mother is one of the mightiest, but she has no chariot."

He cleared his throat. "Indeed. I stand corrected."

Persephone was relieved that he wasn't too proud to admit when he was wrong.

A ruckus on the land below drew their attention.

"What's happening down there?" Persephone leaned over the edge.

A crowd of people had gathered around the altar in Aulis. The king stood over a prisoner with his blade at the back of the prisoner's neck. The prisoner was a maiden in a bridal gown.

Persephone gasped. "A bride is to be slaughtered?"

"It's Agamemnon," Hades said. "He's going to kill his own daughter as a sacrifice. Does he really believe this will help him win the war against Troy?"

"Let's do something!" Persephone insisted.

"What do you propose?"

Persephone could think of nothing as the prisoner's wails reached her from below.

"I can't bear to watch." She closed her eyes and pressed her face into Hades's chest, shivering against him. How could a father kill his own daughter, for any reason? For a brief moment, Persephone missed her mother's arms. At least, the goddess knew her mother would never harm her.

Hades wrapped his thick arms around her and held her close as Agamemnon brought his blade across his wailing daughter's neck.

It was so cruel and barbaric. How could mortals be so heartless?

"Take me down to Tartarus," Persephone whispered. "I've seen enough of the upperworld."

"You must be joking."

She lifted her unhappy face to his. "Do I look like I'm joking?"

"As you wish." He held her in one arm as he steered his black stallions down toward the nearest chasm.

Persephone screamed and clung to Hades when a giant monster leapt from the dark waters of a sinkhole and screeched at them. It had nine long necks with dragon heads. Each head had an enormous mouth full of sharp teeth.

"Hello, Hydra," the lord of the Underworld said calmly as he swung the chariot past the sinkhole and down into the depths of the earth.

"What was that?" she asked when they were some distance away from the beast.

"That was Cerberus's sister, the Hydra, another one of my guards."

"Oh." She patted her chest and caught her breath. "Well, then. You really do keep interesting company."

Hades parked the chariot, unbridled the horses, and removed his helm, willing it back to his rooms. Then he gave her his arm and led her, by god travel, to one of the deep pits of Tartarus.

"What interests you here, my lady?" Hades asked when they had arrived.

"Seriously? Do you have to ask?" She thought he would know the answer to his question.

"It's a dark and dreary pit full of gruesome souls, guilty of the most heinous acts of crimes against the gods and humanity," he said. "Why would anyone choose to come here?"

"Because it's satisfying to see justice served," she said, thinking of Agamemnon and of what he had done. She hoped one day to see him here. "Like you said, 'Life isn't fair, but death is.' I like that."

He looked rather pleased with her, which brought heat to her cheeks. To cover up the blush, she turned from him and asked, "Why do you suppose Agamemnon and his men are so bent on destroying Troy?"

"Aphrodite's vanity has caused it," he replied.

She whipped back around to face him. "If you mean to say that this is Aphrodite's fault, then I must strongly disagree."

"Eris may have caused discord among the goddesses with her apple trick, but Aphrodite sealed the fate of the mortals when she promised Paris a woman already married to another. Of course, it's Aphrodite's fault."

Persephone crossed her arms and lifted her chin defiantly. "Humans have the power to act or not on their feelings. If Helen left Menelaus for Paris, she must have had little love for her husband."

"Are you saying you condone a wife's betrayal?"

"In some cases, especially if she had no say in the marriage. From what I understand, her suitors drew lots for her, and *chance* picked her husband."

He pushed his dark brows together. "Are you saying her marriage vows meant nothing?"

"They meant nothing if she was forced into them. A woman should have as much control over her fate as a man, but I look down from Mount Olympus all the time and am appalled at the way women are used. They are treated as spoils of war, as property, as trinkets."

"Your mother has shown you these things."

"Yes, and I'm grateful to her. I love my mother."

"Then why are you here, hiding from her?"

She wanted to say because she loved his company, but she bit her tongue. "Perhaps I should leave." She would never pretend to believe one thing or another just to win his approval.

"Perhaps you should."

She wanted to cry. She had believed him to be different from the other men and gods. His talk of justice had wooed her.

"Tell me something first," she said.

He clenched his jaw and gazed down at her. "I'm listening."

"Do the judges down here consider the gender of each soul before sending it to Tartarus, or to Erebus, or to the Elysian Fields?"

"Gender has no bearing on their judgment," he said.

She stepped closer to him and glared at him, feeling his breath on her face. "Then death truly is more just than life."

She turned on her heels and god-traveled away, deciding that she did not need him or his chariot.

CHAPTER TEN

King Tantalus

Demeter didn't want to accompany the other Olympians to celebrate with the Lydian king the twenty-fifth anniversary of the Olympic Games, founded by the king's son, Pelops. She wanted, instead, to lead a raid on the Underworld and recapture her daughter from the clutches of her misogynist brother, Hades.

But Zeus had insisted they must all attend on the old king, since his grandson, Agamemnon, the son of Pelops, was about to wage war on Troy. Zeus and the other gods believed the Olympic Games would create a diversion for the old man and his kingdom while so many descendants prepared to march to their deaths. Even her brother, Poseidon, had come from the depths of the Aegean Sea to join their company. In fact, all were present, save Hades, whom Demeter most wished to see.

The gods dispatched in five different chariots from Mount Olympus. Since Demeter had no chariot, she rode with Hephaestus and Aphrodite. The god of the forge attempted to make cheerful conversation along the way, but both goddesses were quiet and distracted, and so the ride was likely dull for him.

A servant of Tantalus greeted the gods at the gates and, while the chariots were attended to, ushered the divine guests into his master's castle, where a huge golden table full of goblets and trays of grapes awaited them. Dozens of servants quickly pulled out the chairs and helped the deities to their seats. Each god and goddess was given a goblet full of the king's best wine.

Demeter did not particularly like the old king. He had once stolen ambrosia from Olympus to serve it to his court. He had also bragged about his special relationship with the gods and had revealed more than one of their secrets. But Demeter had not objected when Zeus had asked them all to accompany him, because she had hoped, and still hoped, to get his help in saving her daughter.

As the gods were served and beckoned to eat, Demeter went through the motions of pretending to enjoy herself. She wanted to get the festivities over with so she could enlist the help of her brothers and sisters, and she didn't pay close attention to what she put into her mouth and ate. Had she not been so distracted, she would have realized the horrible truth of what she was about to ingest. It wasn't until it had entered her stomach that she paused, looked around the table, and realized what the other gods had already known.

"This is an outrage!" Zeus thundered.

The old king, who sat opposite Zeus at the other end of the long table, quivered in his chair. "Are you not pleased, my Lord?"

Poseidon stood, full of tears over one of his favorites.

They had been served Pelops, Tantalus's own son.

Zeus angrily collected all of the parts of Pelops and ordered Ares and Hermes to take Tantalus as their prisoner. "I'll ask the Fates to restore Pelops!"

Poseidon pounded a fist on the table. "What of the old king? He should go to Tartarus!"

"Hear, hear!" several gods chimed in.

"We'll take him to Hades immediately!" Zeus agreed.

Demeter saw an opportunity. "Lord Zeus, let me go, too, so I may provide the Fates with a piece of ivory to use for the part I've eaten."

Zeus allowed it. She followed him, Ares, and Hermes, along with their prisoner, into Zeus's golden chariot. Poseidon returned to the sea to vent his anger on the tumultuous waters, and the other gods hastened back to Mount Olympus. All were disheartened by what Tantalus had done. Even Demeter had begun to wonder if the mortals didn't perhaps deserve the years of destruction that they were about to endure when Agamemnon and his men reached Troy.

As they flew through the evening sky, Zeus turned to Demeter and said, "Your sadness must come to an end, dear sister. The unending winter must break. Barren lands and bitter cold will only make the war among the mortals longer and more miserable for all."

"Then help me get our daughter back from Hades," she said. "While we're there, have a word with him yourself."

She held her breath and waited for Zeus's reply. He seemed to consider her request for a long time. Just as they broached the chasm and delved into the depths of the Underworld, she heard him grunt, "Indeed."

Relief swept over her.

In another moment, Hades met them at the gate, guarded by Cerberus. They stood just across the river.

"To what do I owe the pleasure of your company?" Hades asked.

Demeter noticed that Persephone was not with him.

Zeus explained what had happened back in Lydia.

Tantalus fell to his knees on the riverbank. "Please have mercy on me."

"That's for the judges to decide," Hades barked at Tantalus before he flew across the river and drove his sword through the old king's heart.

Hermes took Tantalus's soul to Charon as the waters of the Acheron swallowed the body.

Once that was done, Zeus said, "And one more thing, Hades. I need you to return Persephone to her mother. The Trojan War cannot be fought on barren lands in bitter cold. You'll have to choose another."

The corners of Hades's mouth twitched into a frown. "I do not have her. I swear on the River Styx."

CHAPTER ELEVEN

In Aphrodite's Confidence

Persephone tugged the hood of the cloak a little further over her eyes as she followed Aphrodite and Thalia from the dining hall toward Aphrodite's chambers. Artemis glanced their way, but the goddess of the hunt did not seem to notice anything unusual. Everyone was still dismayed over what had happened at the palace of King Tantalus. Persephone was glad not to have been among them—though she had been tempted to wear Algaea's robe as she was doing now and attend on Aphrodite in the eldest Grace's place, just to have a chance to see the lord of the Underworld.

Had he been thinking of her as much as she'd been thinking of him?

But when she'd asked Aphrodite which of the gods had been in attendance, she'd learned that Hades hadn't been among them, so it was good that she had stayed behind.

According to the Fates, Hades and she would choose to wed one another, but after hearing his attitude about the cause of war among the mortals, he seemed too obtuse to be her lifelong partner.

But maybe she was meant to change that. She hoped so.

As soon as they were in the privacy of Aphrodite's chambers with the door closed, Persephone pulled the hood from her head and asked, "How long before Zeus and my mother return from Hades?"

"You'll be gone before they arrive," Aphrodite said. "I want you to go at once."

Persephone frowned and lifted her brows in surprise. "I thought you wanted to help me."

"And I have. For two weeks, I have hidden you as one of my Graces from all the other gods, including your own mother, and I haven't required an explanation. But now I need you to help *me*."

Persephone bit her lower lip. She should have expected this. Hadn't her mother warned her that all gods and goddesses were selfish? They only extended a favor when one was needed in return. "What would you have me do?"

Aphrodite began to pace along the marble floor in front of the fluffy white couch where Thalia had taken a seat. The goddess of love wrung her hands as she said, "There's a maiden near one of my most sacred temples. Her name is Psyche."

"I've heard of her," Persephone said.

Aphrodite's face turned red. "You have? What have you heard?"

"Only that she's beautiful."

"They say she is as beautiful as I," Aphrodite said. "And some have even begun to worship her in my place. I just got Helen carried off, and now I have this new beauty to contend with." The goddess of love stopped pacing and stood as if in a trance. "My own people no longer love me."

"Of course, they still love you," Thalia interjected. "They'll never stop loving you."

"Thalia's right," Persephone said. "The people are just frightened right now because of the war and will cling to any symbol of hope they can find."

"Aren't you planning to help the Trojans destroy the Greeks anyway?" Thalia asked. "Last we spoke on the topic, you had pledged your loyalty to Paris of Troy."

"Not *destroy*," Aphrodite corrected. "*Defeat*. There's a difference." Then she added, "And it's nothing personal against the Greeks—they are my beloved people, and I expect their continued worship. I made a promise to give Helen over to Paris, and it's not my fault if the Greeks feel the need to take her back."

Persephone joined Thalia on the fluffy couch. "Did Helen *wish* to go to Troy?"

"It's hard to say," Aphrodite admitted. "She seemed taken in by Paris's charm and good looks. I asked my son, Cupid, to aid her feelings toward Paris."

Persephone sank against the back of the couch, sorry for her harsh words to Hades. Maybe he'd been right in his assessment of Aphrodite's part in the war. She seemed to care more about her reputation than the well-being of her people. This is the first Persephone had heard that Cupid had used an arrow of Eros on Helen.

"I want you to go to Kythira," Aphrodite said to Persephone. "I want you to kill the maiden they call Psyche."

Aphrodite wanted her to kill?

"And if I refuse?" Persephone asked, mortified.

"I will expose you to your mother."

Persephone imagined how bitter, hurt, and resentful her mother would feel when she learned that her daughter had been hiding from her. At some point, Persephone was going to have to face Demeter, but she needed time to think of a plan, of some excuse for her absence. She couldn't ever let her mother know the truth. Demeter would never recover.

"How do you want me to do it?" Persephone asked Aphrodite.

Hades Despairs

Beneath his helm of invisibility, Hades turned from Aphrodite's couch and clenched his jaw. Was Persephone really the kind of person to kill another without just cause? He couldn't believe it. This wasn't the Persephone he'd come to know. His heart ached with disappointment and betrayal. She knew how he felt about murder. Didn't she care?

If she were a mortal, he'd be forced to avenge the death of the innocent Psyche.

He'd only just arrived on Mount Olympus when he'd spotted Persephone in the disguise of the eldest Grace. The other gods had been fooled, but they hadn't the advantage of the helm. He had realized when Demeter had come looking for her daughter in the Underworld that Persephone must be here, on Mount Olympus, hiding. It wasn't hard for Hades to figure out that she'd solicited the help of another god or goddess. Luck had been on his side when he'd spotted her entering Aphrodite's chambers. He'd managed to squeeze in behind her just before the goddess of love had bolted her door shut.

He'd come looking for Persephone because he had given her argument—about a woman's right to choose her own spouse—careful consideration and had come to the conclusion that she was right. He had hoped to find her and to persuade her to come back with him. He'd admired the way Persephone had stood up to him, unwilling to bend her convictions to please him. He wanted a partner with a mind of her own.

But now that he'd seen what she was willing to do, he was sickened by the thought of spending eternity with her. Had he misread her all this time? As the lord of the dead, he did not take murder lightly. The other Olympians might not think much about using their own interests to justify killing a mortal, but Hades had a special responsibility to make sure the unjust treatment of souls was avenged. If a murdered soul had no one to seek vengeance on his or her behalf, Hades did the deed himself. But when the murderer was a fellow god, there was little he *could* do. This was distasteful and highly unsatisfying to Hades.

And Persephone knew all this. She knew how he felt. He couldn't believe she'd so easily disregard his feelings, his philosophy, and his principles just to be in Aphrodite's good graces.

Yet, as he gazed on Persephone's beautiful face, he hoped she would not go through with it. Clearly, she was mortified by Aphrodite's request. Maybe Persephone planned to deceive the other goddess. He clung to that hope as he continued to eavesdrop.

Aphrodite had begun to pace again. "I asked my son to make her fall in love with the most vile, ugliest man on Earth."

Hades frowned. This was the goddess the people loved above all the others? The mortals wouldn't even say his name, and yet they built temples for Aphrodite.

"And has he?" Persephone asked.

"I thought he had," Aphrodite replied. "But months have passed since then, and she's still unwed. Even her less beautiful sisters have married. The people continue to travel for miles to have a look at this girl. The soldiers leave their camps once a day just to gaze at her!"

Hades rolled his eyes.

"You should appear to them yourself," Thalia suggested to Aphrodite. "One look at you will make them forget all about Psyche."

"She needs to be punished for her attempts to be worshipped in my place," Aphrodite said. "To seek to be like the gods, that is one of the unpardonable sins, is it not? She belongs in Tartarus."

"Isn't that for the judges of Lord Hades to decide?" Persephone asked.

Hades caught his breath. So maybe Persephone cared about his principles after all. Maybe she wouldn't go through with the murder and was only mollifying Aphrodite to avoid conflict.

"I want you to go to her tonight," Aphrodite said. "I want you to offer her some of my beauty. Tell her you've stolen it from me. If she refuses to accept it, she will be spared. If she accepts, my wrath will be unleashed upon her the moment she opens this box."

Persephone took the small black box in both of her hands and gave the goddess of love a solemn nod.

Hades followed Persephone as she god-traveled from Aphrodite's chambers on Mount Olympus to the peak of Mount Kythira. He felt as though his future happiness hung in the balance.

CHAPTER THIRTEEN

Psyche's Misery

Persephone dimmed herself as she appeared to the young woman known as Psyche. The maiden sat on top of a rock on the highest point of the island overlooking its southern shores. The winds blew Psyche's long wavy hair, the color of ebony. Her skin, too, was dark—a deep bronze—and when she lifted her tear-stained cheeks, she revealed two stunning emerald eyes.

"Don't be afraid," Persephone said as soon as she had made herself visible.

Psyche's eyes widened. They were filled with tears. "You're not a dragon."

Persephone tucked Aphrodite's black box of beauty beneath one arm and laughed, hoping to lighten the mood. "Are you expecting one?"

"Well, yes," the girl said solemnly.

In another effort to cheer up the girl, Persephone said, "You really are as beautiful as they say. I think even more so than Helen."

"And look what good that did," the girl snapped. "People are going to die because of her."

Persephone was taken aback by the girl's lack of respect, especially when the goddess was only trying to make her feel better. "How dare you take this tone with me? Do you know who I am?"

"It doesn't matter," the girl said, again without reverence. "Because if you think for one minute that beauty is a blessing for us mortals, you're wrong. And if I can anger you enough to kill me before the dragon comes, then good for me."

"Why would you say such a thing?"

"Beauty has done nothing but curse me with jealous sisters who hate me and with parents who live in fear that princes will draw us into battle over me. My father has tried to marry me off, but the suitors have stopped asking for my hand. They want only to look at me, and then they leave."

Persephone pressed her lips together, wondering what mischief Aphrodite had caused this poor maiden.

Psyche continued her tale: "My father was so distraught, that he made a journey to Delphi to seek advice from Apollo. He was told to bring me here and leave me—that I was to be married to a fearful dragon, stronger than the gods."

Persephone gawked. "That can't be!"

"I would kill myself if I didn't fear being punished for it in the afterlife," Psyche added, trembling like a blade of grass in the wind. Tears streamed down her lovely cheeks. "Please, Goddess, will you do it for me? Kill me before my dragon husband comes for me! Please!"

Persephone could only imagine how such a deed would be viewed by the lord of the Underworld. Just the thought of him scowling at her again made her shiver. The last thing she wanted was to make him angrier at her. If she was going to be by his side for all eternity, she hoped she could somehow regain his respect and admiration.

But Persephone couldn't turn her back on poor Psyche.

She had an idea. She held Aphrodite's box in both hands and said, "You see this? This was given to me by Aphrodite."

Psyche frowned. "That's not who addresses me now?"

"No. My name is Persephone. I'm the goddess of spring."

Psyche's eyes widened again, like the two perfectly round emeralds Persephone had fondled in the chambers of Hades. "Will you help me, Goddess?"

"Aphrodite sent me here to give you her box of beauty. I was to tell you not to open it, but to return it to Aphrodite's temple, unmolested. It was to be a test, designed to see if you could obey, or if your vanity would get the best of you."

"More beauty is the last thing I need," Psyche said. "She need not fear my opening it."

Persephone lifted a finger in the air. "But listen. She told me that if you dared to open it, her wrath would kill you on the spot."

"Then please give it to me now," the maiden begged. "Let me open it and end my misery."

"I wasn't meant to reveal that to you."

"As much as I hate to disappoint the goddess, I'm anxious to open her box. Please, I'm begging you, give it to me."

"I will give it to you," Persephone said, filling with dread. She did not like to see Psyche so anxious to give up her soul. "But first allow me to tell you what I know of the Underworld." Persephone told her about the judges, about Tartarus, Erebus, and the Elysian Fields. She told her about the Lethe River, the river of forgetfulness.

"Nothing sounds more marvelous to me," Psyche said.

Persephone wondered if her own longing to return to Hades had colored her depiction of his realm.

"But none of us knows our fate," Persephone said. "You might have been meant for some calling, some purpose, and, by opening the box, you'll never fulfill it."

More tears slipped down the cheeks of the maiden. "The oracle said I'm to be married to a dragon—a fierce beast with wings. I'm frightened, Goddess."

"Only the Fates know with certainty," Persephone said. "The oracle could be wrong."

"My sisters despise me," Psyche said. "My parents are afraid for their kingdom. I have nowhere to go. Please give me the box."

Persephone sucked in her lips and paced around the mountaintop. She wanted to help the poor girl, but she hated to see her end her life. If only her mother were here. Demeter would know what to do.

The thought of her mother helped Persephone come to a realization. Each person should be in charge of her own destiny—not controlled by another. As her own eyes filled with tears, Persephone stopped pacing and handed the black box to Psyche.

Just then a shriek filled the sky above them as an enormous flying beast descended toward the island. Persephone sprawled out her arms and placed herself between the beast and the girl, but the dragon swept both her and Psyche up in its iron claws and carried them away.

CHAPTER FOURTEEN

Demeter Wanders the Earth

Demeter flew to the gates of the Underworld where Cerberus stood guard. She demanded that Hades appear. She was sure that her misogynist brother had deceived her on some kind of technicality when he had sworn on the River Styx that Persephone was not there with him.

"Hear me, Hades!" she bellowed again from the riverbank outside of the gates. "I want my daughter back!"

But Hades did not come.

In a few moments, old Charon and a boat of souls neared the gates from the Acheron, and when he reached the Styx, she cried, "I need to see your lord."

"He's not at home," the old boatman replied.

"Where can I find him?" she asked.

"I do not know."

Helios had said that Hades had abducted Persephone. Was her daughter now forever lost to her?

Full of anger and sorrow, Demeter flew to the earth, wondering if she might find some way to kill herself. The pain of losing her daughter forever was too great. She'd rather die and go to the Underworld, where she could be with her daughter.

Demeter wandered around, disguised as an old woman, until she came into a pretty village on a hillside. Near its center was a well, and it was surrounded by a stone bench. Demeter sat and took comfort by the well, covered her face in her hands, and wept.

After some time, four girls came to fill their jugs, and when they saw Demeter weeping, they asked if she needed help.

"I don't think anyone can help me," Demeter said. "My daughter has been stolen from me by the lord of darkness."

"Oh, no!" the youngest cried. "She's dead? You poor thing!"

The little girl put a hand on Demeter's shoulder.

"The people in this village are kind," the oldest said. "Anyone would take you in, but you would make us happiest if you would come and stay with us for however long you need to."

Demeter smiled at the girl and was surprised by her kindness. "Thank you. But first go and ask your mother if she has room and enough food for me."

The girls left with their jugs and, in a half hour, they returned without them, skipping.

"Our mother says yes!" the youngest cried before they'd reached the well.

Each girl had a smile for Demeter and something else besides—an orange, a feather, a flower, and a walnut.

"Please say you'll come and be our grandmamma," one of the middle girls said as she handed over her present.

"Our mother just had a baby and is stuck in the house all day," the girl who had not yet spoken said. "She would love to have your company."

"She said so?" Demeter asked.

All four girls nodded.

Demeter was moved by their enthusiasm. They didn't even know who she was and yet they were so welcoming to her. She stood up from the bench and allowed them to crowd around her and take her by her arms.

The girls giggled and talked the whole way home, asking about her favorite color, her favorite food, her favorite thing to do. Demeter tried to answer as best as she could, though she had to make things up since her real answers would give away her identity.

After a while, they came to a small house on the edge of the village. Demeter was appalled by its condition. The exterior was badly worn, and it seemed too small for such a large family. There were no flowers in the garden, and the door had a hole at the bottom of it.

Waiting inside with a baby in her arms was the mother. She smiled warmly at Demeter and said, "Welcome to our humble home. My name is Metaneira, and this is Demophoon, my newborn son. Come inside and sit with us by the cozy fire. I'll have my daughters bring you a glass of honey-sweet wine and a bowl of spicy lamb stew."

Demeter was at once smitten with the baby. "May I hold him?"

"It would be an honor!" Metaneira said as she handed her precious bundle to the goddess whom she thought was just a lonely old woman.

Demeter couldn't believe the members of this household would treat a stranger with such kindness. Her pleasure made flowers bloom around the house. No one noticed yet, but they would soon, though they wouldn't understand the cause. Demeter also fixed the hole in the door while no one was looking, and she reinforced the entire house with magic, to keep the place from falling down. But mostly, she sat by the fire and held the baby boy, and sang to him, and was reminded of the days when Persephone was a baby.

CHAPTER FIFTEEN

The Red Dragon

Persephone held onto Aphrodite's black box of beauty with one hand and to Psyche's hand with the other as the majestic red dragon carried them over Kythira toward Mount Olympus. His head was the size of a man, his body the size of two men, and his tail the size of three. His bright, red-feathered wings were beautiful. She was less afraid of the dragon than she was of being discovered by her mother.

Maybe Demeter had sent the dragon to find her.

Maybe Apollo's oracle had seen a dragon coming for Psyche, but it had been meant for Persephone all along.

"Where are you taking us?" Persephone demanded. "And do you know who I am?"

The dragon circled the peak of Mount Olympus and then landed on a nearby cloud. A golden castle towered over them, and a stream, bordered by grass and flowers, flowed around the perimeter of the castle. The dragon set Psyche and Persephone down in the grass between the castle and the stream.

"I won't hurt you," he said hovering above them as his flapping wings created a strong current that lifted their hair and made them stumble. "I am here to protect you, Psyche. Inside, you'll find a servant waiting to attend to your every need."

Without waiting for a reply, the dragon flew away.

Psyche dried her eyes with her fists. "What should we do, Goddess? Should we do as he said?"

Persephone had the power to leave and to take Psyche with her, but where would they go? She wondered if this might be a good place to hide from her mother while thinking of a plan. The dragon had said he'd protect Psyche. Unless he was lying and this was a trap, one of the gods must favor the girl and want to protect her from Aphrodite. Persephone wondered who it could be.

"Let's go have a look inside," Persephone said.

Inside the golden castle doors, they found a long banquet table already spread with plates of food and goblets of wine.

A satyr was dressed in the robes of a servant, and, without a word, he stepped forward and pulled out a chair for each of them.

Psyche sat across from Persephone and plucked a golden spoon from the table.

"This could be a trap," Persephone warned. "The food could be poisoned."

"I hope it is," Psyche said before she dipped the spoon into a bowl of soup. After swallowing some, she said, "Mmm. Poison must be delicious."

Being a goddess, Persephone didn't need to eat as often as mortals, but the wine looked inviting, so she decided to have some. "The wine is delicious, too." It reminded her of the wine of Dionysus. Could that be the god who'd sent the dragon?

After the bowl of soup, Psyche ate a leg of lamb, steamed vegetables, and salted rice. She didn't hold back. Persephone knew that as the daughter of a king, Psyche never went hungry, but this food was likely better than anything the girl had ever eaten.

Once Psyche had finished eating and Persephone's goblet had been emptied for the third time, Psyche said, "I'm sleepy now. I wonder if there's someplace where I could lie down."

The satyr was at her side in an instant. He gave her his arm, and, without a word, led the girl from the room.

Persephone was left alone at the table for only a few moments when Cupid appeared in the chair where Psyche had just been sitting.

"Cupid?" Persephone asked in surprise. She'd forgotten how beautiful he was. His blue eyes gleamed on his young, beardless face beneath dark brows. His brows, along with his golden curls, had a subtle tint of red on the very tips of each hair, making it seem as though his hair and brows were smoldering. "So, you're the one behind all this. You sent the dragon?"

"I *was* the dragon. I'm the one who carried you here."

"You saved Psyche from your mother. You disobeyed her."

"Indeed."

Persephone smiled. "We have something in common, then."

Cupid lifted the dark ember that was his brow. "And what's that?"

"You have to swear on the River Styx to tell no one. If you agree, I'll help you save Psyche from Aphrodite."

"I swear," he said without hesitation.

"I've run away from Demeter. She would never let me out of her sight for more than a few minutes. I felt like I was suffocating. Do you understand?"

"I'd heard that Hades had abducted you."

"We said that to spare my mother's feelings. No one must know the truth, and you swore."

"Your secret is safe with me. But you do realize that mortals are suffering? With your mother's despondence, nothing on earth can grow. Do you have a plan?"

"I want to win back the heart of Hades," she said. "When we last spoke, we had a disagreement."

Cupid grinned. "I can help you with that."

Persephone shook her head. "It's something I need to do on my own. But maybe I could hide here until I figure out how to carry out my plan?"

"Of course."

"Now tell me how I can help you," Persephone said.

Cupid took a sip of wine from one of the golden goblets. Then he said, "When my mother sent me to make Psyche fall in love with the ugliest man alive, I wasn't expecting to be taken in by her beauty myself."

"Maybe you accidentally pricked yourself with one of your arrows."

He chuckled. "I don't think so, but maybe."

"Was it an *instant* attraction?" She was thinking of the way she had felt the first time she'd looked at Hades. At first, she'd been afraid of him; but later, after she'd studied him, she'd found him interesting and beautiful. More than his beauty was the promise of thrilling adventures she'd come to associate with the lord of darkness. He was the opposite of her mother in almost every way. Before long, she hadn't been able to get him out of her mind.

"Yes," he said. "But it was more than that."

"What do you mean?"

"I've seen countless beautiful girls in my life," he said. "So it wasn't just her physical beauty that struck me—no pun intended."

Persephone laughed.

"I think it was her sadness," he said. "She loves her sisters so much, even though they're cruel to her. And she loves her parents and worries about them and their fears. She doesn't like to be the cause of anyone's pain or discomfort. She's unselfish and forgiving to the very people who make her sad, and I think that's what I love about her."

Persephone frowned. Had she been selfish in wanting to leave her mother to pursue her own happiness? And had she been wrong to do so? As quickly as she had asked herself these questions, she thought of the answer: No. She was not wrong. While being unselfish was admirable, pursuing one's freedom was, too. Persephone was right to leave her mother's overprotective clutches to find a life of her own.

"So why not confess your love to her and be done with it?" Persephone asked. "Why disguise yourself as a dragon and avoid revealing your true identity?"

Cupid took a deep breath and exhaled slowly. He seemed to be carrying a very heavy burden in his heart. "You might not understand, since you've rarely left your mother's side, but if you had traveled all over the earth among mortals as I have, you would know how difficult it is to tell when mortals genuinely care about you. So many of them just want to use you, because they know there are advantages to being favored by a god."

"So, you want to test her love for you?"

"She doesn't love me yet," he said. "She doesn't even know I exist."

"When you first saw her…"

"I made myself invisible."

"Oh." Persephone took another sip of wine.

"I want her to get to know me without knowing who I am. And if she falls in love with me without knowing I'm a god…"

"Surely she suspects as much."

"I want her to think I'm a dragon."

"What?"

"I want her to think I'm a beast. If she can fall in love with me as a beast, then I'll know that I can trust her love."

This sounded like an interesting experiment. "How can I help?"

CHAPTER SIXTEEN

Hades Combs the Sea and Sky

Beneath his helm, without his chariot, Hades followed Persephone from Mount Olympus to the mountain peak on Kythira and eavesdropped on her conversation with Psyche. He filled with relief when he saw Persephone wouldn't kill the girl. He admired her for giving the maiden a choice. He'd been about to approach them, to add his own advice to the melancholy Psyche, when the red dragon descended from the clouds and captured its victims. Hades followed them to a bank of clouds above Mount Olympus, but when he tried to pursue them into the clouds, an impenetrable wall held him back.

Hades tried not to panic as he flew around the clouds, searching for an entrance or a weak spot. He attempted to drive his sword into the haze, but he was held back. Then he conjured a spear and flung it with all his might against the fog, but the spear fell from the sky. Then he tried a gentler approach by feeling all around the entire fortress with his hands, hoping for a door or gate of any kind. When he found none, he decided to seek out Hermes. Maybe he would know something about this red dragon, since, as the fastest god, he interacted with all of the others on a regular basis as their messenger.

He decided to god-travel back to the Underworld to summon Hermes rather than to call him to the bank of clouds above Mount Olympus. He didn't want to risk exposing Persephone's whereabouts to Demeter. If Demeter knew her daughter had been abducted by a dragon, the goddess would only further tighten her grip on her daughter's life.

"You called, my lord?" Hermes asked after he had appeared.

Hades blinked. The god truly was fast. "I was wondering if you've ever heard of a red dragon that flies around Mount Olympus."

"No. I can't say that I have."

Hades sighed. "I'm sorry to have beckoned you here for nothing, then."

"To find out about monsters, you might ask the Old Man of the Sea and his wife," Hermes suggested. "They are, after all, the parents of most of the beasts."

That was true. Cerberus and the Hydra came from them. "Good idea. I'll head over there."

"I wouldn't recommend going alone, Lord Hades. They have an old grudge against all Olympians, and they like to taunt and play with us, to our detriment. Shall I go with you? I'm always up for a challenge."

A grin spread across Hades's face. He wasn't used to camaraderie with the other gods. Only Hermes was ever friendly to him, but he'd never offered to join Hades for an adventure. "Shall we take my chariot?"

A moment later, the two gods stood in the chariot as Swift and Sure raced from the Underworld up into the sky over Greece. They flew to the west, toward the Ionian Sea, near the island of Ithaca, where Phorcys, and his wife, Keto, dwelled in their castle at the bottom of the ocean.

In an effort to make small talk on the way, Hades turned to Hermes and said, "I heard Athena wears Medusa's head on her shield."

"Perseus didn't let us down, that's for sure."

"You know Medusa was an innocent, don't you?" Hades asked.

Hermes shook his head. "It has nothing to do with me."

Hades made no reply.

"Have you seen the baby horse with wings that flew from Medusa when Perseus killed her?" Hermes asked.

"A horse with wings?"

"Yes. A little baby horse, white as a cloud. Zeus named him Pegasus."

"I hadn't heard."

"Zeus has been trying to distract Hera with the little guy."

"So he can deceive her again?" Hades accused.

"I think he wants to protect his son, Hercules. Hera keeps trying to kill him. When she's not making trouble for Dionysus, she keeps herself busy tormenting the poor man."

"I think she's succeeded in driving him mad," Hades said. "His children have recently joined my kingdom, killed by their father's hands. When I went to avenge them, Hercules begged me to punish him."

"And did you?" Hermes asked.

"His labors will soon begin," Hades said. "I sent him to a king who knows the proper way to punish criminals."

"It's interesting to me, Lord Hades, that you can see the innocence in Medusa and not in Hercules."

"It's interesting to me that both my brothers bring pain and suffering to humankind, and yet *I'm* the one whom mortals most fear." Hades was particularly angry with Poseidon for his part in creating the Minotaur, whom Theseus had recently killed.

This time Hermes made no reply.

Hades decided to change the subject. "So what do you think of the Greeks' plan to destroy Troy?"

"I hope they succeed," Hermes said. "As much as I admire King Priam, it was wrong, what his son Paris did."

"Do you know how the other gods stand?"

"As far as I know, there aren't many supporting Troy. Aphrodite is, because she's loyal to Paris. And Ares will always follow Aphrodite."

"You know of no others?" Although Hades was neutral, he was interested.

"I heard Artemis was behind Agamemnon's sacrifice."

"The sacrifice of his daughter?" The outrage he'd felt when he and Persephone had witnessed it returned, but he suppressed it.

"That's the one. I heard Artemis replaced Iphigenia with a doe at the last moment."

"Good for Artemis." Now he wouldn't have to avenge the girl's murder. "Sounds like she favors the Greeks."

"I don't think so. I heard she kept Iphigenia and is making a lover out of her."

"She might still favor them yet," Hades said.

"I doubt it. And I have the same feeling about Apollo."

"Interesting." Hades plunged his chariot into the Ionian Sea.

As they passed an underground volcano, a giant black octopus shot toward them and startled the stallions. The chariot wavered while Hades attempted to regain control of Swift and Sure.

"And I thought chariot travel was safer!" Hermes complained as he threw a spear at the beast.

Hades pulled on the reins. "It is. Just a bit…rocky at times."

As the octopus sank to the ocean depths, releasing a trail of blood, Hermes said, "That was my favorite spear."

"We'll come back for it."

With the attack behind them, they sped in the chariot toward the castle of Phorcys and Keto when they were suddenly intercepted by Poseidon riding in his chariot behind his three white steeds.

Hades slowed his stallions, and the two chariots now moved side by side.

"I told you to warn me before entering my domain!" Poseidon growled at Hades.

"An unreasonable request," Hades said matter-of-factly. "Over seventy percent of the earth's surface is your domain."

"And yet you make it impossible for any but Hermes to enter yours," Poseidon said as his long, sun-bleached hair drifted around his face.

"Because only the dead go there," Hades pointed out. Gods and mortals alike were always trying to steal the dead back to the world of the living. "Do you notify Zeus each time you take your chariot to the skies?"

"State your business," Poseidon demanded, his turquoise eyes narrowed. "Why are you here?"

"Shouldn't you be off making more mischief for the Trojans?" Hades taunted. He'd heard that Poseidon favored the Greeks and was behind the greatest Achaean warriors.

"You forget the power of my trident!" Poseidon threatened.

"If I'd worn the helm, you never would have known we were here," Hades said. "But I didn't wear it, and that was a courtesy to you."

"We've come to see the Old Man of the Sea," Hermes said. "It has nothing to do with you, Lord Poseidon."

"Thank you, Hermes," Poseidon said kindly. To Hades, he said, "Now that wasn't so difficult, was it?"

Without waiting for Hades to reply, Poseidon and his chariot sped away.

CHAPTER SEVENTEEN

Persephone Helps Psyche and Cupid

Persephone walked with Psyche along the stream that surrounded Cupid's magnificent castle in the clouds—a gift from his mother, he'd told her.

"You seem less unhappy since we've been here," Persephone said. "Are you not frightened of the red dragon?"

"Not at all. Are you, Goddess?" Psyche turned her stunning emerald eyes to Persephone.

"I suppose not. He seems kind." Persephone picked up a large stone and tossed it into the stream, to see how far she could throw it. With her goddess strength, she threw it as far as her eyes could see.

"He's very kind. He tells me he loves me and wants to marry me." Psyche chose a stone and she, too, threw it into the water. It didn't go far, but it skipped three times on the surface before sinking.

"That's a neat trick!" Persephone said, delighted.

"My father taught me. Want to learn?"

"Please."

Psyche chose another stone. "You need a flat rock, like this one. And you should hold it like this. Then give it a slight backspin as you aim to skim the surface." Psyche skipped the stone along the surface. Persephone counted five skips this time.

"That's remarkable! Let me try!"

They threw rocks all afternoon. It was such a small thing, but Persephone loved learning to do it without godly power. She was coming to realize how much the small things added to one's quality of life—another reason to find a way out of her mother's clutches.

After a while, Psyche said, "I'm getting hungry. Do you mind if I go in for some supper?"

"I'll go with you." Then Persephone asked, "So do you love the red dragon back?"

"I know this sounds crazy, but I think I do. I've never known anyone so kind and so concerned about my wellbeing. My parents love me, but even their love is dull compared to his."

"They did leave you stranded on Kythira," Persephone pointed out.

"Only because Apollo's oracle commanded them to."

Persephone linked her pale arm with Psyche's bronze one, giving it a little squeeze. "You shouldn't love someone just because he loves *you*." Persephone thought of Hades. She hoped her interest in him wasn't the cause of his interest in her. She hoped he truly liked her personality. Yet, after their last argument, he probably dreaded the Fates' prediction that he would marry her. "You want to be sure you love him, too. Have you had a chance to get to know him?"

"Let's see. He loves flying more than anything—after me," Psyche said. "Next, he loves horses. He says he sometimes transforms himself into one so he can run among the wild horses on earth. He thinks love is the most important virtue, and we've actually talked for hours about what we both think love is. It's not an easy concept to define."

"You've learned a lot about him these past days."

"He's even come to my bed at night, just to hold me."

"How is that possible? Isn't he too big for your bed?"

"He transforms into a man, I think."

"What do you mean you think?"

"He keeps the room dark and won't let me look at him."

"And you don't mind?"

"Maybe a little. He's just so kind. It shouldn't matter what he looks like, right?"

"Right." Persephone was pleased to see Cupid's plan working.

"Oh, and he also adores his mother—though, when I asked who she was, he said he couldn't tell me. But I don't mind. I trust he has his reasons."

Persephone nodded. "I'm glad you're fond of him."

"There's only one thing keeping me from giving him my heart," Psyche admitted as they reached the twin doors of the castle.

"Oh? What's that?"

"I miss my family, but when I ask the dragon if he'll take me home for a visit, he refuses. How can I fully love someone who wants to keep me from my family?"

"Hmm. Let me have a word with him. Maybe I can change his mind."

Psyche surprised her by falling to her knees and hugging Persephone's feet. "Thank you, Goddess! Thank you ever so much!"

While the satyr servant attended to Psyche's dinner, Persephone roamed around the castle looking for Cupid. Not finding him at home, she prayed to him, and he appeared to her in his natural form in one of the back chambers of the castle.

Persephone shared what she'd learned about Psyche's feelings. "Maybe if you take her to see her family, she'll consent to marry you."

Now it was Cupid's turn to surprise Persephone. He took her in his arms for a tight embrace before releasing her. "Thank you, Persephone! I'll do it!"

<u>CHAPTER EIGHTEEN</u>

Demeter Loves Demophoon

Demeter was sitting beside the cozy fire with Demophoon bundled in her arms when his mother, Metaneira, returned home with a basket full of corn and potatoes.

"It's the strangest thing," Metaneira said as she set the basket on the table and took off her coat. "Crops are failing all over the lands. Neighboring villagers are starving. But our little farm has had the best harvest of my life. I've just been to market, where I sold corn and potatoes by the bushel! Dozens of them!"

"It pleases me to see you so happy," Demeter said.

Metaneira smiled. "You brought us this good fortune. The gods must favor you."

Demeter held the bottle of goat's milk to the baby's lips. "Your baby has grown bigger these past few days. His strength is remarkable."

"And that is your doing, too," the mother said. "You've been a wonderful blessing to us, dear."

Metaneira's daughters burst through the door with their jugs full of water.

"It's so cold out there!" the youngest said.

"It's never this cold!" the oldest said.

"But it's nice and warm in here," Metaneira pointed out. "Take off your coats and warm yourselves by the fire."

The girls sat on the floor at Demeter's feet and begged her to tell them another story.

As Demeter nursed Demophoon with the goat's milk, she said:

"A long time ago, before people walked the earth, there lived only gods. The primordial beings, such as Chaos and Nyx, gave birth to others, and eventually Uranus, the sky, ruled them all. He was a cruel husband to Gaia, the earth, and an even crueler father to the Titans and Cyclopes and other monsters he begat. He imprisoned most of his children in Tartarus. Gaia wanted her children to overthrow her husband, but the only one brave enough to do it was Kronos. Gaia gave him a sickle and a hiding place, and then she called Uranus into the room. That's when Kronos ambushed his father and castrated him. Uranus fled from the earth and Kronos became the new ruler.

"Kronos provided many years of peace, but he returned most of his brothers and sisters back to the pit in Tartarus, and, because of a prophecy that a son would overthrow him, he swallowed his children whole as soon as each was born. The first of these were three sisters—Hestia, Demeter, and Hera. Then came two brothers—Hades and Poseidon."

The girls gasped.

"What is it?" Demeter asked.

"We never say his name," the youngest girl said.

Demeter frowned. "Who's name?"

"The name of the lord of darkness," the oldest said. "But please, go on with your story and my sisters and I won't interrupt again."

"When a third son was born—Zeus—Rhea, their mother, had an idea. In place of the baby Zeus, she gave Kronos a rock swaddled in blankets. Kronos swallowed it whole.

"While Zeus was secretly raised by nymphs in a cave on Mount Ida, the other five children of Kronos grew to adulthood in the belly of their father. As babies and, later, children, they delighted one another by playing games; but, as they grew older, it became crowded, and they irritated one another. They all but despised one another by the time something caused their father to vomit them out. They soon learned that their youngest brother, Zeus, had come back for them. He'd given their father an elixir that had set them all free."

"Lord Zeus!" The youngest daughter clapped her hands. "He became king of the Olympians!"

"Yes," Demeter said. "With the help of his sisters and brothers, Zeus freed the Titans and Cyclopes and other children of Uranus, hoping they would all help overthrow Kronos; but not all of them supported Zeus. Some remained loyal to their brother, even though he had been cruel to them.

"The war between Zeus and Kronos lasted for ten years," Demeter continued. "It was a horrible time for all of them. The earth became barren and ravaged as one battle after another was fought. To multiply their force, Zeus had relations with two of his sisters and a handful of Titans. One of his sisters, Demeter, agreed out of obligation. The other sister, Hera, fell in love with him and wanted to marry him. Their children—Ares, Eris, Hebe, and Hephaestus—along with some of Zeus's children—Athena, Hermes, Artemis, and Apollo—joined forces with their parents and finally succeeded in trapping Kronos and his loyal Titans in the pit of Tartarus. Zeus charged the loyal Titan Prometheus with forming humankind and the animals of the earth out of clay, so there would be subjects to rule over, and then the three Olympian brothers drew lots to decide who would rule the three domains—Sky, Sea, and Underworld."

"Zeus got the sky!" the youngest called out.

"And Poseidon the sea!" said the second to the youngest.

"And you-know-who rules the Underworld," the second to the oldest said with a shiver.

"The reason we don't say his name," Metaneira explained from the pantry, "is that we fear he will take us as his subjects."

"I don't blame you for fearing him," Demeter said. "You are wise to avoid him."

Then Metaneira turned to her daughters and said, "Now you girls go get cleaned up before supper." To Demeter, she said, "Let me take my son. I'll bathe him and bring him back to you shortly."

"I can bathe him," Demeter said, holding the baby close.

The mother frowned. "I don't mind doing it, my dear. I rarely get the chance to hold him as it is."

"I'll do it, Metaneria. That way, you can get on with making the supper."

Metaneira nodded, but Demeter could see she'd hurt the mother's feelings.

As Demeter bathed Demophoon at the basin in the back of the house, the youngest daughter entered the room to offer her help.

"Can you take the jug of water back to your mother for me?" Demeter asked, pointing to the water she hadn't used on the infant.

"I'd be happy to." As the girl was about to leave the room, she turned back to Demeter and asked, "Are you going to keep my baby brother for yourself?"

"Of course not, child," Demeter scolded. "He belongs to your mother."

The girl apologized and left the room.

After supper, Demeter thought it would be wise to allow Metaneira to hold her own son. She didn't like the suspicions that seemed to be growing among the members of the household. Demeter cleaned the supper dishes while the family visited around their fire. Metaneira's husband, Celeus, had just returned from his hunt, and the girls begged him to tell them about his adventures.

When the supper dishes were clean and the stories were finished, Demeter asked if she might once again hold Demophoon. The mother kissed her baby's forehead before handing him over—sadly, it seemed to Demeter. The goddess realized she had allowed herself to grow too fond of the baby and was hoarding him as she had her own daughter.

Her heart still ached for Persephone, but in her efforts to divert her heartache, Demeter couldn't rob this mother of her time with her child.

As the mother stood to ready herself for bed, Demeter whispered, "I won't remain in your house much longer. You'll have your baby back soon."

The mother either didn't hear Demeter, or she pretended not to hear, as she ordered her daughters to bed. Then Metaneira told Demeter goodnight before she followed her husband to their bedroom.

Alone with the baby, Demeter took a vial of ambrosia from her robes and anointed it all over Demophoon's sweet skin. If she was to spare him from death, tonight was the night she must make him a god. As she anointed his skin, she sang the song she'd sung to him each night:

Sweet little cherub, don't you cry.
Sleep will be coming, and soon you'll fly
Up to the stars and into the night.
A kiss for Selene and all is bright.

Then, holding the baby in one hand, she stoked the fire with the other, and then she kissed Demophoon on the forehead.

"You will become like me, sweet boy," she whispered. "And then, when your family has long since died, you will still walk the earth, until you're ready to join me on Mount Olympus."

She swaddled him more snuggly in his blanket and then reached down to place him in the flames in the hearth.

Behind her, Metaneira screamed. "No!"

Demeter jumped. She'd been so consumed with what she was doing, that she hadn't noticed the mortal enter the room.

Metaneira rushed to Demeter's side and ripped Demophoon from the goddess's arms. "How could you? How could you want to kill my baby?"

CHAPTER NINETEEN

A Trap

Hades steered his chariot around the underwater volcano and past the reef to the deep abyss, where they plunged thousands of feet into the deep, deep, dark sea. At the very bottom was an old castle of rock—simple and covered in barnacles. It was nothing like Poseidon's crystal palace, which was grand and supreme in beauty and scale. And the deep abyss here was devoid of marine life, unlike the region of Poseidon's abode, where dolphins, sharks, and colorful fish—not to mention mermaids—dwelled.

Hades brought the chariot to the old wooden door. When no one opened it, Hermes leaned over and rapped on it with his fist.

Speaking of mermaids, there was Keto at the door. The half-woman-half-fish opened it a crack and gave them each a once over. "To what do we owe the pleasure of your visit?"

"We wanted to ask you and your husband about a red dragon who flies over Mount Olympus," Hades said.

"Have you heard of one?" Hermes asked.

"I have not," she replied.

"Is your husband at home?' Hades asked. "Perhaps he has."

"Yes. He's home. Please, come in. But I have no one here to tend to your horses."

"They'll be okay for a moment," Hades said. "We won't take up much of your time."

She gave him a gleeful smile that he found off-putting as she opened the door and led them inside.

To keep the gods from floating, Keto handed them each a bag of rocks. Then they left the antechamber and found Phorcys sitting at a banquet table in front of an empty plate.

"Are we interrupting your supper?" Hermes asked.

"Not at all," the half-man- half-fish replied. In addition to a fish tail, he had a pair of pincers at his waist. "It seems we have very little supper these days."

"Not to worry," Keto said to her husband as she offered Hades a chair at the table. "I believe our guests bring us good fortune."

Hermes took a seat beside Hades, across from Phorcys.

"I'll be back in a moment, dear," Keto said to her husband. "They are asking about a red dragon." With that, Keto left the room.

"He flies above Mount Olympus," Hades added. "I've never seen him before. Have you?"

"A red dragon?" the Old Man of Sea repeated. "Let me think…Our Ladon, as you know, is a one-hundred-headed serpent dragon, but he's *green* and you're looking for *red*. Our nine-headed Hydra might be called a dragon, too, but…how would you describe her color? A yellowish gray? Chimera has a dragon's *tail*, but you would have recognized *her* by her lion and goat heads. And her tail isn't red. And, let's see, I wouldn't describe Scylla as a *dragon*, even though her six long necks and grisly heads are dragon-like. She's more like a *crab* with her ferocious pincers and tentacles. The six dog heads at her waist are just a bonus. We're quite proud of her."

"I'm familiar with your children," Hades said when he could finally get a word in edgewise. He felt as though Phorcys was wasting his time.

"But I haven't even mentioned Echidna and Charybdis," the old man complained.

A commotion near the entrance alarmed Hades. He turned to Hermes to see the same look of concern cross his face.

Swift and Sure snorted and whinnied in a panic.

Hades dropped his bag of rocks and conjured his sword as he swam to the front door with Hermes close behind him.

Keto, Chimera, and Echidna had surrounded Hades's stallions. Chimera had her lion's mouth wide open and was about to sink her fierce teeth into the side of Swift's neck when Hades brought his sword down across Chimera's mane. The lion head separated from the rest of the monster and floated a few feet away. Blood filled the area around them.

Keto screamed.

Chimera's goat head shrieked with pain before her whole body went limp.

Echidna, a half woman and half snake, swung her enormous snake tail toward Hades and wrapped it around his body.

Hermes raised his sword, but before he could stab Echidna, Scylla appeared and picked him up in her pincers.

Phorcys then came out and, seeing Chimera's lifeless, decapitated body, cried, "What have you done to my daughter!" He scooped her up—all of her—and carried her into the castle.

With Hades imprisoned in the coils of Echidna's tail and Hermes hanging from the end of Scylla's pincers, Keto was free to remove the chariot from the horses.

"Please don't take this personally," Keto said to Hades as she grabbed the reins of Swift and Sure and led the horses toward her castle. "We haven't eaten in days."

<u>CHAPTER TWENTY</u>

The Betrayal of Cupid

The castle was quiet. Unlike Mount Olympus, where the sun al-ways shone, night had come over the bank of clouds. Except for the light from Selene--the moon goddess—Persephone's room was dark. She folded back the covers on her bed and lay down. She hadn't needed sleep in the weeks she'd been Cupid's guest, but she missed Hades and hoped she might see him in her dreams.

"Please, Hermes," she prayed as she pulled the bedcovers to her chin. "Send me a dream about the lord of darkness."

She lay there with her eyes closed for a very long time, but neither sleep nor dreams came. As she sat up in frustration, she was startled by a terrifying wail. It came from Psyche's bedroom, but it didn't sound like the girl. It sounded like…Cupid?

Another cry rang out. Persephone flew to Psyche's bedchamber. From the door, she saw Cupid lying on the bed in his natural form, but dimmed, writhing in pain. Psyche stood beside him. She held a lamp with one hand and covered her mouth with the other.

"I'm so sorry!" Psyche cried to Cupid. "What can I do to help you? The oil from the lamp! I didn't mean to spill it on you!"

Persephone froze, unsure of what to do. Should she interfere or stay put?

"I trusted you!" Cupid growled at the frightened girl. "I thought you trusted me!"

"I do!" Tears fell from the girl's eyes, and the lamp shook so much in her hand that Persephone feared another oil spill.

"You lie! I asked you to wait! I wasn't ready for you to see me yet!" Cupid covered his face and moaned.

"But you're so beautiful." Psyche fell to her knees beside the bed. "Why hide yourself from me?" She reached out to touch the golden curls on his head.

He flinched from her touch. "I needed to know if I could trust you."

"My sisters, they…"

"If you love them so much, go back to them!" Cupid shouted.

"Please," Psyche begged. "I don't know your name, but I love you. Truly, I do. My sisters said you might not be what you said you were."

"I'm not," the god said, panting and writhing. "I *was* someone in love. *Now*, I'm someone with a broken heart. Please go!"

"How? How can I leave you?"

Persephone stepped further into the room. "I'll take her home. Can you go to Apollo for help?"

"I think so," Cupid said to Persephone. "Thank you."

Cupid vanished.

Psyche set the lamp on the bedside table and put her face in her hands. She knelt over the bed, her face in the bedcovers where Cupid had been lying moments before. Persephone filled with anger.

"How could you do this?" Persephone asked. "You've ruined everything for him and for yourself." She was as angry at herself as she was at Psyche, because she had convinced Cupid to allow the girl to visit her family. This betrayal wouldn't have happened had the girl's sisters not planted doubts in Psyche's head.

"I just wanted to see what he looked like," Psyche said. "And why shouldn't I?"

"You said yourself that it doesn't matter," Persephone snapped. "He was giving you a chance to prove it. And you failed."

Psyche held her open palms toward Persephone. "What should I do now, Goddess? I will do whatever you say!"

Persephone took a deep breath, and, as she exhaled, the anger left her body. The girl had made a mistake, but there was no reason to chastise her further. "Go home and pray to him. Pray to him and to his mother."

"I still don't know who they are."

"Cupid and Aphrodite, the gods of love and beauty."

Psyche's mouth fell open and she stared back at Persephone in silence for many seconds. Then she hugged herself and murmured, "Oh, what have I done? What have I done?"

Persephone put a hand on the girl and god-traveled to Psyche's kingdom. She left Psyche at the palace doors and said goodbye before disappearing, but she hovered above the city, to be sure the girl was welcomed.

The king and queen were shocked to see their youngest daughter returned. They seemed less happy than Persephone had expected. They weren't like Demeter at all. They wanted their daughter to find a husband and to move on.

Full of sadness, Persephone turned away. She missed her mother, and she missed Lord Hades, and she wasn't sure where to go from here.

CHAPTER TWENTY-ONE

Demeter Reveals Herself

How could you?" Metaneira cried again as she held her baby over her shoulder. The baby wailed with fear. His mother bounced him and patted him and kissed his little head. "It's okay," she whispered to her son. "I've got you now, my sweet lamb."

Demeter was mortified by Metaneira's accusation. "I would never kill Demophoon! I love him as if he were my own child!"

"You must be mad." The mother stared at Demeter with wide, frightened eyes. Her voice and body trembled as she patted her boy. "I saw what you were going to do. If I hadn't come in when I did…"

"Your son would be immortal, like me."

Metaneira jerked back her head. "What did you say?"

Demeter transformed into the beautiful, slender, youthful woman that she was—but she kept her radiance dimmed, so as not to burn the mortal's eyes and kill her. Demeter's old robes were replaced by a purple gown of silk. Her corn-blonde hair fell in braids across her back. A crown of diamonds sparkled on her head above her golden-brown eyes.

In spite of Demeter's precaution at keeping her radiance dimmed, her transformation startled the woman, and the mother fell back and toppled to the floor. Her baby fell from her arms and struck his head on the brick hearth. The baby's crying came to an abrupt halt. Blood poured from his head.

"No!" both women screamed.

Celeus rushed from his bed to see what the commotion was all about. His daughters peered down from their loft, rubbing their sleepy eyes.

"What's happening?" the husband cried.

Demeter had taken Demophoon in her arms, had covered his wound with his blanket, and was trying to breathe the life back into him, but Hermes had been too swift. He'd taken the baby's soul before Demeter had noticed him.

With her eyes full of tears, the goddess glared at each member of the unfortunate family. "I am Demeter, goddess of the harvest."

"A goddess?" Celeus asked. "Here, in our house?" He fell to his knees.

Demeter saw the girls above them drop to their knees as well.

Metaneira was already on the floor at Demeter's feet, sobbing for her son. She said nothing.

Demeter looked down at the poor woman. "You were good to me while I was feeling low, and I thank you for that. But now Demophoon is dead."

"No!" the mother cried. "Please! It can't be! Oh, no, no, no!" The woman beat her breast and rocked herself to and fro at Demeter's feet.

The girls above broke into sobs, too.

"Can't you fix him?" the youngest asked.

"We'll do anything you say!" Celeus said. "Please save my son!"

Demeter glanced across the room at the hurting father and then looked up at the darling girls, their faces twisted with despair. Then she returned her gaze to the mourning mother at her feet. This is not what she had hoped for this family. "I'll take his body to Lord Hades and beg for his soul to be returned."

Metaneria kissed Demeter's feet, again and again. "Thank you, dear Demeter. Thank you so much!"

"While I'm gone, tell the rest of your villagers to build a cabin for me—a temple—at the base of the mountain, one mile east of here. Once it is built, I'll return, and you'll know if Demophoon lives again."

"It will be done, Goddess," Celeus promised. "And we will pray to you and to the other gods—night and day."

Demeter held the lifeless baby close to her as she left the cottage and god-traveled to the gates of the Underworld, some distance from Cerberus, where she waited on the riverbank, once again for Charon to appear in his boat.

When she saw the old man nearing the gate on his raft full of souls, she spotted Hermes among them. He held Demophoon's soul in his arms.

"Hermes!" Demeter shouted. "Give that soul back to me at once, before the body becomes cold."

Hermes gave her a look of surprise. "Demeter? Is that you?"

"The soul you carry in your arms," she repeated. "Please give it back to me."

Hermes glanced all around. Demeter saw the look he exchanged with Charon.

"You'll have to take this up with Lord Hades," Hermes finally said. "I don't have the authority."

"Tell him I'm here," she said. "Please tell him to let me inside the gate."

Hermes frowned. "I'm afraid he's tied up at the moment."

CHAPTER TWENTY-TWO

Tied Up

Hades pressed with all his might against the thick coils of Echidna's serpent tail. She responded by tightening her grip.

"When my parents were dethroned by you and your brothers," Echidna said, "you left them with few resources. This castle is condemned, and nothing lives around here."

"There's an entire sea full of food," Hades said, though he could barely breathe, and not because of the water. The coils of the monster's tail pressed against his lungs.

"Yeah, right!" Scylla screeched. "Poseidon hoards the sea for himself."

"You and your sister Charybdis rule the Messina Straight," Hermes argued, still dangling from Scylla's pincers. He swung his legs through the water but could gain no purchase. "Poseidon seldom interferes. And I should know. I constantly bring the dead to Hades from that region."

"We're more fortunate than our parents," Scylla pointed out.

"I bring them food when I can," Echidna said. "But it's not enough."

"And you just happened to visit at the wrong time," Scylla said with a smile.

"Or the right time." Echidna tightened her grip. "Depending on your point of view."

Scylla laughed in that terrifying screech that was her signature sound. The dog heads at her waist yelped, too.

"I wonder if it's gall, stupidity, or desperation that drives you," Hades said. "Whatever it is, you should fear backlash from the Olympians."

"The other Olympians don't care about you and your horses," Echidna sneered. "I've seen the way they treat you."

At that moment, Hermes multiplied into fifty—something only he of all the gods, save the Fates, was capable of doing, because he was death and sleep and a messenger for all and had to be at many places at once. He attacked Scylla until he was free of her, and then he strangled Echidna while freeing Hades. Phorcys appeared at the door, but he backed away when he saw the massive army Hermes had made.

Once free, Hades swam into the castle. Keto held a knife at Sure's throat. Before she could pierce his flesh, Hades conjured and threw a dagger. It landed squarely in her left eye. She screamed, dropped her knife, and groped her face in pain. Hades rounded up Sure and Swift and led them back to the chariot. Hermes integrated into one beside him, and, together, they drove away.

Hades steered the chariot to the old volcano and to the dead octopus at the bottom of the sea. "Your favorite spear."

Hermes swam to retrieve his spear and returned to the chariot. "Wouldn't want to leave this behind."

Once they were in the air flying over Greece, Hades said, "Well, you wanted an adventure."

"True." Hermes frowned.

"Not what you had in mind?"

"It was great. I love battling monsters." There was no trace of sarcasm in Hermes's speech.

"Then what?"

"You're wanted at home, and I don't think you'll be pleased with what awaits you there."

Hades didn't need to ask for an explanation, for in the next moment, they descended into the chasm and followed the river to the gate where

Cerberus stood guard. Demeter was waiting for them on the riverbank with a babe in her arms.

"I need his soul," she said before he'd brought his chariot to a halt. "His death was an accident. It shouldn't have happened. You've already taken my daughter. You can't have Demophoon, too!"

Hades gave Hermes a nod and said, "Thanks for your help. You can go. Tell Charon to continue on."

"What?" Demeter cried. "Will you not give me one ounce of respect?"

Hades offered a hand to Demeter and invited her into his chariot. "Sit with me. I harbor no ill feelings toward you, and I hold you in great esteem."

Demeter refused his hand. "I don't believe you! I know you have my daughter here against her will, even though you swore. It had to be on some technicality that you made that oath. You are a clever god, and you know how to manipulate language. You broke my heart when you took her, and now you're breaking it again by refusing me Demophoon!"

"If I could give him to you, I would," Hades said. "I swear it."

"What prevents you?" she asked.

"The Fates."

"But Pelops. Why were you able to bring Pelops back and not Demophoon?"

"The Fates require a trade. I took Tantalus to replace his son. If you know someone who would die for Demophoon, then you can have him back."

Demeter frowned. "Who would give his life for that of an infant?"

"I only know of one kind of person who would do such a thing," he said.

Demeter's face turned white, and tears filled her eyes. As she nodded, she barely choked out the words he knew would come from her lips. "A mother."

"Protect the baby's body with ambrosia to ensure a successful resurrection," Hades said. "I'll give you the boy's soul when you bring his mother to me."

Hades couldn't bear to look at the grief-stricken face of Demeter. He wished there was something he could do for her to make her feel better.

As if she'd read his mind, she asked, "May I see my daughter before I go?"

"If I could show her to you, I would," he said cryptically. He didn't want Demeter to know that her daughter had been abducted by a red dragon. "She's detained at the moment."

"What? Is she safe?" Demeter asked. "Tell me the truth, Hades. Swear to me that my daughter is in good hands."

Since he couldn't swear it, he said nothing and sadly drove his chariot through the gate. He felt Demeter's cold stare on his back, but he didn't turn to look at her again.

CHAPTER TWENTY-THREE

Apollo

Persephone was nervous about showing up on Mount Olympus after her weeks of hiding in Cupid's castle, but she was finally ready to face her mother. Seeing the way Psyche had been ill-received by her parents had made Persephone grateful for her mother's love.

At the gate, she said, "Spring, Summer, Winter, and Fall, please open the gate, so that I, Persephone, Goddess of Springtime, may enter."

The clouds parted, and she flew past the fountain and up the palace steps to the main hall, anxious about what her mother would say.

She was noticed by Zeus immediately. Only Hera and Hestia were in the room with him.

He stood from his throne. "Dear child, where have you been?"

"We've been looking for you," Hera said, though Persephone didn't sense concern in her voice. It sounded more like jealousy.

"Should I get you some ambrosia?" Hestia asked. "You seem pale."

"No, thank you," Persephone said to Hestia. Then to Zeus she said, "I needed time away from my mother, but I'm ready to see her now. Where is she?"

Zeus crossed the room and put a hand on her shoulder. He was her father, but he felt more like a king. "I don't know. We haven't heard from her in weeks, and most of us have been too busy with the war to look for her."

"Oh, no." Persephone bit her lip. "This is not good."

"No, it isn't," Zeus agreed. "Her despondence is affecting the soldiers."

"Not to mention their families," Hera added.

"She's neglected her duties," Hestia explained. "There are no crops. The cattle are dying off."

"And the bitter cold isn't helping," Zeus pointed out.

Persephone fought off tears. People were suffering because of her. "What should I do?"

"Ask Apollo if he can see your future." Zeus returned to his throne. "Maybe he can shed some light on the situation."

"Do you know where he is?" she asked.

"In his chambers with Cupid," Hera said.

Persephone turned and headed for the door of the god of truth and light, of healing, and of music. As she lifted her fist to knock, she heard Apollo say, "Come in."

She opened the door to find Cupid lying on a golden couch staring at the water in Apollo's fountain. A tiny white colt with wings lay in his lap like a puppy, and Cupid was petting the creature.

Apollo sat upright on another couch across from him, beckoning to her to have a seat beside him. His quiver of silver arrows lay across a small table between the two couches, and his silver bow lay at his feet. In the corner of the room, three muses entertained them with music. Polyhymnia played the lyre, Euterpe the flute, and Terpsichore the harp.

"Come," Apollo said to Persephone. "I know why you're here."

"Thank you," she said, sitting beside him.

Apollo's dazzling green eyes reminded her of Psyche's, though they looked at her from a fairer face, and they were framed with lighter-colored curls. His hair wasn't as yellow as hers or Cupid's, but it wasn't black, either, matching the golden-brown tone of his sister's. His sculpted nose and chin, along with his perfect lips, made him the most beautiful of the gods—though all were beautiful, including Cupid.

And Hades.

Her memories of being in the arms of Hades brought a rush of heat to her face. She shook her head, shoved the memories deep down, and focused on Cupid.

Although his skin had healed from the accidental burn, Persephone could tell his heart had not.

"Hello," she said to him.

He gave her a subtle smile but said nothing as he continued to pet the tiny, winged horse.

"Cupid." Persephone scooted to the edge of her seat to lean closer to him. "Please. You've got to shake yourself out of this. Psyche made a mistake, brought on by her meddling and overbearing sisters. You should forgive her and have pity on her. She loves you. And, her parents…they don't seem to love her nearly as much as you do."

"Her father is visiting my oracle now," Apollo said. "He's asking what he should do with her, since the dragon apparently didn't want her."

Cupid moaned but said nothing.

"What will become of her?" Persephone asked Apollo.

"My vision isn't clear," he said. "I see her at the feet of Aphrodite."

"Let's not talk about it," Cupid said. "I'd rather talk about why *you're* here, Persephone. You didn't come to check on me."

Persephone frowned. "I didn't need to. I knew you were in good hands. I'm the one who told you to come here, remember?"

Cupid returned his gaze to Apollo's fountain and said nothing.

"I know where your mother is," Apollo said to Persephone. "She's near Delphi, at a village near my temple."

"What? Why is she there?"

"She's about to do something…tragic," Apollo replied.

Alarmed, Persephone jumped to her feet and asked, "What is she going to do?"

"Maybe it would be better if I showed you."

A moment later, Persephone sat beside Apollo in his shining chariot as they flew across the Grecian skies toward Mount Parnassus—the villagers called it Mount Kronos—and the city of Delphi.

From the sky, Apollo pointed to a building being erected a few miles west of his temple. "The villagers are building that cabin for your mother."

"I wonder why."

"She plans to live there among them, away from the rest of us," he said. "She's suffering from a serious bout of depression. If she were mortal, she'd probably have killed herself by now."

Tears pricked Persephone's eyes. "I love my mother, but her attachment to me can't be healthy."

"No."

"She rarely lets me out of her sight."

"Which is why you lied about being abducted by Hades?"

Persephone's mouth fell open. Once she had recovered from the shock that he knew the truth—*of course he would know the truth!*—she said, "I beg you to keep that to yourself. I wanted her to believe it to spare her feelings."

Apollo led the chariot toward the earth. "You should tell her how you feel."

"It would break her heart even more. I do love her, but I need to live away from her, at least part of the time. I'm at the age where I need to make my own life, find a husband, have my own children. But she's so afraid a male deity will abuse me or, worse, swallow me."

"She lived for many years in the belly of her father," Apollo pointed out as he brought his chariot to a halt near his temple, but the people gathered there were unaware of their invisible presence.

"She told me," Persephone said.

"Only Hestia endured it longer than your mother did. Both of them were terribly affected by it. Neither wants anything to do with a husband. Hestia refuses to have children of her own. Demeter only agreed to have you to help propagate the Olympians."

"Hera was in there with them."

"And she was so grateful to Zeus for freeing her, that she loves him more than anyone. But even she distrusts husbands and fathers, especially those in power." He stepped from the chariot and then turned to offer her his hand.

She took his hand and stepped from his chariot onto the rocky landscape. "Can you see my future? Can you tell me what to do?"

"I see you with the lord of darkness," he said. "And, although I see some happiness, I see a profound sadness—a horrible betrayal."

"I can't believe it!" She clutched her hand to her heart and held back tears.

"Fly with me over to the small village of Arachova. Let's eavesdrop on your mother."

CHAPTER TWENTY-FOUR

Metaneira's Choice

Demeter carried the lifeless Demophoon in her arms as she flew from the Underworld back to the village near the base of Mount Parnassus, where she saw a crew of men already at work on her temple. She flew further west to their small village and found Metaneira at home sobbing, while her daughters attempted to console her.

As soon as Demeter entered the house, Metaneria leapt to her feet and rushed to the goddess. Her four daughters were close at her heels.

"Is he alive?" she cried peering at the baby in Demeter's arms.

"My baby brother!" the youngest girl said. "Is he safe?"

"Not yet," Demeter said to them gravely.

"Not yet?" the oldest daughter asked.

Metaneira looked expectantly at Demeter. "So he will be soon?"

"Maybe. It's not that simple," Demeter said.

"Please, dear Goddess," the second to the oldest begged. "Explain it to us!"

At that moment, Celeus entered the house. He fell to his knees just inside the door.

"You've returned! Do you have my son?"

His daughters fell to their knees as well, following their father's example. Only Metaneira remained standing, her face close to the lifeless baby.

"He's still not alive," Metaneira said. "She's about to explain, aren't you, dear Demeter?"

"I saw Hermes with Charon on the raft as they were entering the gates of the Underworld," Demeter said. "Cerberus growled at me, so I remained at a distance, and I cried out to Hermes to give me Demophoon's soul."

"And what did he say?" Metaneira asked.

"He said I had to wait for Lord Hades, so I did."

At the mention of Hades's name, the four girls gasped.

"We don't say his name in this house," the second to the youngest reminded Demeter.

"Please, Goddess," Celeus said. "Continue."

"The lord of darkness told me there was only one way he could return Demophoon's soul."

"And what is it?" Metaneira asked anxiously.

"Someone must take his place."

More gasps filled the room.

Metaneira fell to her knees, clinging to Demeter's legs.

Everyone in the room, including Demeter, was crying.

In another moment, Metaneira said, "I'll do it."

The four daughters jumped to their feet and crowded their mother.

"Please, don't, Mamá!" the youngest cried. "You can't leave us!"

"No, Mamá! I won't let you!" the oldest said.

"I'd rather die than let you do it!" the second to the youngest said.

"No, Ophelia! It can't be you, either!" the second to the oldest cried. "Mamá please! Demophoon is in heaven. Let him stay!"

"I agree," Celeus said, climbing to his feet. "My beloved Metaneira, I'm so sorry for your grief. I feel it too. But you'll break my heart beyond repair if you do this thing."

Metaneira stood, and, unsteadily, went to her husband. She cupped his face in her hands as tears streamed down both of their cheeks. "I love you. I don't want to leave you. But my instinct is to save my son. Can you understand that?"

"Your daughters need you, too," he said.

"That's true, Mamá!" the oldest cried. "Oh, please! Oh, please don't go!"

Demeter's heart was breaking, too. She hated Hades for making her do this. Surely, as the lord of the Underworld, he could have thought of a better way.

Metaneira turned to her daughters and embraced each one. "Listen to me, my sweet little lambs. I love you more than life itself. And I would do this for *any* of you."

"No!" they cried.

"You are all old enough to help your Babá, yes?" their mother said through her tears. "And you will take good care of your baby brother? You won't blame him for my death? He is innocent, you know."

"Mamá, please!" they begged.

Metaneira turned to Celeus. "If I don't do this thing, I will be miserable for the rest of my life—knowing I might have saved my son. If I hadn't been given this choice—if he'd died and there was nothing I could do—I might have moved on. But knowing I could save him…it will kill me if I don't. There's no question in my mind. I need to do this."

Celeus gave Demeter an accusing glare. His eyes told her that he blamed her, but he said nothing.

Demeter couldn't stand to be in the presence of the grief-stricken family a moment longer. "You must choose," she said. "The body is growing cold."

"I have no choice," Metaneira said. "Take me to the Underworld."

As Demeter god-traveled with the baby and his mother away from the village, she tried to ignore the wails and cries of the family members left behind.

CHAPTER TWENTY-FIVE

Hades in Delphi

Hades hadn't been in his chambers long when he was struck by an idea. The girl on the mountaintop that had been taken with Persephone by the red dragon—Psyche was her name—she had said that the oracle at Delphi—Apollo's oracle—had instructed her father to bring her to wait for the dragon. If that was true, then Apollo may know who this dragon was.

Hades quickly checked on all the regions of his kingdom. There were twenty-three new souls in Tartarus, including Tantalus, awaiting their punishment, but Hades had no time for them right now. He wished, as he had many times before, that he had help from other gods in his kingdom. Hermes had too many responsibilities, and Charon could never leave his raft. The judges were always too busy judging. And even though the Fates had the power of disintegration so they could spin, measure, and cut the threads of every soul, they loved their games of luck and would never consent to help him. Frustrated that he still hadn't found Persephone, he returned to the main room of his palace and summoned Hermes once more.

"Yes, my lord?" the swift Hermes asked.

"Find Apollo and ask him about the red dragon, will you? Then report back what you can."

"I will do it." Then, as swiftly as he had appeared, Hermes vanished.

A moment later, Hermes reappeared. "Apollo knows who the red drag-on is, but he swore to keep that information secret."

Hades hopped from his throne and paced the room before ap-proaching Hermes and saying, "That dragon took someone I love."

"Apollo said the beast was friendly," Hermes said. "And you know he can't lie."

Hades took a step back. "Indeed. This is a mystery."

"Is it Persephone you're worried about, my lord?"

Hades lifted his chin. "Do you know where she is?"

"I'm not at liberty to say."

Hades took a fistful of Hermes's cloak and pulled him close. "But she's safe?"

Hermes lifted both arms in the air. "She is. I swear."

Hades released Hermes and returned to his throne, wishing Perseph-one could hear his prayers. *Do you intend to break my heart?* he asked her, doubting she would hear.

Then, to his great surprise and relief, she replied: *No, but I intend to protect mine.*

The gods could rarely reach one another telepathically from great distances because of all the fortification wards they carried on their bod-ies, protecting them from one another. This was why Hermes was their messenger. So it was unusual that Persephone could hear him—unless she wasn't very far away.

Are you safe? I saw the red dragon take you. I followed but couldn't get through the clouds.

I'm safe, Persephone answered.

May I know where you are?

Yes.

To Hermes, Hades flashed a grin and said, "You may go."

Hermes disappeared.

After Helios had already dropped below the mountains in the west, Hades took his chariot across the dark night toward Mount Kronos, also known as Mount Parnassus, to the Oracle at Delphi, which was situated almost directly above his underground palace. The region had another name: it was called the omphalos, or navel, of Gaia, because it was the center of the earth, and the sacred place Zeus went to speak to their grandmother.

From his chariot in the sky, Hades noticed villagers below leaving what appeared to be a partly constructed temple at the base of the mountain to the west of Apollo's temple. Then he saw Demeter among them, and he wondered what she was up to. Was she aware that Persephone was only a few miles away? Was Demeter plotting to reclaim her daughter?

Then he saw Apollo's chariot, parked and abandoned below. He brought Swift and Sure to a halt beside Apollo's bright red mares, wondering where he and Persephone had gone to. He didn't sense them in Apollo's temple.

I'm here, beside Apollo's chariot, he prayed to Persephone. *Where are you?*

Meet us in the cave behind the oracle, Persephone said.

Her tone was somber. Maybe she was still angry over what he'd said about Aphrodite being to blame for the Trojan War, or about the disgraceful way Helen had broken her marriage vows.

Hades passed the old oracle, who sat on the tripod over the chasm, where Apollo's inspirational mist informed the old woman of the future. He saw Psyche and her father among the mortals gathered there with their torches in the night to hear what Apollo had to say. Above the oracle was Apollo's cave. Hades flew to it and found the god of light embracing Persephone, who sobbed against his chest.

Blood rushed to Hades's face, and jealousy squeezed his throat. "Has something happened?"

"How could you?" Persephone asked, looking up at him through wet lashes. "How could you break my mother's heart?"

CHAPTER TWENTY-SIX

Demeter at the Gate

Demeter god-traveled with the mother and baby to the riverbank near the gate of the Underworld and called out for Hades. "I've done as you asked! I've brought you the mother!"

"I'm frightened," Metaneira said through a chattering jaw as she looked across the river at Cerberus. "Will you stay with me until the very end?"

Demeter squeezed the mother's hand. "I will stay with you for as long as I'm allowed."

"Will I be able to see Demophoon before I go? Just once, to say goodbye?" She glanced at his lifeless body cupped in one of Demeter's arms.

"I will ask. It's not up to me."

Metaneira kissed the goddess's hand. "Thank you."

The enormous black iron gate screeched open, and Demeter thought about making a run for it—racing inside to find Demophoon and Persephone and taking her chances against Hades—but before she could commit to the idea, Charon emerged from the gate with an empty raft.

As soon as he passed the threshold, the gate screeched closed behind him. Cerberus watched attentively.

"Where's Hades? I need to speak with him!" Demeter shouted from across the river.

"He's not at home."

"What?" Demeter was outraged. "How can he call himself the lord of the Underworld if he's so seldom here?"

Charon said nothing in reply but slowly pulled his pole through the river.

"What about Hermes?" Demeter asked. "Can't he help me?"

"He hasn't yet come with the next batch of souls," Charon remarked.

"Is there no one in charge down here that can help me?" Demeter complained.

Again, Charon did not reply.

"He's a man of many words," Demeter muttered beneath her breath.

"What's wrong?" Metaneira asked, her teeth still chattering. "Is something amiss?"

"I guess we'll just have to wait," Demeter said with a tinge of anger she couldn't suppress, not even for the frightened woman. How she hated Hades. He'd abducted her daughter, he'd refused to allow Demeter to see her, and now he was destroying a family dear to her heart.

"I don't know how much longer I can take this," Metaneria said. "I may just die of fear right here and now."

"Wait, that's it." The idea that came to Demeter was horrific, but it was worth giving it a try. What did she have to lose?

"What?"

Demeter conjured her dagger. "The surest way to get a god of death to come to us is to force his hand."

Metaneira's eyes grew wide. "Is it time, then?"

"I'm afraid so, my dear," Demeter answered. "But it will be quick. One sharp pain, and then it'll be over. Then you'll be free."

Metaneira nodded, though her teeth continued to chatter. "I'm so afraid. Do you suppose you could sing to me, like you did as you rocked Demophoon to sleep?"

Tears now spilled down Demeter's face as she smiled at the woman. "I promise to look after your baby and to protect him as if he were my own."

Metaneria didn't say it, but she unwittingly prayed, *Isn't that what you always wanted?* Aloud, Metaneria said, "I would be forever grateful, Goddess."

Demeter sang her soft tune as she raised the dagger.

Sweet little cherub, don't you cry.

Sleep will be coming, and soon you'll fly

Up to the stars and into the night

A kiss for Selene and all is bright.

As she sang, Demeter drove the dagger into Metaneria's sweet heart, and by the time she'd reached the final word, Metaneira's body had collapsed onto the riverbank.

Quickly, Demeter removed her dagger from Metaneira's chest and drew a circle in the mud around Metaneira's unconscious body. Then she marked the four cardinal points and stood inside the ring, as Hecate had once taught her to do. Neither Hermes nor Hades would get the mother's soul until a deal was made.

CHAPTER TWENTY-SEVEN

Fear and Rage

The hair stood up on the back of Hades's neck as he gazed at Persephone in Apollo's arms. For the first time in his life, he was afraid.

He hadn't been afraid as a child when he'd realized his own father had swallowed him.

He hadn't been afraid as a man when his brother saved him and, together, they fought against their father and the other Titans.

He hadn't been afraid as a lord when he became master of Cerberus, the Hydra, and the dead.

But that look on Persephone's face—she was horrified by him, thinking he'd intentionally broken her mother's heart—frightened every fiber of his being. This was the woman with whom he was destined to spend eternity, and before they'd even visited the marriage bed, she already despised him.

"It's not what you think," Hades said gently.

"Then educate me," she demanded.

Hades glanced at Apollo, who stroked Persephone's hair. The healing god was trying to comfort and calm the goddess, but he was only filling Hades with jealous rage.

Hades bit back the rage and said, "You give me too much credit if you think I get to decide who lives and who dies."

"What he says is true," Apollo said. "Only the Fates decide."

"But you're the one who told my mother that she could make a trade," Persephone said to Hades.

"Because the Fates allow it," Hades said. "And because she begged me to help her. Don't you see? I was trying to *help* your mother."

"It only made things worse," Persephone accused. "The family might have healed from the loss of the infant, but those girls and their father…you should have seen their suffering. You should have heard their cries. If you had, you'd never make such deals."

"I didn't demand the trade," Hades said, the rage and frustration rising in his throat. "I let your mother know it was an option. She could have decided to let things be. She wanted to save the baby because she'd come to hoard him and his love in the same way she does you and yours."

Persephone's mouth dropped open.

Hades heard Demeter calling to him from the gate below. "I must go. Your mother wants to make her trade."

"Take me with you," Persephone insisted.

<u>CHAPTER TWENTY-EIGHT</u>

Persephone's Third Descent

Hades was silent as he drove Persephone in his chariot, and she wasn't sure what to say, so she stood silently beside him.

"You were right," he said at last. "A woman has the right to choose her husband. What I said before about Helen and Menelaus…I was wrong."

Persephone's throat felt like sand, and the heat left her face. She struggled for the right words to explain that she, too, had been wrong to so quickly defend Aphrodite without having all the facts. And she'd been wrong again when she'd assumed Hades had been the cause of her mother's heartache.

"I don't know what to say," she finally admitted.

He turned and met her eyes. "Say you love me."

She glanced at his mouth, recalling the pleasure his lips had given her not long ago—too long ago. But what of Apollo's warning of a betrayal? Would Hades break her heart? Only the Fates knew the future with certainty.

Then, before she could answer him, he kissed her.

She closed her eyes, which filled with tears—but they were tears of joy. The feel of his breath against her revitalized her senses. She yearned to be back in his arms like she'd been on Mount Thor as they'd watched with smiling faces the sparkling Northern Lights.

Before either of them could say anything more, they'd arrived at the gate and Demeter.

Hermes and Hecate were there with her on the riverbank, where she stood close to the fallen figure of Metaneira. Demeter still clutched the body of Demophoon in one arm.

Hades helped Persephone from the chariot.

"Is the mother dead?" Persephone asked him.

"It doesn't appear so. Let's go see what's going on."

They joined Hermes and Hecate, outside of a ring Demeter had drawn around her and Metaneira.

"What's going on here?" Hades asked.

"That's what I'm trying to figure out," Hermes replied.

"Persephone!" Demeter cried. "Oh, I'm so relieved to see your precious face! Are you okay? Have you been harmed?"

Tears streamed from Demeter's eyes, and Persephone felt the cold, hard clench of guilt. "I'm fine, Mother. Truly."

Demeter narrowed her eyes at Hades. "I knew you were lying to me! I knew you had her all along!"

"Why have you drawn this circle?" Hades asked, ignoring her accusations.

"To parley with you."

"Be careful," Hecate warned her. "Are you sure this is what you want to do?"

"Hades has already promised to return the soul of Demophoon if I give him Metaneira's."

"That's true," Hades acknowledged.

"Before I allow Hermes to carry off this poor mother's soul," Demeter said, "I want Demophoon's soul back, and I want his mother to be able to say goodbye to him."

"You do realize that when her body expires, nothing can hold back Death?" Hermes asked.

Demeter pointed her bloody dagger to the ground. "This is a powerful circle."

"And an unnecessary one," Hades said.

Hecate took another step closer. "It won't hold back Death. Nothing can."

Hades lifted his chin. "Hermes, bring me Demophoon. He's in the Elysian Fields."

Hermes vanished.

"Listen to me, Mother," Persephone said. "I think this is a mistake. The family needs *her*!" Persephone pointed to Metaneira's unconscious body. "Let the baby go."

"She's made her choice," Demeter said. "She wants to do this for her child, just as I would do anything for you! In fact, I would give Hades *both* souls and mine, too, if he would release you from this hell!" Then she added, "But don't you worry. I'll find a way to free you. Zeus even said Hades will have to give you up!"

"But I love him," Persephone said.

Persephone heard the slight intake of air by Hades. She'd surprised him, but he was keeping it well hidden from everyone else.

Demeter gawked. "What? I don't believe you."

Hermes appeared with Demophoon's soul.

"It's true." Persephone took Hades's hand and clutched it in her own. It was large, and hot, and strong. She never wanted to let it go.

"You must be under a terrible spell," Demeter said. "I can't imagine anyone wanting to be here, with *him*!"

"Be careful," Hecate warned softly.

"Please don't say such things," Persephone said.

"Do you want to make this trade, or not?" Hades asked angrily.

"Yes!" Demeter pointed her dagger at Hades. "But let Metaneira say goodbye to her son! And then let me say goodbye to my daughter!"

Hermes glanced at Hades, who nodded.

Hermes took the soul of Demophoon and placed it inside the baby's body. The baby gulped for air and then began to wail. Demeter dropped her dagger, pulled a bottle from the folds of her silk gown, and nursed him. His cries became soft, sweet suckling sounds.

Persephone squeezed Hades's hand, happy to see the baby alive again, and happy to see her mother's joyful expression. She knew it would be hard for the family to lose their mother, but at least the boy would live.

Then Hermes lifted the airy soul from the body of Metaneira and pointed her in the direction of her son. At first, the woman seemed confused, but then when she gazed upon the face of her baby, a smile lit up her transparent face. She leaned over and kissed her son on his forehead before Hermes led her away, where Charon and his raft were waiting.

Demeter sang the song she used to sing to Persephone when she was a little girl:

Sweet little cherub, don't you cry.
Sleep will be coming, and soon you'll fly
Up to the stars and into the night.
A kiss for Selene and all is bright.

"I love you, Mother!" Persephone shouted as the memories of her childhood swept over her. She did love her mother, and she did want to be with her, but not constantly.

Demeter met Persephone's eyes with a smile that was at once joyful and sad. "I've missed you more than you can know. If only I could have you back. If only there was something I could do to break whatever spell he's put you under. I promise I'll get Zeus to help me again!"

Persephone walked up to the very edge of the circle Demeter had drawn in the sand. "Come out of there and embrace your daughter."

Demeter raced toward Persephone and wrapped her one free arm around her daughter, embracing her with the baby between them. Then she wept against Persephone's shoulder. "My love for you is more than I can bear. You are my sweet, precious girl, and I love you so much. I've always been so grateful that you were born to me."

Tears rolled down Persephone's face as she clung to her mother, remembering her scent and the comfort of her arms. "Oh, Mother! I love you, too."

Demeter ran her fingers through Persephone's hair. "It worries me so, knowing you are down here in this repugnant place where all the dead dwell. And I don't trust *him*. How can I have any peace of mind? I'll be nothing but a ball of nerves for the rest of time, unless I get you out."

"You could come and visit me," Persephone suggested, though she worried her mother would move in with her and control her life again.

"Here?" Demeter said. "There must be another way."

"What if *I* visit her?" Hecate offered. "I could let you know how she is."

"You would do that?" Demeter asked her old friend. "Could you bear it?"

"I don't mind the Underworld," Hecate said. "I've served Lord Hades many times by gathering the lost souls. I help them find their way."

Hecate glanced at Hades, who gave her a nod of approval.

"That would give me some peace of mind," Demeter said. "But shall I really never see my daughter outside of this dreadful house of dead? Can I never spend delightful days strolling with you in the sunshine, baking bread in our beautiful rooms on Mount Olympus, or singing together in the great hall as Apollo plays his golden lyre?"

An idea came to Persephone. "In six months, I'll come and stay with you on Mount Olympus."

Demeter lifted her face and studied her daughter's expression. "How is that possible? Why can't you come with me now? If no spell is holding you here, come with me this instant!"

"Because…" Persephone took a deep breath. Should she tell her mother the truth? Should she tell her she needed to get away from her smothering love at least part of the year? Should she say she needed to live her own life? Or did her mother need a gentler touch?

Hades cleared his throat. "She can't go now because she ate my pomegranate seeds."

"What?" Demeter looked back and forth between Hades and Persephone.

"That's right," Persephone said, hiding her relief. *Nice job, quick thinker*, she said telepathically to Hades.

"But what does that mean?" Demeter asked.

"It means I have to stay here with Hades for six months out of the year, every year." She smiled at Hades. "One for every seed I ate."

"But for six months of every year, I get you back?" Demeter asked.

That seems too long a time for a wife to be away from her husband, Hades said to Persephone telepathically.

I know, but it's the best I can do. I love her, and soon she'll have to give Demophoon back to his family, and she'll be all alone. I'm all she's ever had.

So be it, Hades said. *If that's the only way I can have a happy wife, I'll take what I can get.*

Persephone's heart filled with even more love and desire for Hades.

"Yes, Mother," Persephone finally said. "For half of every year, you'll get me back."

Demeter kissed her daughter's cheek. "I'll be counting the days."

<u>CHAPTER TWENTY-NINE</u>

Light in the Underworld

Hades opened his eyes and wondered how long he'd been asleep. Persephone was still curled up beside him in his bed with the blanket half on and half off her slight but curvy form. She was still asleep with her face turned toward him, her cheek in the crook of his arm. She was breathtaking with her long lashes, slightly up-turned nose, and pink, full lips—utterly kissable. Her creamy skin and long, soft hair begged to be touched. He took a deep breath and breathed in her sweet scent. She smelled like lilacs.

So this is what happiness felt like.

In the two weeks that she'd been in his kingdom, this was the first time they had slept together.

She yawned and stretched her arms, and he blanched when she hit him in the jaw. She was stronger than she looked. His chin smarted for a moment.

Then she opened her eyes. "I'm so sorry! I didn't mean to punch you!"

He laughed and rolled onto his back. "I needed to be knocked back into reality."

She hugged his chest and lay there, making him want her again.

"This *is* reality," she said. "Isn't it? Or am I still dreaming?"

He kissed the top of her head. "It feels like a dream."

"Then let's never wake up."

He stroked her hair. "I've neglected my duties too long."

"I can help you. Isn't that what a wife is for?"

"You might not enjoy this work."

She lifted her face to meet his eyes, resting her chin on his chest. "What work?"

"Tantalus is waiting to be punished, along with a few others."

"Is Agamemnon there yet?" she asked. "Because I wouldn't mind helping with *him*."

He chuckled. "Not yet. But I heard Artemis saved Agamemnon's daughter at the last moment."

"Really? How?"

"By replacing her with a doe."

"Poor doe."

"Lucky Iphigenia."

"I still want to wring his neck. Even if he didn't kill his daughter, he intended to."

"Good point. Maybe one day you'll have the opportunity."

She sat up with the blanket draped around her shoulders, and he immediately missed the feel of her against him. "To Tartarus then, dear husband?"

"Let's go."

Before he'd climbed out of bed, Persephone clutched her abdomen.

"What is it? Are you ill?"

Her face was full of bewilderment. "No, not ill. I think…Can it be? So soon?"

"What? What is it?"

"I think I'm pregnant!"

Hades's jaw dropped—nearly to the floor.

She smiled up at him from the bed. "That was fast!"

"I can't believe it." He wanted to shout. He'd never felt so much joy in his life. Was this allowed? Was one person allowed to feel so happy? He swept her up in his arms, cradling her as if he were holding their child. "Tell me what you need. More pillows? Ambrosia? Soft slippers for your feet?"

She laughed and hugged his neck. "I'm only pregnant, not an invalid. Put me down, you silly thing."

He kissed her before setting her on her feet.

"Now let's get to work," she said as she slipped on her silk robes. "I can't believe I've been here for two weeks and have done nothing but played when there was work waiting for you. You should have spoken up."

He put on a fresh pair of trousers. "If we couldn't take a proper honeymoon, what's the use of being gods?"

He'd wanted her to see all of his favorite places around the world, including a few special places in his kingdom.

"I suppose you're right," she said smiling up at him. "I'm just eager to show you how useful I can be."

They went to Tartarus to deal with Tantalus.

"What do you have in mind for him?" Persephone asked.

"He tried to feed his own son to the gods," Hades said. "He has a sick appetite that should never be quenched."

Hades conjured a bunch of grapes and made them hang in the air, just above the old king's reach.

"That should teach him a lesson," Persephone agreed. "What is it with kings and their eagerness to sacrifice their children?" Persephone rubbed her abdomen.

"Our children will never know that pain," Hades said. "I guarantee it."

"Don't be too sure about that," came a voice from around the corner. It was Tiresias talking to them from the seers' pit beyond the wall where the Phlegethon did not flow.

"Who said that?" Persephone asked.

"Don't mind him," Hades said. "It's just old Tiresias. Have you heard of him?"

"No, I don't think so."

"He speaks in riddles about the future."

"Why is he here?"

"Prophesizing is one of the unpardonable sins," Hades explained. "Only the Fates know the future, and they don't like it when mortals play god."

"But what about Apollo's oracle?" she asked.

"It's the one exception, only because Apollo is a god of prophecy and can choose to guide humankind."

Persephone nodded. "I see."

"So do I," Tiresias called. "I'm blind, but I can see."

"Let's go ask him what it is he wants to say," Hades suggested. "He seems to know something about our children."

Persephone grabbed Hades by the hand and held him back. "No. As the Fates say, nothing good can come from knowing the future. I don't want to hear it."

He had a feeling she knew something—something foreboding. He leaned down and kissed her. "As you wish."

Her expression changed.

"What is it?"

"Psyche. She's praying to me from the gate. Why would she be here? I wonder what's happened."

"Let's go find out."

Together, they god-traveled just outside the main gate.

Psyche waited on the riverbank, where Demeter had stood just two weeks ago.

"Aphrodite sent me," Psyche called out across the river. "The goddess asked me to bring back her black box of beauty—the one she gave you before you found me on Kythira. Do you have it?"

"Yes." Persephone conjured it and then flew to Psyche's side. Hades remained beside Cerberus, not wanting to frighten the mortal.

"Do you know why she asked you to come for it instead of asking me for it herself?" Persephone asked the girl.

"She's testing me—or punishing me. Or both."

"But why?"

"It turns out Cupid still loves me and wants to marry me," Psyche said with a hopeful smile. "But his mother wants to make sure I'm good enough for him—that I'm trustworthy."

That sounded like a reasonable idea to Hades. He thought of his child growing in Persephone's womb. He'd want the same for him or her.

Persephone handed the box over to Psyche. "Remember not to open it. Her beauty is there, but beside it is a curse."

Psyche nodded. "I remember, Goddess. Thank you." Then she dropped to the ground at Persephone's feet. "Please help me, however you can. You helped me before, and I'm grateful. But if there's anything more you can do to help me be with my one, true love, I'd be eternally grateful."

Persephone glanced across the river at Hades, who only shrugged. He was just learning about love himself. What could he do?

"I'll do what I can," Persephone said. "Now go."

CHAPTER THIRTY

Spring Returns

Persephone clung to Hades as he drove them in the chariot across the Grecian skies to Mount Olympus. She couldn't believe six months had already passed them by. She held him so close, so tightly, that for a moment she worried she'd become her mother and was smothering the person she loved. She loosened her grip, but as soon as she had, he pulled her against him and kissed her.

In another moment, they arrived at Mount Olympus, her home for the next six months.

"If you need me—for any reason whatsoever," he said, wiping a tear from her cheek, "I'll be here. If you can't reach me through prayer, send Hermes."

"Thank you," she said.

"And take care of that baby of ours," he said with a slight catch in his voice. She could tell he was hurting even though he fought to hide it from her.

"I will," she said. "But what if it comes while I'm here, away from you?"

"This is the best place to birth a child," Hades said. "There's no safer place on earth."

He kissed her again and again. She didn't want to leave his arms, but she knew it was time.

She stepped from the chariot and stood near the gate as her tears spilled from her eyes.

He tapped the reins against Swift and Sure and sped away.

As soon as Persephone walked inside the gates of Mount Olympus, her mother was there, waiting for her with open arms.

"My precious girl!" Demeter cried. "I'm so happy to see you! I've missed you more than you can possibly imagine!"

Together they entered the main hall. Not many of the other Olympians were at home—including Hera, which was a surprise. Zeus was there, along with Hephaestus.

Hecate was waiting for Persephone in Demeter's rooms with her polecat, Galin, beside her. Hecate and Galin had gone to visit Persephone twice during her six months with Hades, but, both times, Persephone had felt as though the goddess and her familiar were spying on her. Persephone had kept her distance from her mother's friend *and* her scrawny weasel.

"Welcome home," Hecate said with a friendly smile.

"This isn't my home anymore," Persephone replied.

A few days after Persephone's arrival, Aphrodite knocked on Demeter's door and invited Persephone to her chambers to discuss something important. When Demeter asked what it was about, Aphrodite snubbed her by saying it was a private matter.

Persephone followed Aphrodite, into her beautiful rooms and, as she took a seat on the fluffy white couch, said, "Thank you. It's only been three days, but I needed a little break from my mother."

Aphrodite narrowed her eyes and took a step toward the couch. "I heard what you did. You betrayed me at Kythira. You told Psyche the truth about my black box of beauty."

"The poor girl was miserable." Persephone held up her palms. "She wanted to die. If I remember correctly, you wanted that, too. I simply told her how she could manage it."

"It was supposed to be a test."

Persephone crossed her arms. "She didn't want more beauty; I can tell you that. Besides, *your son* stopped her from carrying out her plan—not me."

Aphrodite sighed and linked her fingers together. "Yes. I know."

Persephone was about to change the subject when Aphrodite sat in a chair across from her and said, "You might be interested to know that Psyche *did* open my box this time."

Persephone jumped to her feet. "Oh, no! Is she dead?" Persephone had come to care about the mortal girl.

Aphrodite rolled her eyes. "Of course not. My son's in love with her. I couldn't let that happen."

Persephone shivered. "I can't believe she opened it. Do you think she intended to kill herself?"

"Oh, no. She wanted more beauty."

"But she said beauty was a curse."

"That was before a *god* told her he loved her. Now she's just like the rest of us. She'll do anything to hold on to her power."

Persephone took a step back and shook her head. "I'm not like that."

Aphrodite laughed. "Of course not. Instead, you've found a delightful way to shirk all responsibility."

Anger flared in Persephone's chest. "How dare you?"

"I've heard about your little arrangement. You spend six months in the Underworld bedding that sexy lord of darkness and the other six months appeasing your sick mother up here, baking bread and listening to music. You don't actually have any responsibilities of your own."

Persephone straightened her back and balled her fists. "That's not true. I'm the goddess of spring."

"So?"

"Everyone knows that lovers love best when spring is in the air. They wouldn't even have flowers to give one another if it weren't for me."

Before Aphrodite could say another word, Persephone added, "And now I'm *more* than Spring. Now I help avenge those mortal souls who need avenging. I help Hades punish evildoers in Tartarus."

Aphrodite's eyes widened. "Why, that's repulsive!"

Persephone took a few steps toward Aphrodite and looked down at her with a hard, cruel smile. "And necessary. So have a little respect."

Then she god-traveled from Aphrodite's chambers back to her mother's.

A few weeks later, Apollo and Hermes had been giving a concert, accompanied by the muses, for Zeus, Hephaestus, Aphrodite, Hestia, Demeter, and Persephone when Hera returned to Mount Olympus. Hestia had told Persephone that the queen of the Olympians had been worried about her golden apple tree ever since Eris had stolen an apple from it. Even though the tree was guarded by Ladon, the one-hundred-headed serpent dragon, Hera—according to Hestia—went to station Atlas's three daughters—the Hesperides—at the tree for extra protection. While Hera was gone, she made mischief for the Trojans, whom she despised because of Paris's answer.

As soon as Hera saw Persephone, she said, "You're back."

"Yes."

Hera pushed back her green velvet hood and smoothed her fiery red hair from her face. Then she looked Persephone up and down. "My goodness, that was fast."

"My mother didn't think so. I guess she was more eager to see me than you."

Hera wrinkled her brow. "What are you talking about?"

"My return to Mount Olympus. What are *you* talking about?"

"Your pregnancy. Didn't you know?"

The music stopped, and everyone rushed over to congratulate Persephone. She hadn't meant to keep it a secret; she'd only been worried about how her news would be received, since the Olympians had little love for her husband. It turned out that they were all happy for her.

Except for her mother.

Hera put her hand on Persephone's barely swollen abdomen. "You have three daughters in there, my dear."

Persephone smiled and tears rushed to her eyes. "That's wonderful! I thought I felt more than one. I'm beginning to sense them. Oh, thank you, Hera!" Persephone embraced the queen. Then she asked, "Do you have any idea when they'll be born?"

"It's different for every god and goddess," Hera said. "In fact, they may not all be born at once. One may come, and, weeks later, another. You never know—though Apollo might."

Persephone glanced at Apollo, who stood between Zeus and Hephaestus.

A flash of concern darkened Apollo's features. "I don't see their actual births," he said with a frown.

"But you do see *something*." Persephone said anxiously.

"Not clearly enough to know what it means," he replied.

"Well, now," Hephaestus said. "I've made something for you, and this is as good a time as any to give it." He presented her with a golden crown—not as big as Hera's, but just as lovely. "As the queen of the Underworld, it seemed fitting that you have one."

"Thank you," Persephone said, noticing her mother's frown.

Hephaestus placed it on her head, and Aphrodite surprised her with a kiss. Persephone should have been overflowing with delight; but, Apollo's reaction to her question had her worried.

Sensing her concern, Zeus put an arm around Persephone and kissed her cheek. "Don't worry, my dear. All will turn out well for your babies, I'm sure." He patted her abdomen gently.

"Now, now," Demeter said. "Let's give Persephone some room to breathe."

Persephone was touched by her father's display of affection, but Hera was noticeably changed by it. After the other gods had returned to their thrones to hear more concert-playing, Hera lingered near her and whispered, "If you ever allow Zeus to kiss you like that again, I'll make trouble for you."

CHAPTER THIRTY-ONE

Hades Goes to Troy

After he'd taken Persephone back to Mount Olympus, Hades returned to the Underworld, and the first thing he did was pay old Tiresias a visit. He followed the winding path down, down toward the seers' pit. The iron gate scratched against the rocky floor and ceiling when he opened it. This pit was the only place in Hades's realm where the Phlegethon did not flow, and thus it remained in complete darkness. Yet, Hades could clearly see with his godly eyes the hunched figure of the prophet lurking in the farthest corner.

"You, there," Hades called. "I'd like to have a word with you."

The blind prophet turned toward his lord and shuffled across the pit.

"What were you trying to tell me the other day, old man?" Hades asked.

The prophet's transparent form was bowed, and he had saggy breasts and eyeless sockets. "It was a mistake. I meant nothing by it."

"Don't lie to me," Hades said. "You spoke out of turn, and now you're trying to cover it up. But there was something you saw—something about my children."

"It was you I saw, Lord Hades," Tiresias said. "I saw you committing an evil deed against your babe while it was still in the womb."

Hades blanched. "You must be mistaken." He would never bring harm to his own child.

"No one ever believes me." Tiresias threw up his arms and shuffled away, back to the shadows.

Hades was tempted to call the old prophet back, to force him to explain what he'd seen, even though Tiresias always spoke in riddles; but, then he remembered Priam's daughter, Cassandra.

Everyone was familiar with Cassandra's story: Apollo fell in love with her many months ago and gave her the gift of prophecy; but, when she didn't return his affection, he retaliated by making it so that no one would believe her. When Cassandra tried to warn her father about what would become of Troy, he thought she had gone mad, and he locked her away in a cell in his castle.

If Priam had killed his innocent daughter, Hades would have had to avenge her death by going after him. Hades was glad the king was an honorable man.

And now he wondered what Cassandra might have to say about his unborn child.

Nothing good ever comes from knowing the future.

Hades wrestled with the idea of going to Troy. On the one hand, he knew more harm than good could result from seeking answers; but, on the other hand, the Fates had told him about his future wife, and look how good that had turned out. And shouldn't he do everything in his power to protect his unborn child? Plus, he could check out the status of the war first-hand while he was there. Although he wasn't rooting for one side or the other, he was curious about the greatest war in modern history.

Yes. He would go to Troy.

He decided to leave his chariot behind and, instead, god-traveled to an area not far from the city walls. Under the protection of his helm, he was invisible to more than the mortals who were engaged in battle all around him; he was also invisible to the gods.

And it was a good thing, because Ares was there with the Trojans, guiding their spears into the hearts of the Greeks. And Athena was there, too, blocking Ares's efforts, so that almost an equal amount of bloodshed occurred on both sides.

Hermes was among them as well, ushering all those souls to Charon and his raft.

That was the one good thing about war: it multiplied Hades's kingdom by filling it with slayed heroes—the best kind of souls. They were the most honorable.

Hades supposed that if he ever had to defend his kingdom from attack, the sheer number of souls he had at his command would prevent any power from overwhelming and dethroning him. Yes, the best souls to people his kingdom were the fallen noble warriors.

Hades's attention soon fell on Hector. The oldest of King Priam's sons, he was noble and valiant—in Hades's opinion. Hector had never wanted this war. He had wanted to force his less noble brother Paris to return Helen to her husband. That would have been the right thing to do.

But Paris had refused, and Priam had stood by his son. What could a father do? Hades wondered if Priam felt guilty for making his wife, Hecuba, send Paris away as an infant to be raised by a she-bear on Mount Ida in an attempt to avoid a prophecy that he would one day bring down Troy.

Nothing good ever comes from knowing the future.

Hades shuddered at the thought of Tiresias's accusation and could think of nothing that would motivate him to harm his own baby—unless that baby was a threat to its mother. Was Persephone in danger?

He needed to find Cassandra.

The city walls were massive. He tried to imagine the days when Poseidon and Apollo built them. The two gods had been stripped of their powers and sentenced to a year of servitude among mortals for plotting to capture Zeus. How ironic that today these very walls protected Poseidon's enemies. Hades wondered if the prophetic Apollo had possessed any kind of inkling about the threat that these walls would one day endure in the days that he built them.

Hades slipped past the guards and flew over the wall and into the city of Troy. Although bereft of its men, who'd gone to defend the neighboring areas, the city was otherwise untouched by battle. It glistened under Helios in the morning light, and the marketplace bustled.

The city was crowded with women, children, and old men, but Hades managed to navigate through them toward the palace gates. He flew past another set of guards and then entered the castle proper. Now he just needed to find the cell where Priam held his daughter.

"Mother, please don't cry," came a voice below him.

Along with the voice, he heard weeping. He followed the winding stone stairs to the dungeon. Two women stood on either side of a door made of iron bars. The one on the inside was the beautiful Cassandra, trying to console her mother. The one on the outside was Queen Hecuba, and she seemed inconsolable.

Cassandra spoke to her mother again. "There's nothing to be done. Treasure every moment you have with your children. We will all be dead to you in ten years. But you, my sweet mother, you will live forever, though it will be a life you could never imagine."

"Why do you say such terrible things about you and your siblings?" her mother asked.

"Because they are true."

"And what kind of life could I possibly have without my children?"

"You will take the form of a black dog," Cassandra said. "And you will serve Hecate and Lord Hades."

Hades flinched with surprise, and Hecuba turned her eyes in his direction. She stared through him for many seconds before returning to her daughter and saying, "Please stop this nonsense. If you would only stop, I might convince your father to set you free."

"I'm only in here because no one likes to hear the truth."

Hecuba shook her head sadly before kissing her daughter's hand through the iron bars of the door and walking away—up the stone steps in the direction from which Hades had come.

When he was alone with Cassandra, he removed his helm.

Cassandra screamed.

"I'm not here to hurt you," Hades said calmly. "I need your help."

Hecuba ran back down the steps.

Hades returned the helm to his head.

"What's wrong, my dear?" Hecuba asked breathlessly.

Cassandra took a few deep breaths and shook her head. "I'm okay, Mother. I, I thought I saw something." She looked in Hades's direction.

"You really know how to make a mother worry."

"I'm sorry. Will you please stay with me? I'm frightened."

"Nothing can harm you in there. I wish I could stay all day with you, but I have duties to attend to." Hecuba kissed her daughter's hand once more and left.

"Are you still here?" Cassandra asked once she was alone again.

"Yes. But you aren't going to scream again, are you?"

"That depends on who you are and what you want."

He grinned beneath his helm. "My answers are likely to provoke a scream."

She squeezed the iron bars with both hands. Hades could tell she'd become frightened again, as she was trembling. "I saw you coming," she said softly. "You're Lord Hades."

"Indeed." He removed his helm.

She fell to her knees and turned deathly pale.

"I'm not here to take you," he said. He didn't bother explaining that he wasn't Death. "I've come to ask you about a prophecy. It was told to me by someone who speaks in riddles and makes little sense."

"I'm not sure I can help you. No one ever believes me," she said meekly.

"He seems to have the same problem."

"No one likes to hear the truth."

"He told me I would one day bring harm to my unborn child," Hades said. "But I would never do such a thing. So I came here to ask you what you see. I'm worried my wife will be in danger. It's the only way I can imagine I ever would try to…" He couldn't finish the sentence.

Cassandra slid her hands up the bars and slowly pulled herself to her feet. "I do see you reaching inside the womb of a goddess who lies beside you."

Hades couldn't believe it. "What else do you see?"

"I see two of you," she said. "One of you lies beside the goddess while another of you travels across the sky in your chariot."

"What does that mean?" he asked, maybe with too much desperation in his voice.

"I don't know. I can only tell you what I see."

"And the goddess? Is she in danger?"

"I see sadness. And overwhelming heartbreak."

CHAPTER THIRTY-TWO

Hecate's Promise

Demeter took her daughter's hand and stopped her from leaving her rooms. "Wait."

"But, Mother, Hades is just outside the gate."

"Don't you love me?" Demeter asked as tears filled her eyes. She glanced back at Hecate, who gave her a reassuring nod.

"Of course, I do!" Persephone embraced her mother, and Demeter shuddered against her as the tears fell down her cheeks.

"Tell me you'll miss me," Demeter said, unable to stop herself from stroking her daughter's hair. She was filling with panic, worried this might be the last time she would ever see her daughter again. What if the lord of darkness went back on his word and never let Persephone leave the Underworld again?

"I *will* miss you. I love you very much." Persephone pulled away to look at Demeter's face. "But you must understand that I'm anxious to see my husband."

Demeter pursed her lips. "Perhaps if he were any other husband."

Her daughter heaved a heavy sigh.

"What if you give birth while you're down there, among the dead? What kind of place is that to nurse your babies?"

"It's as good a place as any," Persephone assured her.

"Who will help you deliver them?" Demeter insisted. "Maybe I should go with you."

"No. I don't think that's a good idea."

Demeter lifted her brows. "You want to get away from me."

"No, of course not, Mother." Persephone took both of Demeter's hands. "I just know how unhappy you'll be."

"I'll be unhappy anywhere without you," Demeter pointed out.

"Ask the Muses to cheer you up, or Aphrodite's Graces."

Demeter could barely breathe. The idea of being seen by the other gods in her agitated state was appalling to her. No, she wouldn't stay on Mount Olympus. If she couldn't be with her daughter, she'd go to her new cabin near Demophoon.

Hecate crossed the room and placed a hand on Demeter's shoulder. "I could go with her until the babies are born."

She turned to her friend. "Oh, my dear Hecate! That might make the next six months bearable." To Persephone, she said, "Hades won't object, will he?"

Demeter detected a hint of disappointment in her daughter's face as she said, "Of course not. Now let's not make him wait a moment longer."

Persephone led the way into the great hall, where the other gods stopped what they were doing to bid her farewell. Hephaestus stopped polishing his shield, Apollo stopped playing his lyre, Hermes put down his pipe, Hestia wiped her hands on her apron, and each came to kiss Demeter's daughter on the cheek. When it was Zeus's turn, Persephone turned her head, and Zeus's kiss landed on her hair.

Instead of apologizing, Persephone raced to Aphrodite for a kiss. Demeter noticed Zeus had taken offense at being snubbed, but he said nothing. Hera, on the other hand, seemed rather pleased. The queen followed Persephone and got her kiss, too.

At the gate, Demeter thought she might faint. How had her life come to this? What other mother in the whole wide world had to watch her daughter die again every year?

Persephone waved once more as she stepped through the gate. Demeter could see the chariot waiting on the other side, but she made no effort to look upon the lord of darkness.

Hecate and Galin were about to leave too, when Hecate turned once more to embrace Demeter. "It breaks my heart to see you so unhappy."

"Don't let anything bad happen to her."

"I won't. I promise."

C H A P T E R   T H I R T Y - T H R E E

Persephone's Fourth Descent

There they are again, Persephone said telepathically to Hades. *I'm telling you, they're spying on us.*

She and Hades were soaking in a hot pool. Hades had his arms wrapped around her neck and was making up for lost time. His kissing was amazing, but Persephone did not like having an audience. It seemed like every time she turned around, Hecate and Galin were following her. And there they were, at the end of the tunnel, poking their heads around the corner.

Just ignore them, Hades said as he moved his lips down her neck.

The babies kicked again. Her belly had grown the size of a watermelon, but its shape was constantly shifting. Her feisty daughters romped around as though they were kicking a ball—and right now, that ball was her kidney.

She and Hades had come to this secluded place to avoid the influx of dead from the Trojan War. Charon and Hermes brought in new souls by the dozens. Many of them went straight to Erebus to heal, but there were plenty deserving of torment that were sent to the pits of Tartarus.

It was her job to help her husband punish them.

But she and Hades hadn't been in the mood. They'd been neglecting their duties since she'd first arrived three weeks ago. Their responsibilities were piling up. Hades didn't seem too worried right now as he moved his tongue around her ear, but she was anxious and unable to relax.

If only we had the helm, she said, glancing down the hall again at Hecate and her scrawny weasel.

Hades snapped his fingers, and the helm appeared. He put it on and continued his process of kissing her ear.

Now that they were invisible, she relaxed against her husband and sighed. "That's better," she said, returning his kisses.

Just remember that you can still be heard, he warned.

She'd forgotten. *Let's sneak away, someplace where we can't be found.*

We could go back to my—our—room, he suggested.

She smiled up at him, and in less than a minute they had god-traveled to their bed.

Hades lay on his back and pulled her to him, but her belly got in the way, and the girls were still kicking up a storm.

Persephone caressed her belly and whispered, "Settle down in there."

"I still can't believe we'll soon have three daughters," Hades said gently as he moved his hand alongside hers. "I can feel them moving."

"Believe me, I can, too." And the pain was becoming a bit too much.

"Have you decided what we will call them?"

"I'd like to name them after three flowers that grow near the chasm where we first met."

He beamed down at her. "And which are those?"

"Megaera, Alecto, and Tisiphone."

He kissed the top of her head.

Just then, there was a knock at the door. "Persephone? It's Hecate."

"Can you believe her?" Persephone complained. "She's getting to be as bad as my mother."

"I need to talk to you," Hecate called through the door. "It's important."

Hades brushed the hair from Persephone's eyes. "Maybe you should hear her out."

When Persephone sat up, she felt a streak of pain along her back and abdomen. It took her breath away.

Hades flew from the bed to kneel before her, but she couldn't even look at him, so great had the pain become. She closed her eyes and moaned.

"Are you okay?" he asked her.

"You're going into labor," Hecate said from the door. "That's what I've been trying to tell you."

A rush of water fell between her legs.

Hades went to the door and opened it. "Come in."

"Sometimes I can sense the future," Hecate said. "I'm sorry I've been a pest all day, but I sensed your babies were coming."

Another shooting pain wrapped itself around Persephone's body. She held her breath and bowed over, waiting for it to pass.

"Help her," Hades said to Hecate. "Please."

CHAPTER THIRTY-FOUR

The Birth of the Triplets

Hades watched on with a feeling of terror as Hecate and Galin helped Persephone lie down on the bed. He should have been full of joy and excitement over the fact that his daughters would finally be born, but he feared he was destined to bring one of them to harm. And as much as he wanted to be at Persephone's side, he forced himself to hang back in the shadows.

He stiffened when she cried out in pain. He'd never felt so helpless.

"Dear, Persephone," Hecate said softly. "Bite on this cloth and see if that helps."

"And open your legs," Galin said. "Wider."

"I'm afraid they're all three trying to get out at once," Hecate said. "Maybe it would be best if you went to sleep."

"Should I call Hermes?" Hades asked from the shadows.

"Please do," Hecate replied.

In another moment, swift Hermes was there. "Yes, my lord?"

"I need you to put Persephone into the deep boon of sleep," Hades commanded.

Hermes moved to the bedside and touched Persephone's forehead. Her moaning ceased.

In the next instant, Hades shuddered at the sound of ripping flesh. Then came the squeals of infants as all three babies flew up—one from between Persephone's legs, another from a rip in her belly, and a third from Persephone's mouth. The baby girls flew in a circle around the room and then disappeared.

Hades rushed to Persephone, who lay in a pool of her own blood, looking as though she'd been torn apart by the Maenads. Even though her mouth and body were already beginning to heal from where they'd been ripped, Hades was frightened that she might need more care.

"Can you help her?" he asked Hecate, who, along with her weasel, was busy soaking up the blood.

"It wouldn't hurt to call Apollo," she replied.

Hades turned to Hermes. "Can you bring him to us?"

"What about the babes?" Hermes asked. "Shouldn't I go after them?"

"I'll hunt them down," Hades said. "You get Apollo and bring him here."

"I can do both," Hermes said before he vanished.

"I'll be back as soon as I can," Hades said to Hecate.

Before leaving his domain, Hades reached out with his senses, hoping to detect the triplets somewhere in the Underworld. When he didn't, he god-traveled to the upperworld and soared across the sky, using his hawk-eye vision to scan the earth for his daughters.

Although he hadn't known what to expect, he never, in a million years, would have guessed that the babies would fly away as soon as they were born. Where had they gone to? And were they together? Or scattered?

He hoped they hadn't been summoned by another deity bent on swallowing them. It occurred to him that Zeus or Poseidon might feel threatened by the expansion of the Underworld pantheon. Would either go to such lengths as to swallow his newborn children?

Combing the land, sea, and sky for hours, Hades saw no sign of his runaways. Just as he was about to weep with an overwhelming sense of gloom and hopelessness, Artemis appeared beside him.

"Apollo said you might need help."

He'd never been happier to see her.

They decided to split up—he'd take to the lands and she to the sea. He flew closer to land near the North Pole. His plan was to fly east to west in a southern spiral—as many laps around the globe as was necessary—until he found them.

As he flew, he came to understand how Demeter must have felt as she had scoured the earth for Persephone. Then the sympathy he felt was quickly replaced by suspicion and dread. Had Demeter done this to him?

CHAPTER THIRTY-FIVE

Demeter's Winter Cabin

There was a pain in the pit of Demeter's stomach that wouldn't go away. As much as she tried to remind herself that her daughter was not dead—only gone for a little while—her fear that Hades had deceived her overwhelmed her.

When the only thing a mother ever loved was her child, when a mother had nothing else in the world she cared about, how should she proceed once that child was gone?

How to proceed?

The tears overpowered her as she fought to hold them back. She felt pathetic and weak as she sat there in her winter cabin, trembling. She despised herself for her weakness and lack of motivation. People were praying to her from all over the earth—soldiers injured and dying in battle cried out for solace, for a blessing, for an end to their pain. Metaneira's daughters—not far away—cried prayers to her at night as they tossed and turned in their beds. And she heard Demophoon bleating like a little lamb, missing his mother and missing Demeter, too. How could she comfort any of them when she herself could find no comfort of her own? She felt as if she'd fallen into a pit of gloom and was floundering, fighting for her life and sinking into a sea of despair. Not for the first time, she wished she could die. At least the pain would be over.

As dull as her senses had become from the despair enfolding her, they sparked to attention when she felt the lord of darkness nearing her door.

Why had he come? To taunt her? To tell her she would never see her daughter again?

Full of anger and hatred she flung the door open. "What do you want?"

"Persephone delivered the triplets."

"You didn't come all this way to tell me that news. Has something happened?" She held her hand over her heart and braced for the worst. "Is Persephone hurt?"

"She's recovering. Hecate and Apollo are with her now."

She took a deep breath of relief. If Apollo was with her, she was at least in good hands. But this still didn't explain Hades's appearance at her door so far away from Mount Olympus. "What else? You've come to say something more, I'd wager."

"Our daughters flew away as soon as they were born. I've been scouring the lands looking for them."

"Well, how ironic?" She hadn't meant to say that aloud. Then she realized why he'd come. "You think I summoned them here, don't you?"

"It crossed my mind."

"We're not all scoundrels, you know. Most of the Olympians don't go out of their way to break one another's hearts."

"I never intended to hurt you, Demeter. The Fates told me Persephone would become my wife."

Demeter shuddered, not sure if she should believe him. "So you thought it was okay just to take her?"

"Do you have my daughters or not?"

"I wish I did, but I don't. So go look for them and leave me be!"

CHAPTER THIRTY-SIX

Persephone Awakens

When Persephone opened her eyes, she was alarmed by the faces looking down at her: Hecate, the weasel, Apollo, and Hermes.

Where were her babies? And where was her husband?

"What's happened?" she asked. That's when she felt the pain searing her lips. In fact, her entire body was a giant ball of pain.

"Drink this tonic." Apollo helped her lift her head from her pillow so she could swallow it down. It tasted like pomegranates. "This will help speed up your recovery."

Hecate stroked Persephone's arm. "It's always more difficult with multiples, but you'll be yourself again soon."

"I want my babies," Persephone said. "Will you bring them to me?"

Hermes frowned. "They're sleeping now. We'll bring them to you soon."

Apollo's face turned bright red, and that's how Persephone knew something was wrong. "Apollo? Are my babies okay?"

"I can't see them," he said. "I don't know."

Persephone tried to sit up—but the pain. She lay back down. "Someone tell me what's going on."

"The girls flew away as soon as they were born," Hecate said. "Lord Hades has been searching for them."

Hermes lifted his chin. "I've disintegrated into the thousands and am searching, too."

"Artemis is swimming the seven seas," Apollo said.

"I can't lie here." Persephone fought back tears. "I have to go look for them, too."

She tried once more to get up, and although the pain had lessened, it was still too great to move. She couldn't believe this was happening. Before today, she'd imagined so many different scenarios of how the delivery of her triplets would turn out, but she never once thought they would leave her as soon as they were born. Didn't they love their mother?

For the first time in her life, she had a true glimpse of what her mother must be feeling.

I love you, Mother, she prayed. *I hope you know that I've always loved you.*

Persephone? Are you recovered from the births? Demeter replied telepathically.

How did you know?

Hades was here looking for them.

Persephone sat up, able at last to bear the pain. *I'm much improved and am leaving now to help with the search.*

Hermes interrupted Persephone's prayers. "I've found them! And you won't believe what they're doing!"

CHAPTER THIRTY-SEVEN

The Kindly Ones

Hades had just passed the southern tip of Norway during what must have been his tenth revolution around the world when Hermes suddenly appeared beside him.

"I've found them. They're a few miles outside of Troy."

Now that was a surprise. "What are they doing there?"

"You'll have to see it to believe it. Follow me."

They god-traveled southeast and, in less than a minute, appeared on the edge of a battlefield not far from Troy.

"Look there." Hermes pointed.

Hades followed the line of the other god's finger toward the battlefield where fallen soldiers lay dying. Among them were his babies. But what were they doing?

"They're consoling the wounded," Hermes explained. "I found them here when I came to collect the dead."

Athena suddenly appeared beside them wearing her full battle armor. "Hermes told me that those infants are your daughters," she said to Hades.

"That's right," Hades said. "They were born a few hours ago. They haven't yet nursed at their mother's bosom."

Her gray eyes sparkled when she said, "It seems they made it their very first mission to come here and give blessings to the dying. The wounded warriors have taken great comfort from them and are calling them the Kindly Ones."

"Just look at them," Hermes said in awe.

The palest babe, with her white-blonde curls, placed her plump little hands on either cheek of an injured soldier. "Bless you," she said in her infant's voice just before she kissed him. "May you go in peace, knowing you served your brothers and sisters in the noblest way possible."

"Thank you, Cherub of Mercy," the fallen man cried.

The red-skinned babe, with hair like flames, knelt a few yards away over the body of another fallen soldier. She put her little hand on the soldier's forehead and said, "Bless you, and may you find peace in the Elysian Fields in my father's kingdom."

"Bless you, too, Kindly One," the soldier said.

Athena brushed a tear from her cheek. "These are my men, defeated today by the Trojans with the help of Ares and Aphrodite. More Greeks are coming, and we will eventually bring down our enemies, but today was a great loss. The Kindly Ones have helped my people to endure."

The darkest babe, with chocolate skin and hair the color of ebony, pulled an arrow from a man's leg and wrapped the wound with a bandage. "Bless you," she said as she worked. "You will heal today and fight again tomorrow."

"Thank you, Kindly One," the soldier said. "And tomorrow, we will win."

Hades watched on as his baby daughters, still naked since leaving the womb, flew from soldier to soldier to bless them as they died, or to encourage them as they healed. He was pleased by the fact that they had been born with a purpose. They knew what they were meant to do. That wasn't true of all the gods. Discovering the unique way in which to serve the world and its inhabitants could sometimes take years. But his three little girls flew from the womb ready to serve.

They were the Kindly Ones, the bearers of blessings to the wounded and dying.

Persephone soon appeared with Hermes, Apollo, Artemis, and Hecate. It took all of Hades's strength to hold back his wife, to keep her from interfering. He told her what he'd discovered and comforted her as best as he could, assuring her that their babies would return to her when their duties were finished. Once she understood what their daughters were meant for, she beamed with pride. The gods all watched the three little angels doing their work. They were a lovely and magical sight to behold—beacons of hope in a war-torn field of dead.

CHAPTER THIRTY-EIGHT

Seven Years Later

As the years wore on, Persephone saw less and less of her daughters. They came home to the Underworld every so often to eat and sleep, but they spent most of their time on the battlefields—not just those of the Greeks and Trojans, but in other parts of the world as well.

When they did come home, Persephone took turns holding each one in her arms, singing lullabies, and telling them stories about the Titans and the gods and goddesses of Mount Olympus. She tried to teach each girl to sew, or to bake, or to play a musical instrument, but they had neither the inclination nor the talent to learn.

During the spring and summer, while Persephone lived with her mother on Mount Olympus, she rarely saw her children at all. They came during their second year for the marriage of Cupid and Psyche and brought joy to all of the Olympians on that day. All three girls wore pretty dresses and flowers in their hair and carried baskets of rose petals, which they scattered on the floor before the bride. It was one of the best days for Persephone, to have all three daughters and her mother with her at once. And it was made even better when Hades came to sit on the council that decided to make Psyche immortal.

The next year, Aphrodite gave birth to a set of twins by Ares (which brought great dishonor to Hephaestus, her husband). As with Megaera, Alecto, and Tisiphone, the duties of these new twins became immediately apparent. They flew straight away to the battlefield beside their father and brought fear and panic to the Greeks as they fought against the Trojans. This made the job of the Kindly Ones more difficult as they worked to bring peace to the wounded and dying. The twins became known as Deimos and Phobos.

When the girls turned seven, Athena held a party for them on Mount Olympus, in recognition of their unending work on the battlefield. Persephone had never been happier when she, Hades, and their three daughters were given seats of honor in the grand hall. With the help of Aphrodite's Graces, Hestia prepared an amazing feast which she spread out on the banquet table in the large dining room. Many of the gods and goddesses took their plates back to the main hall, where the Muses delighted them with their concert-playing. Later, the Graces performed a dance, and near the end of the party, Athena gave each of the Kindly Ones a gift.

To Alecto, she gave an adorable black kitten. To Tizzie (short for Tisiphone), she gave a handsome white puppy. And to Meg (short for Megaera), she gave a beautiful parakeet that soon showed he could sing as well as the Muses.

"These shall be your animal companions, immortal, like you," Athena said, her gray eyes shining. "As your familiars, they will bring you comfort when you face the trials of the battlefields to bring blessings to the wounded and dying."

Applause broke out among the gods, and then the gods themselves began to dance as Hermes played his pipe. Persephone had never danced in front of others before, let alone with a partner, so when Hades took her hand and led her to the middle of the great hall beside the other dancing gods and goddesses, her heart sped up with both excitement and fear.

When she looked up at his face as he held her in his arms, swaying with her to the music, there was something in his expression she couldn't quite read. "What is it?"

"I can hardly say." He twirled her under his arm.

"Please try. You have me worried now."

He smoothed back her hair. "Don't worry. I'm merely overwhelmed with emotions—all positive."

She smiled and relaxed the muscles she hadn't realized she'd tensed.

"You've brought so much joy and honor into my life, Persephone. It's more than I ever expected."

"I feel the very same way about you."

As they were about to kiss, Zeus appeared beside them.

"May I have a turn?" her father asked.

Persephone glanced around the room for Hera. The queen was seated at her throne and was watching Zeus like a hawk.

"Why are you suddenly so pale?" Hades asked her.

"I'm afraid I'm not feeling well," she said. "Lord Zeus, do you mind if I sit down?"

Zeus's face reddened as he said, "Of course not, my dear."

She could tell her father felt snubbed once again, even though he tried to hide it by calling out to Ares to engage the god of war in conversation.

As Hades led her back to her seat, Hera came up beside her and whispered, "Well-played, my dear. I shall bestow blessings upon your unborn sons."

Persephone gawked at her queen, utterly speechless.

Hades, who'd overheard, asked, "We're having sons?"

"Twin boys," Hera said. "Congratulations."

Persephone's eyes filled with tears of joy, but when she turned to her husband, he was frowning.

"Aren't you happy?" she asked him.

"Yes. Of course."

He kissed her, but she could tell he was holding something back.

CHAPTER THIRTY-NINE

Avoidance

Hades should have been glad when the day finally came to bring Persephone home from Mount Olympus, but as he flew across the darkening sky in his chariot, he felt nothing but worry.

Two different sources had told him he would bring harm to his unborn babe. He knew he would never do such a thing, but he would be foolish not to take precautions. As long as Persephone was pregnant, he needed to stay away from her.

At first, this wasn't too difficult, for not two days after Persephone's return home, Hercules showed up at the eastern gate to slay the Hydra—why the king in charge of Hercules's punishment had to choose the Hydra, of all monsters, Hades wasn't sure. In his opinion there were plenty of less useful creatures than one of his most trusted guards. Hades worked day and night for one full week to protect the Hydra's body for its resurrection. He had to keep it moist with water from her sinkhole and prevent it from decay. Only one of her nine heads was immortal, so from that time on, the other eight necks sagged to her sides and flapped like wings when she ran.

With that task behind him, he volunteered to help with the Trojan War. When he told Persephone where he was going, she tried to stop him.

"Didn't we say we would remain neutral and not allow the cruelty of men to interfere with our happiness?" she asked him.

He took her in his arms and kissed her on each cheek before saying, "It's hard to turn a blind eye to what's happening, now that Achilles has refused to fight, and the Trojans are attacking them at home. I'm one of the few Olympians not involved. I feel it's my duty to go."

When she continued to frown, he added, "And it will give me a chance to see our daughters in action."

"I could go with you," she said, brightening. "I don't know why I didn't think of it before."

He held her close and kissed her once more. There was nothing he wanted more than to have her at his side. "You need to stay here with Hecate. The boys could be born any day now."

Although she didn't say what was on her mind, she didn't need to. He knew he'd left her wondering why he didn't want to cherish their limited time together, especially when it was true that she could be delivering their sons very soon.

But he didn't want to frighten her with his answer.

A short time later, Hades arrived without his chariot on the beach where the Trojans were headed to attack the Greeks. He found Hera, Athena, Poseidon, and Hephaestus rousing the Greeks from their slumber and encouraging them to prepare for battle.

Hera spotted Hades immediately and flew directly to him. "I hope you've come to help our side."

"I've only come to watch."

"Apollo, Artemis, Ares, and Aphrodite have bolstered the courage of the Trojans. You see that ship there? That's Hector on his way to kill Menelaus."

"Hector is a good man."

"And Menelaus isn't? You've forgotten who was wronged. And to make matters worse, Achilles has gotten his awful mother to convince Zeus to help the Trojans against his own army."

"Why would Achilles do such a foolish thing?"

"To make Agamemnon sorry for dishonoring him. To make the Greeks realize how much they need and depend on him. Oh, he's acting like a child, if you ask me, but if you don't help us against Zeus, we have little hope."

Hades licked his lips—they'd become dry in the sun—and said, "I bet you can find a way to distract your husband long enough for the Greeks to hold the Trojans back."

Hera blushed. "I think you give my female talents too much credit."

"With Aphrodite away from home, I imagine her magic girdle is unprotected. Anyone who wears it…"

"Aha." Hera's blush deepened. "Excellent idea, brother."

He'd wanted to tease her by adding *Why make war when you can make love?*, but he'd had a feeling it would only mortify her and distract her from her mission. As she flew away toward Mount Olympus, he couldn't help but laugh.

Artemis spotted him hovering above the coastline chuckling to himself. He regained his composure as she approached him.

"What did you just do, Lord Hades? I didn't expect you to get involved."

"I'm not involved."

"I saw you give some secret advice to Hera. It looks as though you've chosen a side."

"Not in the least. I assure you."

"Then tell me what you just now told your sister."

"I told her to make love with her husband."

Artemis widened her eyes. "So, you're playing Cupid now?"

"How dare you take that tone with me?"

"You're helping her to distract Zeus, who was about to help us rouse the Trojans."

"It seems you've succeeded on that front without him."

"I searched the seas for hours for your baby daughters. What has Hera ever done for you?"

Although Athena had given his daughters a party and gifts, Hera had done nothing. "What would you have me do?"

Artemis lifted her chin. "Convince Athena and the others to let Paris and Menelaus settle this war once and for all in single combat. The winner gets Helen, and everyone else gets their lives."

This seemed like a reasonable request to Hades. "I'll suggest it, but I can't guarantee they'll agree to it."

"I know." Artemis flew away, back to the Trojan ships not many miles away.

As Hades headed across the beach toward Athena, he spotted Poseidon coming toward him.

"Out of my way, Hades," he said. "Or do you plan to deter me from raising the sea against my enemies?"

Poseidon had a knack for rubbing Hades the wrong way, but instead of bickering with him, he relayed Artemis's idea.

"Menelaus will crush Paris," Poseidon said. "This war could be over by lunchtime."

"Indeed. Shall we take the plan to the others?"

Although an agreement among the gods could not be made before the Trojans attacked, Agamemnon soon caught on to Athena's whisperings in his ear, and he made the offer Artemis was hoping to hear. Before long, the two warriors stood face to face wearing their best armor and holding their sharpest blades. The weapon belonging to Menelaus was crafted by Hephaestus, and this, along with the Achaean's superior strength, made the victory for the Greeks seem imminent. However, Ares had infused Paris with indelible courage, so Hades supposed one couldn't be too certain of a victory for either side.

Hades scanned the crowds of soldiers, which had formed a thick ring around Menelaus and Paris, for signs of his daughters, but since there were no wounded or dying today, the Kindly Ones weren't among them.

Phobos and Deimos were there, however, running through the crowd of Greeks and heading straight for Menelaus.

The two warriors fought bravely for a time until it was apparent that Menelaus would win. Paris had fallen, and Menelaus had raised his sword and was about to bring it down when Aphrodite sprang forward and lifted Paris out of the ring of soldiers in a veil of clouds. Artemis tried to stop her, arguing that the bloody war could finally end, even if it meant a victory for the Greeks, but Aphrodite wouldn't listen, and she carried Paris all the way back to Troy.

Menelaus searched the Trojan ranks for Paris, accusing his enemies of cheating him of his victory. Everyone there was sweating in the hot afternoon sun, their skin burnt and shriveled like rotting tomatoes. When the Trojans swore they didn't have Paris, Agamemnon demanded they return Helen and the war would be over. It looked as though the Trojans were willing to cooperate, but about that time, Hera returned from wooing Zeus and was infuriated to see Paris and the Trojans getting off so easily. She convinced Athena to stir the men into battle. Then she flew directly to Hades and glared at him.

"Why do you look at me like that?" he asked.

"You tricked me."

He wrinkled his brow. "You're mistaken."

"No. You got me out of the way so you could bring the war to an end when you know I want to see every Trojan crushed."

"It was Artemis's idea."

"So now you're on *her* side."

"I'm on no one's side. I told you that."

"Well, I won't forget this," she said, and then she flew away.

Hades had had enough of war for one afternoon. He was about to leave when he spotted his daughters consoling the fallen soldiers. He followed them and was pleased when each of them looked up and noticed him. One by one, they flew to him and kissed him on the cheek.

Hermes was soon there, too, to carry off the souls of the dead. When he noticed Hades flying among them, he came up and said, "I'm surprised to see you here, my lord."

"So am I. I'd rather be anywhere else."

"Why aren't you at home?"

"I have my reasons."

"Then you should join me and my good friend, Dionysus, tonight, for a bit of wine and revelry."

Hades smiled. That was exactly what he needed.

CHAPTER FORTY

Cold Shoulders

Persephone said very little as Hades drove her, along with Hecate and Galin, in his chariot up from the chasm and across the sky toward Mount Olympus. What could she say? In the six months that she'd been home, Hades had spent very little time with her. She was beginning to get the feeling that he'd fallen out of love with her.

It didn't help that her waistline no longer existed and that her belly was once again the size of a watermelon. Although the Kindly Ones had been more active than the twins before their birth, when the boys did kick, it hurt much worse. She supposed her mood had been affected these past months by the anxiety she felt as she anticipated those occasional hard kicks to her innards.

But she would not blame herself for her husband's lack of attention. Her condition was a blessing, not a curse, no matter how unsightly or painful. If he couldn't find it in his heart to love her through her pregnancy, then it was his problem and his loss. She would not beg for his affection.

When they reached the gate, he took her in his arms and kissed her. "I'll miss you, my dear."

Since he'd lost out on so many opportunities to be with her, she wasn't convinced and said nothing.

"Are you feeling well?" he asked. "You don't seem yourself."

"I've felt better."

"For your sake, I hope those boys come soon," he said.

She followed Hecate and the weasel from the chariot and through the gates of Mount Olympus to where her mother was waiting. She walked into her mother's arms and, as the gates closed behind her, she burst into tears.

Demeter lifted Persephone's chin. "Has that scoundrel hurt you?"

Persephone shook her head.

"Then what's wrong?"

"He just hasn't had much time for me lately."

"Good. Who needs him?" Demeter put her arm around her daughter's shoulders as they followed Hecate toward the palace.

Persephone wanted to say, "*I* do. *I* need him," but she kept her mouth clamped shut.

Over the course of the next several days, Persephone noticed that Hera was acting coldly toward her, though she could think of nothing she had done to deserve it. Persephone had made sure never to return Zeus's gaze or to allow him opportunities to kiss her. She'd all but estranged herself from her father because of the queen's threats, and still Persephone received nothing but a cold shoulder in return.

One day, Persephone had had enough of her ill treatment from Hera. The queen had been gone all afternoon, and when she returned, Persephone approached her near the gate.

"What's this?" Hera asked suspiciously. "Why are you out here near the gate instead of inside with the others? Are you waiting for someone?"

"I've been waiting for you."

"Oh? I can't imagine why."

"I think you can. Have I done something to offend you?"

"No, my dear. You've been a perfect peach."

"Then why the cold shoulder?"

"You should ask your husband."

Hera made to fly away, but Persephone caught her by the hand.

"You know I won't see him for many months."

"That's not my problem." The queen pulled her hand away.

Persephone moved in front of Hera, blocking her path. "Whatever he's done, do you think it fair for wives to be held accountable for the sins of their husbands?"

"Perhaps not their wives, but certainly their children."

Persephone clutched her swollen belly as a chill ran down her spine. "But the children are innocent."

"Indeed," Hera said haughtily. "That's what makes harming them such an effective form of punishment for the father." With that, Hera disappeared, using god-travel to get away.

Persephone hovered near the gate, still clutching her abdomen. She wondered what Hades had done to offend their queen. He'd jeopardized the safety of their unborn children while Persephone had worked so hard to steer clear of Hera's wrath. She moved one hand to her heart as a tiny bit of hate for her husband pulsed through her veins. Her love for Hades had once been profound, but now it was weakened by fear and distrust. For a moment she wondered if she wouldn't be better off staying with her mother on Mount Olympus year round.

Just the thought of it brought her to tears. As angry as she felt toward him now, she still loved him and couldn't bear the idea of never being with him again.

CHAPTER FORTY-ONE

Demeter Spies on Hecate

It worried Demeter to see her daughter unhappy. Whenever she asked Persephone why she was so glum, her answers were vague. Demeter did not want to see her daughter fall into the paralyzing grip of depression. Depression had been too good a friend to Demeter—faithfully returning to her every year when Persephone left for the Underworld. Demeter did not want it to become a friend to her daughter, too.

She hoped Persephone's moodiness was caused by the pregnancy, but she feared something more sinister might be at the root. Having no love for Hades, Demeter was sure he'd done something to break her daughter's heart.

One day, while Persephone was walking outside the palace, Demeter took the opportunity to question Hecate.

Hecate sat polishing the brass handle of one of her lamps, which she often used to help people find their way. Galin was curled on her lap, sleeping.

"Do you know why my daughter is so blue, dear friend?" Demeter asked the Titaness.

"Hades wasn't at home much last winter. I think she worries he's lost interest in her."

"Do you think he has?"

"No. But I do think something troubles him."

"Oh, I hope he *has* lost interest in her." Demeter sighed and clasped her hands together. "Then maybe he could be persuaded to let her live here forever!"

"Even if it broke your daughter's heart?" Hecate asked with a frown. "She loves him, you know."

Demeter lifted her hands in the air. "But surely a broken heart can mend."

"That depends on the thing that breaks it. Has your broken heart ever mended?"

"It never has the chance, because it's broken anew every time my daughter leaves."

"Are you saying you would recover if she never came back to you at all?"

Demeter felt sick just by the idea. "No, I suppose not."

They were quiet for a few minutes as Hecate began to polish another of her lamps. Then Demeter broke the silence by asking, "Do you have any idea what troubles the lord of darkness?"

"I have an inkling of an idea—nothing strong enough to mention."

"An inkling of what? Please tell me what you know, Hecate!"

"Let me look into it more thoroughly. Once I can see it more clearly, I'll tell you what I know."

A few weeks later Demeter followed Hecate—as quietly and discreetly as possible—from their rooms and watched the Titaness leave the palace with Hermes. Demeter still had no answers to her daughter's withdrawn and solemn behavior, so she decided to follow them, hoping Hecate might reveal to Hermes the inkling she had about what troubled the lord of darkness.

Waiting outside the gate for the two gods was the winged horse, Pegasus. Demeter could still recall the tiny colt he'd been when he had first arrived years ago after Perseus slew Medusa. He'd been a cute and adorable colt back then, but now he was full-grown and majestic.

Pegasus wore no saddle, but there were saddle bags draped over his back, and attached to them on each of his flanks was a fishing rod. Hermes and Hecate carefully climbed onto his back, too, and then Hermes said, "Let's go!"

The three of them took off.

Demeter followed, wishing she had the helm of invisibility that belonged to the lord of darkness. She changed herself into a hawk and kept a few miles between them, hoping the other gods wouldn't sense her.

Demeter followed them to the northeast across the lands, to a lovely brook amid rolling hills outside of a tiny village. There, Pegasus landed, and Hermes and Hecate dismounted and gathered up their gear.

Hermes tossed Pegasus an apple from one of the knapsacks and said, "Thanks for the ride."

Pegasus whinnied before taking to the sky and flying away.

"You were right," Hecate said to Hermes as she rigged her fishing line with hook and bait. "That was more fun than flight and better than a chariot."

"I promised him half of whatever we catch."

"Sounds fair to me."

Demeter waited patiently in hawk form in a tree on the side of a hill above them while the two gods fished together in the early morning sunshine. They spoke of trivial things, and, after a while, Demeter thought the subject of Persephone would never come up. But as she was about to leave, Hermes said something that made her pause.

"I wish we could do this together all year," he said. "I hate it when you leave Mount Olympus."

"Absence makes the heart grow fonder," Hecate said.

"Are you saying you'd get sick of me if we saw each other year-round?"

Hecate laughed. "We do see each other year-round."

"It's not the same when I'm working with the dead. It's not like this."

Hecate didn't reply. Her rod tip bent, so she jerked it back and reeled in a fish.

"What a beauty!" Hermes said.

Hecate removed the fish from the hook and tied it to a line, the other end of which she tied to a branch near the bank. Then she put the fish back in the water on the end of the tethered line.

Hermes cleared his throat, reeled in his line, which still had bait, and cast it back out again. "I really thought that once Hades had children, they'd take over some of my duties in the Underworld. No god works as hard as I do."

"But you can be in many places at once. Only the Fates share that power."

"I would give it up if I could give up being Death. I loathe that job."

"I have a feeling it won't be yours forever. As you know, I have visions."

"I hope you're right. But I didn't mean to change the subject. I don't want you to go back with Persephone this year. Stay here, with me."

Hecate rebaited her hook and cast it back out. "Come stay with me in the Underworld. I'm sure Lord Hades won't object."

Hermes shuddered. "I can't stand to be there any longer than I have to. How can you?"

"I don't mind it. And I made a promise."

Hermes sighed. "Why did you ever make such a promise, anyway? Did you think of me at all?"

Hecate laid her rod down on the bank and cupped Hermes's face in her hands. "You know how I feel about you, but if it weren't for Demeter, I'd be a Titan prisoner in Tartarus."

"No, you wouldn't. You supported the Olympians."

"Not at first. You see, I nursed Atlas's children."

"The Hesperides?"

"That's right." Hecate stepped back and picked up her rod. "Atlas trusted me, which in turn made me feel loyal to him, until Demeter made me see something."

"Which was?"

"I had my spear up against her back and was escorting her to the pit of Tartarus when she told me telepathically that Kronos was behind me with his scythe and was intending to push me into the pit as well."

"How did you know you could trust her?" Hermes asked.

"I didn't at first, but then I saw his reflection in the iron door and decided not to take a chance on getting pushed in."

"So, what did you do? How did you get away?"

"I whipped around and drove my spear into Kronos's throat. It surprised him long enough for me and Demeter to flee."

"So, you believe she saved you from an eternity in the pit?" As Hermes said this, his rod tip bent, and he jerked it back.

Hermes reeled, as Hecate said, "Yes. And she also helped me to see that Kronos never intended to create the mostly democratic leadership that Zeus has established."

"Mostly democratic?" Hermes unhooked his fish and added it to the line in the water with Hecate's catch.

"Well, Zeus has the final say, but he allows the council of twelve to speak their opinions and cast votes."

"True," Hermes said.

"Kronos was purely a dictator. We're much better off with Zeus in charge."

"Indeed." Hermes rebaited his hook.

"And after that day, I had nowhere to go. Demeter took me in, and we became inseparable until after her daughter was born. I love her and hate to see her so distressed when Persephone returns to the Underworld."

Demeter smiled, and her heart bloomed with love for Hecate. She was about to fly away, when Hecate mentioned Persephone. So Demeter waited on the side of the hill to listen.

"Lately I've been worried about Persephone," Hecate said. "She was happy at first, but I can tell she's hurting."

"Any idea why?" Hermes asked. "Oh, it feels like I'm getting another bite."

"I used a bit of magic to answer that very question."

"I thought you were going to give that up. Doesn't it drive gods mad?"

"Yes, but I was willing to take the chance for Demeter's sake."

Demeter's eyes filled with tears, and she waited anxiously for Hecate to continue.

"So, what did you find out?" Hermes asked.

"I saw something. The vision wasn't clear, and it feels wrong, like there's more to it than what I saw."

"What did you see?" Hermes asked.

"You must swear an oath on the River Styx to tell no one. Like I said, it's an incomplete vision—only an inkling of something."

"I swear."

"I saw Hades beside the sleeping Persephone," Hecate said. "And while she slept, Hades pierced her womb with his bare hand and tried to strangle the baby growing inside her."

Demeter nearly fell from the hillside. She clutched the branch she was perched on and tried not to faint.

"Hades would never do such a thing, would he?" Hermes asked.

"I don't know," Hecate replied. "But I think the tension between the lord and lady of the Underworld has something to do with that vision."

Demeter flew away from the hillside as fast as she could, back to Mount Olympus. There had to be something she could do to protect her daughter from that villain she married, but what?

CHAPTER FORTY-TWO

A Harmless Prank

A few months after Persephone had left with Hecate for Mount Olympus, Hermes came to Hades's main chamber without being summoned. He only ever did this if he had a message to deliver from Mount Olympus.

The first thing that occurred to Hades was that the twins had been born.

"I'm sorry to barge in on you like this, Lord Hades," Hermes said as soon as he'd arrived.

"Has something happened?" Hades asked.

"No, not at all." Hermes scratched his head. "I'm a bit bored at the moment and was wondering if you'd like to join me again on Mount Kithairon."

Hades grinned. The last time they'd gone there together, they'd nearly gotten drunk. The wine of Dionysus was the best in the world.

"You mean you don't spend every spare moment defending the Greeks from the Trojans?" Hades asked.

"Nah. I'm fairly sick of the war by now. So, what do you say?"

He picked at his beard as he considered Hermes's invitation. Hades rarely went out, and his duties had all been attended to. The Kindly Ones weren't at home. Persephone would be gone for another few months. Why shouldn't he go?

"Why not?" Hades finally said.

"Perfect! Shall we go now then? Helios is dropping to the west already."

Hades jumped from his throne. "To my chariot."

Hermes shook his head. "Nah. We'll be faster with god travel. Besides, you shouldn't drink and drive."

Hades clapped his hand against Hermes's back and laughed. "Right, then. Let's go."

A bonfire already illuminated the clearing on the side of Mount Kithairon, where the maenads and satyrs had gathered to celebrate with Dionysus. Helios was still descending, so there was still a bit of light—though all of those in attendance could see perfectly well in the dark.

When Dionysus saw the other two gods making their way through the crowd toward him, his face lit up, and he said, "Well, tonight looks like my lucky night."

Hades tried not to roll his eyes at the mostly naked god who wore a wreath made out of grapevines on his head and a loin cloth at his waist.

Hermes extended his hand and shook the one belonging to the god of wine. "We've come back for more trouble."

"Excellent. I'm glad you're here." Dionysus shook Hades's hand as well. "We outcasts need to stick together."

Although Hades didn't consider himself an outcast and he didn't appreciate being called one, he let the remark go as Dionysus handed him a goblet of wine.

"We're about to begin the dancing!" the god of wine exclaimed as he handed a goblet to Hermes. "If I recall correctly, you had some decent moves the last time you were here."

Hermes guffawed and slapped Dionysus on the back. "Don't you know it?" Hermes slammed the wine down his throat and emptied his cup. Then he ripped off his robes down to his loin cloth and shook his hips for the maenads.

A few of them giggled.

Hades wasn't fond of dancing without his wife, but once he'd drunk down his second goblet of wine, he didn't object to it, either. The satyrs played their pipes and drums, and the maenads moved in their wild, ecstatic, frenzied way. Hades swayed to the beat and closed his eyes, thinking of Persephone. It wasn't long before one of the maenads had taken Hades by the hand to include him in her dance.

The first thing she did was rip off his shirt in one violent jerk.

Since he felt dancing with another woman was not appropriate for a married god, he turned his back to her and reached for another goblet of wine from a satyr attendant. The maenad didn't take that too well. She gave Hades a dirty look and hissed at him. This just made him laugh.

After a while, Hades was bored. He didn't want to dance, and he'd had too much to drink, and it wasn't as fun as he remembered it being. Hermes must have noticed the melancholy on his face, because he stumbled over to where Hades was standing on the edge of the ring, clapped a hand on his now bare shoulder, and said in his slurred speech, "How's about we make some mischief?"

"What do you have in mind?" Hades, eager to do anything else, asked.

"Let's play a trick on Poseidon, shall we? He takes himself much too seriously."

Just the idea tickled Hades's funny bone. He couldn't hold back his laughter. "Ha-ha-HAH! What kind of trick?"

Hermes nearly toppled over but caught his balance before falling on his face. "I don't know. Any ideas?"

Hades scratched his curly black beard and thought for a moment. "He's probably still helping the Greeks on the battlefield, and he won't have taken his chariot."

"Yeah? So?" Hermes asked. "You want to steal his chariot?"

"Why not?" Hades busted out laughing again. "Can you imagine his face...hahaha...when he comes back...hahaha...and finds it missing?" He slapped his knee and lost his balance.

"Ha-ha-ha-hee!" Hermes caught Hades and helped him regain his balance. "He'll go mad! Ha-ha-ha!"

"Let's dress his mares up like maids!" Hades added, feeling giddy. "That will bring him down from his high horse! Get it? High HORSE? Ha-ha-HAH!"

"Dress them like maids?" Hermes repeated in between laughs. "Brilliant!"

Dionysus came up to them through the crowd. "Dress who up like maids?"

Hades giggled as he said, "Poseidon's mares. But, sshhh. Don't tell anyone."

"I hate Poseidon, so count me in!"

Hermes slapped Dionysus on the back. "But you hate everybody...hahaha-hee!"

Dionysus fell over giggling. "So true!"

Hermes mussed up Dionysus's golden curls, upsetting the wreath of grapevines. "It's not your fault, my friend. You can't help what your father did."

"Thank you for that!" Dionysus said before clapping his hand on Hermes's shoulder. "You think you can convince Hera?"

Hermes grabbed his belly and busted out in even more boisterous laughter.

Hades joined him. "Oh, sure he can! Ha-ha-HAH!"

Hermes threw an arm around Dionysus. "You know something? I want you to know this. I've always liked you. Forget Hera. You're a good man."

"I've always liked you, too, Hermes," the god of wine said, putting an arm around the messenger god.

"Are you two going to kiss?" Hades asked in between chuckles.

"So, what's the plan?' Dionysus asked as they huddled in a circle with their arms around one another and their faces close.

"I'll wear the helm," Hades said. "As long as we link arms, you'll both be protected!"

"Ooooh! The infamous helm!" Dionysus said. "How exciting!"

"SShhh. We can't let Poseidon know it's us," Hermes said louder than he realized. "Or we'll all have hell to pay, that's for sure."

Hades conjured his helm and put it on. The wine had made him a little dizzy, but, in his opinion, he was better off than his companions.

Hermes's eyes got wide. "Spooky! It's like you're not even there. You are there, though, aren't you?"

"I'm here," Hades said, causing Hermes to jump at least six inches in the air.

"That's so unnerving!" Hermes said.

Hades reached out and linked his arm with Hermes's.

"Woah!" Dionysus cried, spinning around. "Are you gods still here? Or did you leave without me? Man! Everyone's always leaving me out!"

"Stop crying, Hilda!" Hermes hollered. "We're right beside you!"

Dionysus reached out, but completely missed both gods. "I don't believe you!"

Hades grabbed Dionysus's arm, startling the god of wine, who yelped like a cat before he recognized what had happened.

"This is awesome!" Dionysus said, now that he was under the protection of the helm and could see them both. "Where do I get one of these?"

"Come on," Hades said, ignoring the question, since there was no other like it.

Together, they god-traveled to the east of Greece, to the coast along the Aegean Sea. They landed a bit roughly on a high headland, stumbling all the way to the edge.

"Watch it!" Hermes warned.

The sea raged in the moonlight beneath them.

As they stood overlooking the tumultuous waves, Dionysus asked, "Are we sure we want to get all wet and sticky? My hair never dries well."

"Seriously?" Hades asked, bemused. "Ha-ha-ha! I'll have *my* hairdresser get in touch with *your* hairdresser! Ha-ha-HAH!"

"We can't do our trick otherwise, old friend," Hermes said to Dionysus. "Let's go!"

They jumped from the headland, squealing like girls, and plummeted into the cold, dark sea. With their arms linked, they were forced to swim like mermen, their legs like long tales flapping behind them. Hades sensed the two gods on each end trying to out-swim the other. Even though their arms were linked, it felt like they were racing.

He'd show them!

It was like playing at tug-of-war. He was half-tempted to let go of their arms and leave them in his wake.

But he needed them for, what was it? Ah, yes. Their trick on Poseidon!

When they reached Poseidon's grandiose castle, Hades, who hadn't been there in a long time, was struck by how different it was from the one belonging to Phorcys and Keto. Poseidon lived in a crystal palace full of sparkle and color. It had everything the other castle lacked.

"Woah!" Dionysus said. "Look how it sparkles! Even in the dark!"

"SShhh!' Hades said. Then telepathically, he added, *The helm doesn't make us sound-proof—just invisible.*

Oh, yeah. Got it, Dionysus said.

Since none of the guards could sense them, Hades and his companions easily swam through the door and into the main chamber, where at least a dozen merfolk lounged around on couches, entertaining themselves with jokes and songs. Hades thought what an easy life they must have—free of all responsibilities. But didn't they get bored?

Hermes must have overheard one of their jokes, because he began to chuckle, forcing Hades to clap his hand over the god's mouth. Hermes's gut instinct was to pull away, exposing him from the protection of the helm.

Hades immediately grabbed the god's hand and scolded him telepathically as two merfolk looked suspiciously in their direction.

You're going to get us swallowed by a whale, Hades warned. *To the garage. Lead the way.*

After Hermes's face recovered from having turned a deep shade of red, he led the way through the chamber to a side bay. Since Hermes always traveled back and forth between the gods as their messenger, he was most familiar with the palace.

Riptide, Seaquake, and Crest, stood in their stalls, unbridled from the chariot, which was parked across from them.

This is going to be fun, Hermes said.

Don't leave the protection of the helm, Hades warned as Dionysus was about to unlink arms and move toward the three white mares. To himself he thought, *Man, this god is dense.*

Although he was usually the swiftest god, Hermes was the slowest and clumsiest when he was drunk. Hades watched with dismay as the messenger god attempted to bridle the horses. After dropping the reins, and getting tangled in them, he seemed to have bridled himself.

Dionysus cupped his hands over his mouth to quiet his laughter, but Hades wasn't laughing anymore. He suddenly realized how dangerous this situation had become.

Ah, let me do it, Hades said telepathically. He moved the slow-footed Hermes to the center of their group and put himself on the end.

The mares were spooked by the feeling of being bridled by an invisible presence. They resisted, whinnied, and snorted. Dionysus made wine appear in the cup of his hands and he fed it to the horses. They calmed down after that.

Once the chariot was ready, the gods climbed aboard, putting the entire rig under the protection of the helm. Invisible to everyone else, the chariot flew from the bay and up toward the surface of the sea. Hermes and Dionysus yelped with glee. Hades decided it was futile to tell them to shut up. Besides, Hades had to admit that the thought of getting caught made the whole prank much more exciting. For good measure, he added his own yelp as they broke from the surface and ascended into the sky.

Before continuing on to Mount Olympus, they went to the Underworld to get jewelry, scarves, and hats to put on the mares. He would give his daughters and wife even better ones to replace them.

The three gods laughed each time they added a new accessory to one of the animals.

"Why, don't *you* look lovely?" Hermes said to Riptide in between bouts of hysterical laughter.

Dionysus fell over on the floor. "I just asked this one to marry me! I think we're engaged!"

"Ha-ha-HAH!" Hades cried uncontrollably.

Swift and Sure glared at him from their stalls, but Hades dismissed it. They wouldn't understand.

When the gods were satisfied with the appearance of the mares, they flew the chariot through the chasm toward Mount Olympus—or rather, the mares drove themselves. Hades was seeing double moons and was glad the horses knew the way.

Once they arrived, Hermes left the protection of the helm to open the gate, and he waddled through in such a drunken stupor, that he gave Hades plenty of time to sneak the chariot and Dionysus through to the other side. Then all three rode the chariot to the garage and parked it next to Zeus's, all the while, cupping their hands to their mouths to stifle their laughter.

You go and summon Poseidon, Hades said to Hermes as he and Dionysus climbed from the chariot. *We'll wait here, so we can watch his reaction.*

Hermes started to leave when Hades added, *You might want to put on some clothes first.*

Dionysus busted out laughing.

After Hermes left, Cupid suddenly appeared and stared at the dressed-up mares with an open mouth. Hades and Dionysus froze beneath the helm.

"What's this?" Cupid said to himself.

Neither Hades nor Dionysus could hold back their laughter.

"Reveal yourselves," Cupid demanded, but not without laughing.

Hades removed the helm and put a finger to his lips. "Sshh." (He may have spit.) "Don't worry."

"Be happy!" Dionysus shouted through his snort.

CHAPTER FORTY-THREE

Punitive Damages

Persephone awoke with a start. She felt something. Had it been a dream?

She felt it again. And this time, she was wide awake.

It wasn't the babies. It was Hades. He was here on Mount Olympus.

She threw on a robe over her nightgown and hastened from the room. Down the hall, her mother was forming the dough, which they had made earlier, into neat loaves.

"Couldn't sleep?" Demeter asked.

"No."

"Where are you going?"

Persephone sighed. Even on Mount Olympus, her mother wanted to know Persephone's every move.

"Just for a bit of fresh air. I'll be right back."

Persephone crossed through the main hall. Zeus sat alone on his throne, as the others were either off fighting in the war or on some errand.

"Oh, hello, my dear," he said, standing. "Don't you look ravishing in your night clothes?"

Persephone shuddered. How could a father speak that way to his own daughter?

When she didn't reply, he said, "You look as though you're stealing away to some secret rendezvous."

"I assure you, I'm not. I just want a bit of fresh air."

"Look up, my dear. The sun always shines on Mount Olympus. There's plenty of fresh air to be had in this very room."

Because it was true that the main hall did open up to the sky, Persephone scrambled for an answer. Then, thinking of one, she said, "I need a good walk as well."

She left the hall without turning back and took the rainbow steps down onto the golden-paved grounds in front of the palace. She sensed Cupid in the garage where the chariots were kept, so she flew over and peeked inside.

Cupid stood and stared at Poseidon's three mares. They were outfitted in hats and scarves and…Wait a minute! Those were her and her daughters' hats and scarves and jewels.

"What's going on in here?" she asked Cupid.

When Cupid merely gawked at her, glancing at an empty space across the room, she knew Hades was there beneath the helm.

She turned to the place where Cupid kept glancing. "I know you're here, Hades. Please tell me why."

Hades and Dionysus appeared, each with a finger to his lips.

"Sshh," Hades said with a smile. "We're playing a trick."

"You're shirtless!" Persephone huffed in a loud whisper. "And drunk!"

"Her powers of observation are astounding," Dionysus said in a drunken slur.

Persephone was incensed. How could Hades risk getting on the bad side of any god right now when she was pregnant? She'd already been threatened by Hera. They didn't need Poseidon added to the list of gods wanting to make Hades suffer.

Cupid gave her a sympathetic nod before he left.

She clutched her swollen belly and fought back tears, as she turned to glare at Hades. "How can you be so selfish?"

Her husband's brows shot up. "What? No, no, no. Not selfish. Just having a little fun."

"At what cost?" she asked. "You're already on Hera's bad side. Did you know that she threatened me? She plans to pay you back for who-knows-what by bringing harm to our twins!"

Hades's face turned pale. Then he returned the helm to his head, and he and Dionysus disappeared.

Talk about trying to hide from your problems, she thought. Making himself invisible wasn't going to do him any good. She was about to give him a piece of her mind, when Poseidon came storming into the garage, followed by Zeus, Ares, and Hermes.

"Then how did it get here?" Poseidon raged at Hermes. "And look at my horses! Who would do this?"

Dionysus giggled.

All the gods turned in the direction of the empty space where Persephone had last seen Hades and Dionysus.

"Reveal yourself, coward!" Poseidon bellowed.

When no one materialized, Ares narrowed his eyes at Persephone and said, "I know of only one god capable of making himself invisible to other gods."

"Where's your husband?" Zeus asked Persephone. "Were you speaking to him just now?"

"I was speaking to Cupid," she said, which wasn't exactly a lie.

"Is he the one responsible for this abomination?" Poseidon raged. He rushed over to his horses and removed the hats, scarves, and jewels, throwing them on the ground in the hay. "How humiliating for these good mares! They don't deserve to be so poorly treated."

"Hermes, bring Cupid here at once," Zeus commanded.

Cupid appeared without Hermes having to summon him. "I'm here, my lord."

"Tell us what you know," Ares said.

"Are you responsible for this?" Poseidon asked.

"Or is *she*?" Ares pointed to Persephone.

Before Cupid could answer, Dionysus appeared. "I did it! It was all me, just having a little fun with you, dear Uncle!"

Persephone wondered if her husband was going to let Dionysus take all the blame. At first, she thought the idea cowardly, and she was ashamed of him. But then, she wondered if what she'd said about the babies had made him feel as though he had no choice.

She looked at Dionysus with gratitude. He was going to take the fall to keep her twins safe.

"Don't you 'dear Uncle' me!" Poseidon railed. "How dare you sneak into my fortress and take my chariot? How dare you humiliate my loyal horses?"

"Calm down, Poseidon," Zeus said.

"Calm down?" Poseidon shouted. "I will not calm down! I've been out in the battlefield for days, only to be summoned here to find this nonsense! You need to control your son!"

Ares looked down his nose at Dionysus. "He couldn't have done this alone. He must have had the helm of invisibility."

"I stole it," Dionysus said.

"Show it to us, then," Ares demanded.

Hermes stepped forward. "I'm the one who gave him the helm. We were in on the prank together. Sorry, Lord Poseidon. We had too much to drink and weren't thinking properly."

"Hermes, I'm hurt. You of all people." Poseidon shook his head in disbelief.

"Please, sir," Hermes begged. "Please forgive us."

"So, where's the helm, now?" Zeus asked Hermes.

"It's, uh…" Hermes looked around the room, as if he'd misplaced it.

"No one stole my helm," Hades said, as he appeared beside Persephone.

She blanched, not having realized he'd been standing so close to her.

"Hades?" Poseidon said with his mouth open. "What do you have to say about this?"

Think of the twins, Persephone said telepathically to Hades.

"I'm responsible for this trick, brother," Hades said. "I meant no harm to you. I just wanted to see you get all riled up and flustered. It was wrong of me. As Hermes said, I'd had too much to drink, but that's no excuse. I take full responsibility and will serve any punishment you see fit."

"*Any* punishment?" Poseidon asked.

"As long as you mean no harm to my wife and children," Hades clarified.

Poseidon glanced at Persephone and her swollen belly. "Of course not. They are innocent. But you! This was a low blow! For this, you should be made low, too! I want you to serve six months on earth in the service of a pig farmer. If you act like a pig, you should live with pigs!"

"Six months is too long," Zeus objected. "He has too many duties."

"Three months, then," Poseidon said.

"I will do it," Hades agreed.

"What about Dionysus and Hermes?" Ares asked.

"The idea was mine," Hades said. "Let them go."

"If Hades serves three months on a pig farm, that will be enough to satisfy me," Poseidon said, his anger gone.

In fact, it seemed to Persephone that Poseidon was now giddy. He took a lot of pleasure in imagining his brother among pigs.

"Go home and get your affairs in order," Zeus said to Hades. "I don't care what pig farm you choose but go to it as soon as possible."

"My mother knows a village near Apollo's temple," Persephone said. "I saw a pig farm there. You could check on Demophoon's family from time to time."

Hades gave her a nod and a smile. After so much inattention from him, this little bit of acknowledgement warmed her heart. She also knew he hadn't planned on humbling himself to Poseidon until she pointed out the possible consequences to their children. She was pleased that he'd gone to such lengths to protect them.

Poseidon left with his chariot. Zeus and Ares returned to the palace. Hermes and Dionysus remained behind to shake Hades's hand and thank him for taking the blame.

"I won't forget that you both meant to help me," Hades said. "Thank you."

Hermes and Dionysus left, leaving Persephone alone with her husband for the first time in months.

"I'm so sorry, my love," he said to her. "I've never been more foolish in my life."

She put her hands on his bare shoulders and lifted onto her toes for a kiss.

His kiss was glorious. She sighed and kissed him again.

And then her water broke.

CHAPTER FORTY-FOUR

Hera's Revenge

Hades held his wife in his arms, relieved that his stupidity hadn't caused her or their sons any harm. He carried the prophecy he was given from Tiresias and Cassandra around in his heart like a deep battle wound that wouldn't heal. Even now he was wary of being alone with her in her condition. He was determined to do everything in his power to avoid what the seers had seen. Only the Fates knew the future for certain, and, as they had told him more than once, he was responsible for his own choices.

Persephone lifted her sweet face up to his, and he gladly received her kiss. How he wished he could sweep her up in his arms and carry her back home. Now, because of his foolishness, he would still be serving on the pig farm when it was time for her to return to the Underworld. He supposed the sooner he left, the sooner he could come home.

In his arms, Persephone flinched.

"What's wrong?" he asked.

"My water broke," she whispered. "The babies are coming."

"Now?"

She nodded. "Protect me from Hera. Use your helm."

As he lifted his helm to his head, Hera appeared and snatched Persephone from his arms. They disappeared before he could react.

He roared with anger, shaking his fists and stomping his feet. If he hadn't been drinking, his reflexes would have been quick enough to prevent the abduction. Tears filled his eyes as he reached out to Hecate in prayer.

In the next instant, Hecate appeared in the garage beside him. "What's happened?"

"Hera has abducted Persephone. Can you sense where they went?"

Hecate closed her eyes for several long seconds.

"Well?" he asked, pacing.

"I need my magic." She opened her hand and a small bag appeared.

"What's that?"

"Salt from the sea." She sprinkled it all around the door to the garage.

Hades watched on as Hecate then conjured a lamp and lit it. She stood near the doorway and said:

Mother Asteria in the sky,

Heavenly star-goddess, oh so high,

As I seek the lost Persephone,

Be my third eye.

Hades prayed to Hecate's mother, Asteria, too, hoping it might help the star-goddess to answer. He gripped his helm in his hands so tightly that his knuckles had turned white, only making him more aware of the anxiety and dread gripping him.

At last, Hecate turned to him and said, "Hera's taken her to the garden of the Hesperides, where she keeps her apple tree. Let's go at once."

As they god-traveled, Hades had this horrible thought: Hera planned to feed his twin sons to her one-hundred-headed dragon, Ladon.

When Hades and Hecate arrived at Hera's garden, they found Persephone and Hera in a sword fight beneath the golden apple tree. Ladon's one hundred hissing heads draped from the branches and created obstacles for Persephone, giving Hera the advantage. The three daughters of Atlas had formed a barrier on the opposite side of Ladon and the tree, making it impossible for Persephone to escape. And god travel was too dangerous, especially if Hera had recruited anyone else to be waiting in ambush.

Hades and Hecate conjured and drew their swords. The daughters of Atlas screamed and ran away to hide behind the golden apple tree. Hades attacked Hera, and as soon as Persephone was free, Hecate grabbed her hand and flew away with her.

Hades remained behind to prevent Hera from following.

"I will slice you up and feed you to your dragon," Hades said as he struck his sword against hers. "Isn't that what you intended to do to my unborn sons?"

Hera fought back, unintimidated. "That's what I wanted you to believe, at any rate. I wasn't going to go that far."

He whipped around, and their swords met again. "Why should I believe you? You're so blinded by jealousy that you'll stop at nothing."

Hera struck forward and cut his shoulder. "I can see just fine."

Infuriated, he slammed his sword hard against hers and thrust her back. She fell onto the ground, and he put his sword to her throat. "Swear an oath on the River Styx that you'll leave them alone, and I'll spare you."

She glared up at him with eyes full of hate. "Never."

Just then, a dozen of Ladon's serpentine heads curled around Hade's arms, chest, and legs. He hadn't realized how close he had gotten to the tree and was taken by surprise. His heart never pumped faster as he flailed against the dragon's grip, to no avail. He dropped his sword as Ladon slammed his back against the trunk of the tree.

Hera stood before him, smiling.

He had to think of something to detain her, so he asked, "Why did you and Athena give Paris's judgment so much weight? You know his answer had nothing to do with beauty, don't you?"

"You wouldn't understand," she sneered.

"Try me."

Hera closed her eyes and sighed before opening them again. "After Zeus freed us and we defeated the Titans, I expected more."

"Like what?"

"Equal dominion. I and our sisters fought just as hard and just as bravely as you and our brothers. Did we not?"

"What does that have to do with now, with your blood lust for every living Trojan?" He strained against the dragon but couldn't move.

"When you and Zeus and Poseidon divided up the world among you, the only way for me to gain any kind of power was with my beauty."

"That's ridiculous."

"Yes, but true. Think about it. I used my beauty to gain Zeus's affection, and I became queen. If my beauty is ever jeopardized, I'll lose my power."

Hades glanced up at Ladon. "I think you have more than beauty in your corner."

"Mortals need to be taught a lesson," she said. "That's what this whole war is about, and it's why it's so important. They need to know that it's not their place to judge us—whether it's beauty, or strength, or speed. They should remain silent."

"Zeus *told* Paris to decide."

"He was a poor shepherd then, an unfortunate outcast," she said. "And he should have said he couldn't choose. He should have said it was impossible." She balled up her fist and shook it. "When he chose Aphrodite, he threatened my power—and Athena's power. Our reputations are at stake. And when it comes to beauty, reputation is everything. People most admire what is admired by most."

Hades opened his mouth to object, but Hera disappeared.

CHAPTER FORTY-FIVE

The Birth of the Twins

D on't let go," Persephone said to Hecate as they flew across the sky.

The pain in Persephone's belly and back was almost unbearable. She could focus on nothing but that pain. She was powerless and would fall to the sea below if it weren't for Hecate.

Hecate held onto Persephone's arm, which was draped across her shoulders. Hecate also had her by the waist.

"I've got you," her friend reassured her. "We're almost there."

Persephone closed her eyes and moaned as another wave of pain squeezed her like a vice. When the pain momentarily eased, she asked, panting, "Where are we going?"

"To Asteria, also known as Delos. The island of my mother."

Persephone nodded but couldn't speak as the pain took hold of her again. She'd never been to Delos, but she knew it was the place of Apollo's birth.

As they descended toward the tiny island in the middle of the vast sea, flocks of quail scattered from the trees.

Hecate took her down to the soft warm sand on a flat spot by the shore and helped her to lie on her back. Helios shined brightly down on them, which comforted Persephone as she braced herself for another wave of pain. Then the urge to bear down became irresistible.

"I think one of them is coming," she said through gritted teeth.

Hecate knelt near her. "Yes, my dear. I see his head. Go ahead and push."

Persephone grunted and bore down, again and again, and finally, after many minutes, she had some relief. She looked down and saw Hecate cleaning the baby boy, who now began to cry. He had dark curly hair on his head and the bluest eyes.

"Sshh," Hecate said to him. "We don't want to be found, baby boy. Do you understand?"

The boy stopped crying and nodded.

Persephone opened her arms to him, and he flew to her for an embrace. She filled with joy. Her first babies had flown away from her directly after their births, so she'd been deprived of this important moment of bonding. It was a true pleasure to hold her precious baby, and for the first time as a mother, she completely understood her mother's need to have her by her side. "My sweet baby."

"Do you have a name for him?" Hecate asked.

Persephone hadn't decided. She and Hades hadn't been together often enough to discuss it. "Not yet."

"I'm hungry," the boy said.

Persephone nursed him for a little while until the pain in her belly returned and she knew it was time for the other twin to be born.

"Oh no," Hecate said with her eyes directed to the sky.

Persephone followed her line of vision. Coming toward them was Zeus's eagle.

"Do you think he means us harm?" Persephone asked.

Hecate stood up and drew a circle around them in the sand. "I don't know, but I'm praying to my mother, to Dione, and to Artemis for help, just in case, and I'm placing us in a circle of protection."

The pain of labor wrapped itself around Persephone at that moment, and she cried out. The first baby boy knelt near her head and stroked her hair. Hecate waited to receive the second, glancing up toward the sky as the eagle neared them.

Persephone held her boy's hand, fearing now that the eagle meant to take off with him. "Don't let go," she said to her son, as she bore the birthing pains from the other.

Zeus's eagle swooped down from the sky and grabbed her son's arm with its talons, but the boy held onto his mother and kicked at the bird.

Then, like a shooting star, a rainbow appeared in the sky, and Iris, Hera's messenger, darted out with her shining wings, pointing at Persephone on the island below her. From behind the rainbow, the four dreadful half-bird, half-women that Persephone had ever only seen one other time in her life—the Harpies—charged toward her.

"My magic isn't holding up," Hecate cried. "Dione, please help us!"

A silver face appeared in a wave on the shore. As the eagle used its talons to tug at the firstborn, water shot up and sprayed the bird, along with the goddesses and babe. Once the eagle backed away from the spray, the water nymph became a wall of water that arched over Persephone where she and her baby and Hecate were on the sand. The wall of water formed a protective barrier between them and the Harpies.

"Thank you, Dione!" Hecate cried. "Persephone, push!"

Persephone gave it all she had and bore down, but the baby wouldn't come. She worried the wall of water wouldn't be able to protect them for long, so she prayed to the second boy to please come out.

I'm frightened of that water, her son prayed back to her.

That wave is protecting us, Persephone explained. *She's our friend.*

As the second son slid from his mother, with golden curls on his head and the same blue eyes as his brother, Hera appeared in the wave with her sword and drew on Dione. The wave lost its structure and washed over them, nearly drowning them all.

Persephone sputtered, blinked, and looked around. Her heart stopped beating as she realized she'd been separated from the others. She could hear one of her babies crying, but where were they? She looked up to see both of their naked little bodies dangling in the sky from the claws of a Harpy.

And dear Hecate was dangling from another.

Persephone leapt into the air toward them, her heart pounding and her throat tight with fear. She could barely think, barely breathe. She conjured and drew her sword as one of the Harpies attacked. The half-bird, half-woman screeched as she dodged Persephone's blade. Not far away, Persephone's firstborn was clinging to the heels of her second. The firstborn kicked his legs and twisted his body, causing the Harpy to lose her grip on the second son.

Both babies were finally free and falling through the sky, thanks to the determination of the firstborn, but another Harpy was closing in on them. Persephone raced toward her sons.

Persephone cried out when the Harpy reached them before she had. The beast snatched each boy with its claws and was about to disappear behind the rainbow when an arrow sped through the air and pierced its heart. The beast screeched out in pain and dropped the boys as it fell through the air and into the sea below.

"You can fly!" Persephone screamed to her falling sons, who were just beginning to figure out that they could, indeed, fly.

More arrows shot out, and one pierced the Harpy holding Hecate. As Persephone raced toward her boys, she saw the person who had saved the day. It was Artemis! And by the time Persephone held each boy in her arms, the huntress had shot every single Harpy from the sky.

From out of the water, Hera flew up with her sword pointed at Artemis. The queen of the Olympians had never looked angrier. But Dione, who'd been fighting with her this whole time, leapt from the sea in the form of a giant tidal wave and overwhelmed the angry queen.

This gave Persephone and Hecate just enough time to fly with the babies away from Delos and back to the safety of Mount Olympus, to Demeter's protected rooms.

CHAPTER FORTY-SIX

Time to Go

Hades stood with his back against Ladon's tree as the serpent dragon coiled mercilessly around his arms and legs.

Hermes appeared at his bidding. "Did you call, my lord?"

Hades sighed. "I'm in a bit of bind and…"

Hermes became distracted by the three daughters of Atlas, who had made their way from the back of the tree and had gathered around him. "Well, hello ladies."

The Hesperides giggled at the messenger god's blatant flirtation.

Hades rolled his eyes and commanded his sword to return to his hand. Then he sliced off seven of Ladon's heads before liberating himself and flying to Hermes's side.

"Thanks anyway," Hades said just before he flew away.

The first thing he did, now that he was free, was reach out in prayer to Persephone. When she didn't answer, he tried to contact Hecate, but he still got no reply. So he went to Helios to see if he knew where his wife had gone.

"Look down there," the sun Titan said, pointing.

Hades followed his finger down to the island of Delos, where Artemis was shooting at Harpies and Dione was overwhelming Hera in a giant wave of water as Persephone escaped with Hecate and their newborn sons.

By the time Hades had reached the skies above Delos, his family had disappeared behind the gates of Mount Olympus. He knew that once they reached Demeter's rooms, they'd be safe, so he took the opportunity to thank Artemis and Dione by giving them each a bracelet made of precious stones.

Then he followed Hera to Mount Olympus to meet his family, anxious to see his sons, but the four seasons would not let him pass.

"We were commanded by Zeus to forbid your entrance for the next three months," Summer said.

Full of disappointment, Hades flew home. As long as Persephone was in her mother's rooms, they couldn't communicate, because Demeter had blocked him with powerful wards. Maybe Persephone would think to go outside the palace to pray to him before he had to leave for Delphi.

When he arrived home, he was surprised to find the Kindly Ones sitting in his chamber, each with her familiar on her lap. Although he'd seen them from time to time, it had never been for very long, and seeing them now, in one room rather than flying this way or that way, made him realize how much they'd grown. They were beginning to look like young women.

"You're finally home!" Tizzie cried.

"Now, don't be rude, Tizzie," Meg warned.

"We've been waiting for you, Father," Alecto said.

"Has something happened?" he asked.

Meg put her parakeet on her shoulder and stood up. "Zeus has ordered all the gods to stay out of the war with the Trojans."

"You should see how angry Athena is right now," Tizzie said, petting the white dog in her lap. "The Greeks are losing."

"Both Aphrodite and Ares were wounded by mortals," Meg said.

"So, since they had to pull out, Zeus was worried the Greeks would get too much of an advantage," Tizzie said.

"We don't understand why we can't continue *our* work," Alecto complained as she hugged her black cat. "We weren't supporting one side over the other. Why did Zeus make us leave, too?"

"Can't you speak with him, Father?" Tizzie asked.

"It's really not fair to the wounded and dying," Meg pointed out.

"Life isn't fair," Hades said. "Only death is. And I'm in no position at the moment to negotiate with Zeus."

"Why ever not?" Tizzie asked.

"Tizzie, your manners," Meg said.

Alecto kissed her black cat on the top of its head. "Well, at least we can spend some time helping you here at home, Father."

Hades frowned. "Unfortunately, I have to leave."

"What?" they all three said together.

"Why? Where are you going?" Tizzie asked.

"I made a bad decision, and now I have to pay for it," he said. "I'm going to a village near Delphi to serve three months' labor at a pig farm."

"Oh, that's terrible!" Meg cried. "You poor thing!"

"What abominable work for someone as noble and powerful as you!" Alecto complained.

"Not so abominable," Hades said. "All work is noble, every job important. A king may have higher status than a pig farmer, but the work of one is not more important than the other. Without pig farmers, villagers would go hungry. Don't forget that."

For once, the girls were silent.

"Since your mother won't return for another three months, it's a good thing you're at home," he said. "I need your help."

Their faces brightened. "What can we do?" they asked.

He laughed. "Everything. Keep an eye on Cerberus and Hydra and feed them from time to time. That goes for Swift and Sure as well. Make sure the souls stay in their assigned realms. Keep an eye on the prisoners in Tartarus, especially, okay? And if Charon or the three judges need anything, you'll have to get it for them."

The three girls nodded.

"You can count on us," Alecto said.

"And one more thing," he said. "You might like to know that today your brothers were finally born."

Their faces lit up with joy. "When can we see them?"

"They're on Mount Olympus with your mother. Go quickly, but don't stay long. I leave now for Delphi."

CHAPTER FORTY-SEVEN

Truce

Demeter had just taken the freshly baked whole-grain bread from her oven when she was startled by the sudden arrival of Persephone and Hecate. And in Persephone's arms were her brand-new twins.

She could tell by the looks on everyone's faces that the births had not been joyful.

"Oh, my dears! What's happened?" Demeter cried.

Persephone and Hecate relayed the trauma they'd just endured at Hera's bidding. As she listened, Demeter filled with anger at her sister. What had Persephone ever done to be so poorly treated?

Once she'd helped them all to get cleaned up and resting on her couches, she stormed from her rooms to the main hall in search of their queen.

Hera was not yet at home, but Zeus promised to summon her when his wife returned. Demeter was too angry not to mention to Zeus what had happened.

"Why would Hera go to such lengths to harm our daughter?" Demeter asked him after she'd told him the details.

"So that's why she wanted my eagle," Zeus said. "I honestly had no idea what she was up to, and I can't imagine why she did it."

"I'll tell you why," Hera said calmly as she entered the main hall. She removed the green velvet hood of her cloak and stepped across the marble floor toward her throne beside Zeus. "Hades betrayed me on the battlefield. He needed to be taught a lesson. And that's exactly what I did."

Demeter should have known that the lord of darkness had been the cause of Persephone's troubles, but Demeter would not allow her sister to punish her daughter for the actions of Persephone's abominable husband.

She squared herself to Hera. "No one despises Hades more than I, but…"

"I wouldn't be too sure about that," Hera sneered.

"Let me put this another way, then," Demeter said. "As you know, I don't tend to get involved with the affairs of Mount Olympus. I fought in the war with the Titans and did my part to increase our number." She glanced at Zeus and noticed Hera's face pale. "And since then, I've kept to myself and to my own duties, never contradicting you and your husband on any front, wouldn't you agree?"

Hera arched a brow. "I'd say that's a fair assessment."

Demeter took another step toward Hera. "Well, I may need to remind you someday that I'm just as powerful as you, dear sister. I hope it won't come to that, but if you ever launch an attack on my daughter again, if you ever abuse her in any way, I promise you it will."

Hera smirked. "Your idle threats don't frighten me."

Demeter felt a wave of cold, hard hate for her sister in that moment. She took a deep breath and glared at Hera. "Then let me be more specific. If you ever abuse my daughter like you did today, I will make every single one of your precious golden apples shrivel up and die."

This got Hera's attention. Her face became bright red as she glanced at Zeus. "What? They were a gift from Gaia. You can't touch my golden apples. They're well protected."

Demeter smiled. "I won't need to touch them. Have you forgotten that I control the soil and all that grows from it? There's nothing your one-hundred headed dragon can do to stop me from making the ground beneath him barren."

Hera gasped and then covered her mouth with both hands, which had begun to tremble. Then she said, "I swear on the River Styx never to bring harm to your daughter again."

Satisfied, Demeter turned on her heels and headed back to her rooms and her beloved Persephone.

When she walked into her main chamber, the baby boys were literally bouncing off the walls.

"My dears! My dears!" she said, trying to get their attention.

When that didn't work, she said to Persephone, who was sitting on the couch beside Hecate, "We need to help them burn off some energy. Why don't we ask Dione or Poseidon to give them dolphin rides across the seven seas?"

The younger baby stopped flying around the room. "No offense, but I'll have to pass. After nearly drowning in a wave of water, the sea is the last place on earth I want to be." He turned to his brother, who'd also paused from jumping on the walls, mid-air, to listen. "Wouldn't you agree, bro'?"

"I'm not afraid," the boy said, returning to his game of kicking off from each wall. "I'd love to ride on a dolphin's back."

"Just great." The younger twin crossed his arms and ankles where he hovered in the air. "You saved my life just to leave me hanging."

Everyone in the room laughed.

Persephone stood up and ruffled the golden curls on the younger twin's head. "Maybe we can think of something else to do."

Hecate lifted a finger in the air. "We could ask Zeus if the boys can ride the winged horse, Pegasus, across the sky. It's even better than riding a chariot."

The golden-haired boy sat on Hecate's lap and said, "Flying through the air on a creature with wings? Seriously? After what we just went through?"

Persephone chuckled at her son. He spoke with a delightful sense of humor. "But Pegasus isn't like those nasty Harpies."

"How do we know they won't attack us again?" the golden-haired boy asked with his arms in the air.

Demeter plucked the older twin from the air and sat with him on her lap as she said to the younger, "I've made sure of that. Hera and her entourage will never bother any of you again."

Persephone smiled at her mother, which warmed Demeter's heart.

"Why don't you boys tell us what you'd like to do, other than bouncing around on your grandmother's walls?" Persephone asked.

The older one jumped up from Demeter's lap. "I want to see my father in the Underworld."

"Oh, dear," Demeter murmured.

"Me, too!" the younger one said. "He promised to teach us how to race frogs."

Persephone jerked her head back. "When? When did he make that promise?"

"He spoke to us in our heads," the older one said.

"All the time," the younger added.

Demeter frowned. She'd hoped to protect these boys from the influence of their father.

"Well, he's not in the Underworld at the moment," Persephone said.

"Oh, that's right," the older one said. "We heard."

Demeter lifted her brows. "Oh? Where is he?"

"He's serving a pig farmer near Delphi," Persephone explained. "It's a long story, so don't ask."

Demeter filled with happiness. This was the best news she'd received in a very long time.

"I asked him to check on Demophoon while he's there," Persephone added.

Demeter stood up. "Keep him away from Demophoon. He'll only be frightened."

"Can we go see him?" the older twin asked.

Demeter sat back down. "Demophoon?"

"No, our father," the boy said. "Please?"

Persephone nodded. "I don't see why we can't go for a visit. Then maybe we can decide on names for the two of you."

Demeter scoffed. "I think that after all you've been through, you're entitled to choose names for them yourself."

"It's my choice to include him, Mother," Persephone said.

Demeter stood up again. "Well, before you go, you can at least put some clothes on them. I made them matching outfits using silk fabric Athena gave me."

Demeter went to the back room and returned with the cute little baby blue suits she had made.

The smile on her daughter's face as she accepted the gifts made her so happy that she said, "Maybe I'll go with you to Delphi. I can pay a visit to Demophoon while we're there."

Persephone kissed her cheek. "I'd like that, Mother."

C H A P T E R   F O R T Y - E I G H T

Life and Merriment

If it weren't for the fact that he missed his family, Hades wouldn't mind his punishment. The sunshine, the fresh air, and the hard, physical labor were exhilarating. And when he had showed up dressed as a common laborer looking for work, the pig farmer, named Agathias, had welcomed him and had been gracious and kind. It hardly seemed like a punishment at all.

Hades was working in the pen shoveling the manure into the fertilizer bin, alone with the pigs and his thoughts and the beautiful day, when he sensed a godly presence near him.

"Persephone?" He glanced all around him.

It wasn't until he looked up that he saw them breaking from one of the white fluffy clouds in the gorgeous blue sky. There were seven of them: Persephone, Hecate, the newborn twins, and the Kindly Ones—plus their familiars. They flew toward him with smiles on their faces and landed beside him in the pen.

A few of the pigs snorted and fled to the mud pits in the corners.

Hades dropped his shovel and kissed his wife. "I can't believe you're all here!"

"Neither can I!" Persephone said, smiling.

He lifted both boys in his arms. "I'm glad you're unharmed, no thanks to Hera."

"The bird women tried to eat us," the boy with his mother's coloring said.

Hades chuckled. "I don't think the Harpies would have eaten you."

"I wouldn't let them!" the boy with Hades's coloring said fiercely.

"You know what happened?" Persephone asked Hades.

"I got there right as you were leaving," he explained. "I was held up by Ladon." Then he turned to Hecate. "I owe you one."

Hecate blushed.

"Who's Ladon?" the dark-haired boy asked.

The Kindly Ones giggled.

"He's a dragon," Meg said with her parakeet on one finger.

"Or a serpent," Alecto corrected, as she stroked her black cat.

"Don't be rude," Meg complained.

Tizzie held her white dog in the crook of one arm. "Whatever he is, he's got one hundred heads."

"One hundred heads?" the golden-haired boy repeated. "How did you get away?"

Hades put the boys down and conjured his sword. "With this." He pointed to the blade. "You see? There's still some of his blood on it."

"Dim yourselves," Hecate whispered.

"Now that's an interesting farming tool," Agathias said as he approached them from the barn. "Is this your family, then? Welcome."

Hades sheathed the sword and handed it over to Hecate to tuck inside her robes. "Yes, it is. They won't be staying long."

"That's a shame. My wife has cooked plenty of food, if they'd like to stay for supper."

Before Hades could reply, Persephone said, "How lovely. We'd love to. I have some fresh fruits and vegetables that we can add to your table." She turned her back to the farmer and then turned around once again to face him with a basket full of tomatoes, cucumbers, apples, and oranges.

Agathias's face lit up. "Wonderful! I'll go tell my wife, and I'll see you all inside before dark."

Once the farmer had left, Alecto asked, "We're going to eat with the mortals?"

Tizzie arched a brow. "Are you sure that's wise?"

Meg rolled her eyes at her sisters. "I'm sure our mother and father know best."

"But we want to learn how to race frogs," the dark-haired boy pointed out.

"Well, now." Hades laughed. "What if I show you how to race pigs first?"

"Sounds promising," the golden-haired boy said.

"What name has your mother given you?" Hades asked the one who looked like his mother.

"She hasn't," the boy replied.

"I was waiting for you," Persephone said. "I thought we should name them together."

"Hmm." Hades picked at his beard. "Their names should mean something. Has there been anything notable about them yet?"

"They didn't race away from me, like their sisters did, sure of their duties," Persephone said.

The golden-haired boy smirked. "To be fair, we were a little busy fighting for our lives. Isn't that right bro'?"

They all laughed.

"You're funny!" Tizzie said to her brother.

"He does have a delightful sense of humor," Persephone agreed. "Maybe we should call him Gelos."

Hades smiled as the boy mimicked him by picking at his chin, as if he had a beard, and saying, "Not bad. Not bad at all."

"Gelos it is," Hades said.

"And what about that one?" Alecto pointed to the other boy. "What is he like, Hecate?"

"Well, he did save his brother's life," she turned to Persephone. "Didn't he?"

"Indeed." Persephone mussed the boy's dark hair. "So maybe we should call him Zao, at least for now, until he finds his purpose."

"Life?" the boy asked. "You want to name me life?"

"Do you not like it?" Tizzie asked.

"Like it?" he said. "I love it."

"Then Zao it is," Hades said, patting the boy's head.

"How long will it be before they find their purpose?" Meg asked.

"No one knows," Persephone said. "Everyone is different."

"I have an idea," Alecto said. "Since Phobos and Deimos fly around spreading fear and panic, maybe Gelos could follow behind them and help people find humor when they're afraid."

Persephone embraced Alecto. "That's an excellent idea."

"What do you think, Gelos?" Tizzie asked.

"I think I can work with that," he said.

Zao frowned. "What about me?"

Gelos put one arm around his brother's neck. "Stick with me, bro'. You and I will bring life and merriment to all the boring places of the world."

Hades shook his head and laughed.

But Zao shrugged out of his brother's embrace and said, "I think I'm meant for something else."

"Like what?" Meg asked him.

"I want to save people from danger, like I did today—maybe other children."

"There are plenty who get caught in the crossfire during the war," Alecto pointed out. "Maybe you could shield them from harm."

"Another excellent idea, Alecto!" Persephone beamed. "What do you think, Zao?"

Hades stifled a smile when Zao mimicked his habit of picking his beard, but on a hairless chin. The light in the boy's eyes was answer enough.

CHAPTER FORTY-NINE

A Change of Heart

Demeter was surprised to find Metaneira's daughters gathered with a group of other young women around the well in the center of the village. She rarely saw them when they weren't busy working in the fields outside of their home.

Usually Demeter arrived at harvest time, the busiest time of the year, so she would leave the family to their work and return to the cabin they and the villagers had built for her. Sometimes, if the despair gave her a moment's reprieve, Demeter would try again in the dead of winter and find them huddled around their fire. They were always glad to see her, but once they were older, instead of pleading with her to tell stories, they were eager to tell Demeter theirs.

But today was a beautiful summer's day, when Demeter was usually still on Mount Olympus. So she imagined there was less work to do as she watched the girls visiting with their friends. She hovered above them and listened to what they were saying.

The oldest girl, who was now married, carried her baby on her hip, and said, "We can't leave our father alone for long."

"Where's your husband?" someone asked.

"He went to Kirrha to trade for fish," the second to the oldest replied.

"Since our father is unable to hunt," the second to the youngest explained.

"Why doesn't he hunt himself?" someone else asked.

"Her husband can't see very well," the youngest said. "He always misses his target."

The oldest girl with the babe on her hip blushed bright red.

"And Demophoon is too young to go on his own," the second to oldest added.

"Ten years is not too young," someone said.

"It's too young to go alone," the oldest said.

"Especially with a hurt foot," the second to youngest said.

"But he went anyway," the youngest said.

The oldest shifted her baby to her other hip. "Poor thing. He's sure to be disappointed."

"Aren't you worried about the bears?" someone asked. "Especially if he can't run?"

"Demeter watches over him," the youngest said. "She won't let anything happen to him."

At that moment, Demeter felt a knot in the pit of her stomach, and she flew away to the mountain, where the men of the village often hunted, in search of her precious Demophoon. Why did mortals think they were invincible because they had the favor of a god? Oh, she couldn't blame him. He was only trying to provide meat for his family. But she was overwhelmed by a sense of foreboding as she continued her search.

Less than an hour later, she spotted him on the mountainside. He was down on one knee with his trunk leaning against a boulder, and he was pulling back a bow that was nearly as big as he was. His arrow pointed at a rabbit in a clearing about thirty feet from where he knelt.

When Demophoon shot his arrow, Demeter guided it into the rabbit's head. She remained invisible, so, believing he'd hit his mark on his own, he threw both hands in the air and hollered, "Huzzah!"

Then he climbed to his feet and limped toward his prey. Before he'd gotten very far, however, a lion, which had been hidden in a cluster of bushes, sprang toward the boy.

Metaneira had given her life for her son, and there was no way Demeter was going to let that sacrifice get the boy a mere ten years. She flew to Demophoon, but the lion beat her, and it shoved the boy hard on his back with its front claws. As the lion opened its mouth to tear into Demophoon's neck, Demeter grabbed the beast with both hands and lifted it from the ground. The lion twisted in her arms and caught her face with its claws, but she held onto its struggling form, until she'd reached the top of the mountain, far, far away from the village and its inhabitants. There, she released the beast and told it to stay away from people, or she would return to kill it.

Then, she god-traveled back to the boy, where he lay on the ground, panting, with his bow gripped tightly in one hand, and she revealed herself to him.

He sat up with a look of shock on his face. Then he said, "I knew it was you! Thank you, Demeter!"

She smiled down at him and then swept him up for a hug. "I saw you hit the rabbit. Shall we get it together and take it home to your family?"

"Oh, yes! They'll be so happy to see you!"

She set him on his feet, and together they went to fetch the rabbit.

On the way, he asked, "Did that lion scratch your face?"

"I'm afraid so, but it will heal soon. Oh, look. Is that your rabbit?"

"It's not a lot of meat," he said, "but it's better than none."

"Your father will be proud, but you shouldn't be out here alone with a hurt foot. That lion would have killed you."

He hung his head. "Maybe I could have beaten him up."

She chuckled. "Maybe."

He stuffed the rabbit into his bag and was silent as they headed down the hillside together.

Demeter could tell the boy was struggling with the knowledge that he had nearly been killed, and he was ashamed that he had been vulnerable when he'd been trying to provide for his family. He was ashamed of his weakness and ashamed of his stupidity, and she could also sense the tears that had welled in his eyes and choked up his throat. She knew he didn't want to be babied, even though that was what she wanted to do more than anything else at the moment. So she let him walk in silence and hold onto his thoughts as they made their way toward the village.

Metaneira's family was happy to see her, and not just because she had god-traveled back to her rooms and returned with a basket of her freshly baked bread. They were happy to see her because they loved her as though she were a part of their family. She could sense this in every one of them, except for their father, Celeus, who blamed her for his wife's death.

Neither she nor Demophoon told the story about the lion to the rest of the family. Instead, she listened to the stories of each of the four daughters as she helped them to cook the rabbit stew. Then, when it was time for them to eat, she told them her stories—about the births of the twin boys under Hera's attack and about the punishment of the lord of darkness in the service of a pig farmer.

They all had a good laugh at Hades's expense.

Then, as Helios dipped in his cup to the west, Demeter said her goodbyes and headed home, toward Mount Olympus.

Before leaving Delphi, she decided to look in on her daughter, whom she sensed a few miles away. She found her in a farmhouse around a large table, and all of her family members were there, along with the farmer and his wife. As they shared their meal, they laughed together and told their stories, without revealing their identities to the mortals. And they listened to the farmer's stories, and those of his wife, who'd made children of her animals, since she was barren.

As she watched the lord of darkness show tenderness toward his wife and children, she wondered if she'd been wrong to judge him so harshly. Maybe her brother was worthy of her daughter's love.

She was so moved by the comfort of family from her visit at Demophoon's cottage and from what she was witnessing here at the farmhouse, that she used her powers to make a fertile bed in the barren woman's abdomen, and then she took a seed from the farmer and planted it there so that in nine months' time, they would finally have the child they'd always wanted.

CHAPTER FIFTY

A Different Kind of Night

It was strange to Persephone to return to the Underworld without her husband there, and he would still be gone for another three weeks. Nevertheless, it felt good to be home, and she got to work right away, resuming the duties that the Kindly Ones had so graciously taken over, without complaint, in her absence.

For six more days, she enjoyed her relatively full house with all five children and Hecate at home. The boys explored every nook and crevice of their domain, finding all the secret places where frogs, bats, snakes, and even the Hydra lived. (They quickly learned to avoid the Hydra.) Meg, Tizzie, and Alecto taught them how to get on Cerberus's good side with offerings of cake and apples. Persephone kept an eye on them whenever they went to play with their guard dog, because in all these years, she had never learned to trust him. Watching her boys wrestle the beast while her daughters rode on each of his three heads reminded her of the first time she'd come here, when she'd stolen the helm and spied on Hades with his dog.

To think that was over ten years ago…

But on the seventh day since she'd returned home, Zeus lifted his moratorium on divine interference with the war, and all five of her children flew away to serve. She and Hecate, along with Galin, made good use of their time by punishing the prisoners in Tartarus and seeing to Charon's occasional supper, but Persephone still felt lonely.

Then a week before Hades was due to arrive home, she had an odd experience that she later determined must have been a bad dream. She'd been brushing her hair at her mirror, getting ready to go to sleep, when she sensed a presence and saw a reflection in the mirror of someone standing behind her. She turned to find Hades there in the doorway.

"You're home early?" She leapt from her chair.

He only nodded as she flew into his arms.

Without a word, he carried her to their bed. As eager as Persephone had been to be reunited with her husband, she found him completely altered. His usual playfulness and tenderness and total regard for her comfort and satisfaction were all replaced by what could only be described as brutality. He had his way with her without saying a word, and then he left.

Persephone wondered, as she cried herself to sleep, if the three months of living among pigs had turned him into one.

She didn't see Hades for seven more days, and, if she was to be honest with herself, she hadn't wanted to see him. She felt hurt, used, and confused. And when he finally did come to her again, he behaved as though that horrible night had never happened.

"Where is everyone?" he asked her when he had entered the main chamber, where she'd been eating alone. He was covered in dirt and grime.

"I'm not sure where Hecate and Galin are, but our children have gone to serve in the war. Zeus lifted his moratorium."

"That's disappointing." He dropped his bag on the floor and plucked a grape from the table. "I was hoping to spend more time with them, like we did that night at Agathias's house." He popped the grape into his mouth.

She wanted to ask why he hadn't been eager to see them a week ago, when he'd first come home, but she kept the thought to herself.

"Are you okay?" he asked.

"I've been better," she said without looking at him.

"Has something happened?" He gently laid his hand on her shoulder.

His touch made her shudder.

Hades pulled his hand away. Although she didn't look at him, she sensed his alarm.

"I'm going to the basin to get cleaned up," he murmured just before he left.

He found her a few hours later in the stalls, where she was spreading out hay for the horses. He was clean and fresh from his bath, his curly hair still wet. He asked again what was bothering her.

"You are so hot and cold with me." She dropped her pitchfork and left the stalls.

He followed her down the winding path, past the garage toward their chambers. "What do you mean?"

She stopped and turned to him. "Last fall and winter, you spent very little time with me. I was worried sick that you'd fallen out of love."

"That will never happen." He went to touch her, but she pulled away.

"And then we had that beautiful evening together in the upperworld with our whole family," she continued. "I believed then, at Agathias's table, that you really did love me."

"Of course, I do."

"But then, last week, it occurred to me that being with the children was what had brought you joy. Not me. Because you still showed no tenderness to me, like you used to."

His face paled, and he clenched his jaw, as he seemed to be struggling over what to say. He paced a few steps one way and a few steps back, like a caged animal. Tears welled in her eyes at the thought that he was about to admit that everything she had said was true. Apollo had been right. Hades would break her heart. He no longer loved her.

Finally, he stopped and said, "There's something I need to tell you. I should have told you years ago, but I was afraid."

Tears poured from her eyes as she braced herself for the bad news.

"Do you remember that day, after we were first married, when old Tiresias spoke to us?" he asked.

Fear and dread washed over her. She glanced around, wondering if Phobos and Deimos had come to make everything worse. But she saw no sign of them. She and Hades were alone. "I remember."

"You warned me not to ask what the prophet meant. You said nothing good ever comes from knowing the future."

"That's what the Fates say," she said. "And I believe it."

"I should have listened to you, but, after I returned you to Mount Olympus, I went back to him."

Persephone covered her mouth, dreading to hear what her husband would say.

"He told me that I would one day harm my babe while it was still in your womb."

Persephone felt all the blood leave her face. Suddenly faint and dizzy, she sat down on a rocky ledge that ran between the path and the blazing Phlegethon.

"I hope you believe I would never do such a thing," he said.

She wanted to believe it, but after the way he had treated her a week ago, she wasn't sure anymore.

Hades moaned with frustration and began to pace again. "I would never harm my own child. I promise you. But the prophet's words haunted me. So, I went to see Cassandra behind the walls of Troy."

"Priam's daughter?" she asked.

"Yes, that's the one. Apollo gave her the gift of sight, and when she didn't return his advances, he cursed her, making it so that…"

"No one would believe her," Persephone finished. "I've heard the story. What did she say?"

Hades frowned. "The very same thing."

Persephone covered her face and sobbed.

"But she said she saw two of me," he said. "She spoke in riddles, just like old Tiresias. It made no sense."

Persephone didn't know what to say, though she was crying so hard, she couldn't have said anything anyway.

Hades knelt on the ground at her side. "You must believe me when I say I would never bring harm to you or to any of our children. But I couldn't ignore the visions. That's why I stayed away from you, my love. It wasn't because I fell out of love with you. The opposite is true. I was afraid to be around you as long as you were pregnant."

She wiped the tears from her cheeks and studied his tortured face. She wanted to believe him. He stroked her hair, and she no longer shuddered from his touch. Maybe when he'd come to her last week, he'd been starving for her, having been deprived of her for so long. Maybe that's why he'd been different.

"I've missed you," he said softly. "I could hardly wait for this day to come. I actually didn't mind working for the farmer with the pigs, but I couldn't stand being away from you."

She pushed her brows together and cocked her head to the side. "But you came to me last week."

"What are you talking about? I was still with Agathias last week."

Her mouth fell open. A shiver worked its way down her spine. Had it been a dream then? Had she imagined it?

"Persephone? Are you okay? Please tell me what you're thinking. You're looking at me like I'm some kind of demon."

"It must have been a bad dream," she said through fresh tears. "Last week, you came into our bed chamber and…"

He took her in his arms, and she sank against him, as he gently stroked her hair and kissed her head. "It was only a figment from the Dreamworld, my dear. It wasn't me."

She met his lips with hers and filled with relief. A heavy burden lifted from her.

He swept her up in his arms and god-traveled with her to their bedroom, where he was tender with her again.

<u>CHAPTER FIFTY-ONE</u>

Family

The next day, Hades flew to the battlefields to round up his children and bring them home. He found Hecate and Galin, too, because he considered them members of their family. Once they had gathered together with Persephone and him in the main room of their palace, he told them his new idea.

"That day all of you came to see me near Delphi was the best day of my life," he said.

Tizzie petted the head of her dog, which sat quietly at her side. "Even though you were working with pigs?"

"Don't be rude," Meg said to her sister. Her parakeet squawked, too.

"Even though I was working with pigs," Hades confirmed. "I could have been in the pit of Tartarus, and it wouldn't have mattered."

"Because we were all together," Alecto said, as she stroked her cat. "Isn't that right, Father?"

"That's exactly right," Hades said.

"But I have lives to save," Zao said. "I can't save them all, but I can save some."

"We all have jobs to do," Tizzie said. "We can't help that there's a war going on."

Then Persephone said—but not without kindness, "Let your father speak without so many interruptions."

Hades gave her a wink and then turned to the kids. "I know you're all busy, and I couldn't be prouder of the hard work you do. But from this day on, I want us to meet here once a week and share a meal together."

"That's a wonderful idea, Lord Hades," Hecate said.

"Will there be cake?" Gelos asked. "Because if there's cake, count me in."

Everyone laughed.

Persephone patted Gelos on the head. "There will be cake."

A few weeks later, Hades returned home from avenging the murder of an entire family in a small village not far from Thebes. Hades had first tormented the guilty man in the upperworld before driving his sword through the murderer's heart. Now, Hermes was helping the man's soul to board Charon's raft for the room of judgment, where he was sure to be sentenced to Tartarus. Hades didn't always take pleasure in his work, but bringing justice on behalf of the mother, father, and five children gave him immense satisfaction. As he headed toward his bed chamber looking for Persephone, he realized why this particular case had made him more emotional than usual. The family of seven that had been murdered in their sleep had reminded him of his own family.

When Hades found Persephone sound asleep in their bed, he decided to return to the main room of his palace for a glass of wine before joining her. He hadn't been there, long, however, when Hermes appeared.

"Hecate has asked me to summon you, Lord Hades," Hermes said with a sense of urgency.

Hades leapt to his feet. "Has something happened?"

"Hecate is safe, but something terrible has happened."

"Spit it out, Hermes."

"When Achilles couldn't be persuaded to fight against the Trojans, his best friend, Patroclus, borrowed his armor and went to battle in his place. He wanted the Trojans to think he was Achilles, to make them afraid."

"I know," Hades said. "Patroclus killed a lot of Trojans, but he's here now, in the Elysian Fields."

"Killed by Hector," Hermes said.

"Yes. So?"

"Achilles went mad with rage. He loved Patroclus."

"Yes, I know. Get on with it."

"Hephaestus made Achilles a new set of armor—quite remarkable, too," Hermes said.

"I don't doubt it." Hades wished Hermes would get to his point.

"Well, Achilles killed at least half of the Trojan army, and then he found Hector and killed him, too."

"Killed Hector? Then where is he? Where's Hector's soul?"

"That's the problem. You have to come see for yourself."

"Let's take my chariot," Hades commanded. "With the gods back in the war, it's not safe."

A moment later, they flew toward Troy behind Swift and Sure, with Hermes pointing to the Greek camp.

"Over there," Hermes said.

Down below, Achilles was dragging the dead body of Hector, by a rope tied to his horse, all across the countryside between the Trojan walls and the Greek camp. The transparent soul of Hector was loose from its body, but clinging tightly with both hands, unwilling to let go. Hecate hovered above them, trying to coax the soul away from the body, but to no avail.

"This is disturbing," Hades said.

"And highly distasteful," Hermes agreed. "But how do we put an end to it?"

Hades thought for a moment and then said, "That horse is nearly dead with exhaustion. Take its soul. That will put a stop to it."

Hermes disintegrated and one of him dispatched to take the soul of the horse. As the body of the horse fell over, Achilles leapt from it. Then Achilles cut Hector's body free and dragged it to the outskirts of the camp, allowing it to lie, exposed to the elements, while he himself cleaned up and ate a meal.

Hecate was finally able to get the soul of Hector to follow her to the Underworld, but the soul was restless because the body had been so terribly dishonored.

Hades turned to Hermes. "Go convince Priam to bring a wagon here to the Greek camp."

"Won't the Greeks kill the Trojan king?"

"Tell the king I'll put him under the protection of my helm until he reaches Achilles," Hades said. "I think if he appeals to Achilles as a grieving father, the warrior will hand over Hector's body."

It was a long night, but Hades had been right about Achilles. After Priam brought him to tears, Achilles gave the father his son.

Hades returned to his palace, thinking of his own sons and daughters and wishing he could protect them from all the evils of the world. Even the gods were vulnerable, because, as Achilles had just shown the mortals at war, death wasn't the worst thing that could happen to a person.

Before he reached his rooms, Hades heard Persephone screaming in her bed. He flew to her side. Hecate wasn't far behind him.

They found Persephone lying among bloody sheets, writhing in pain.

CHAPTER FIFTY-TWO

The Birth of Melinoe

Persephone had been in the deep boon of sleep when a sharp pain in her abdomen awakened her. She opened her eyes in time to see a dark figure flee from her bed, but she couldn't be sure if he'd been real or if he'd been a lingering figment from a horrible dream.

And at the moment, she had no presence of mind to analyze what was real and what wasn't, because the pain in her belly had become overwhelming—worse than the pains of labor. When she looked down and saw blood all over her hands and bedcovers, she could no longer hold back her screams.

Hades and Hecate were at her side in an instant with looks of horror on their faces.

"Help me!" she pleaded. "Find Apollo!"

Hades summoned Hermes, who left as swiftly as he'd arrived to seek the god of healing. Meanwhile, Hecate examined Persephone's belly, feeling all around it with her two shaking hands.

"You're with-child," Hecate finally said. "But something's wrong."

Persephone was shocked. She'd had no idea she'd been pregnant again.

Hades summoned Hermes once more. The messenger god arrived without Apollo.

"Bring Artemis, too, if you can," Hades said.

Once Hermes had left again, Hades knelt on the floor beside the bed and held Persephone's hand.

"Help is on the way, my love. Please, hold on," he told her.

She wasn't sure how much longer that was possible. She bit her tongue until she tasted blood.

Hecate lifted the bedcovers and revealed a gash in Persephone's side, as if it had been ripped open, and blood seeped from the wound. Behind the blood, a tiny, crooked hand poked through the gash.

Persephone wailed in pain as the hand pushed out, giving way to an arm, then a shoulder with sagging skin, and finally a ghastly face! Persephone cringed.

Half of the child's face was smooth and black, and the other was white and misshapen. On the white side of her face was a black eye, and on the black side, a white eye. The hair on her head was parted down the middle, and each side of the part matched the side of the face it grew on, so that depending on which way she turned, she looked either all black or all white. Except for the eyes.

As the monstrous child climbed from Persephone's womb, Apollo and Artemis appeared with Hermes, and all three faces showed the same look of horror Persephone saw on the faces of Hecate and Hades, and which she undoubtedly wore on her own face. But this was *her baby*, her own flesh and blood, and it couldn't help how it looked.

Even though she was in pain and disturbed by the child's appearance, Persephone forced herself to smile on the child and to welcome her into the world as Apollo sewed the gash in her side and Artemis wiped the blood from the child's hair, face, and body.

"My sweet little girl!" Persephone said, as the creature continued to look around, distraught. "I'm so happy to have another baby girl!"

"Something hurt me, Mother," the child said in a raspy voice. "Someone twisted me all up and tried to kill me! Was it you?"

Persephone's mouth dropped open. She turned to her husband to find his face as white as a sheet. Tears sprang from Persephone's eyes as she vigorously shook her head. "I would never hurt you! Never!"

Apollo glanced suspiciously at Hades before saying, "Let me take the child to Mount Olympus to examine her more thoroughly with my instruments and determine whether I can help her further."

"Take me with you!" Persephone begged.

"That's not a good idea," Artemis said.

Hecate shook her head. "Artemis is right, my dear. You need your rest. You should stay here in bed."

Persephone started to object. "But…"

"It's okay, my love," Hades said. "You need to let your body heal. I'll go with Apollo and watch over our child."

"I don't think that's wise," Apollo said. "You should stay and comfort your wife, Lord Hades. There's nothing you can do on Mount Olympus."

"Then perhaps Hecate can go," Persephone said, turning to her friend. "Surely the baby will recognize your voice, since we're so often together."

"Mother, I'm frightened," the child said, glancing all around.

"Do you know me?" Hecate said to the girl.

The girl nodded and climbed into Hecate's open arms. As her baby left her side, Persephone was overcome with a bad omen of something truly terrible to come.

"What shall we call her?" Artemis asked as she wrapped a fresh blanket around the trembling child in Hecate's arms.

The only name that came to Persephone was *Melinoe*, because of the stark contrast of the child's dark skin growing beside the white. The uneven melanin was, for now, the most notable thing about her. "Melinoe." She glanced at Hades, who nodded his approval.

"I'll bring her back as soon as I can," Hecate said to Persephone. "Get some rest for now, okay?"

Persephone nodded, in spite of the terrible omen eating her up inside.

"Thank you, Hecate," Hades said.

When everyone but her husband had left the room, Hades leaned over her and stroked her hair. "I swear I did not do this."

Persephone whispered, "I believe you," though she couldn't help but have her doubts. The Hades she knew would never do such a thing, but what if there was a side to him that she did not know? What if that horrible night a month ago had not been a dream? What if the dark figure that had fled from her bed when she had first awakened had been her very own husband?

"Are you still in pain, my love?"

"I hardly know," she said through her tears. "The pain in my heart is greater than anything else. What happened to our baby? What terrible thing caused her to be so malformed?"

"I wish I knew," he said. "Let's hope Apollo can help her."

Persephone closed her eyes and prayed to Apollo. *Save my daughter,* she pleaded as more tears slipped down the sides of her face. *Help her in any way you can.*

CHAPTER FIFTY-THREE

Apollo Accuses Hades

Demeter rushed from her rooms to the main hall when she heard Hecate praying to her. She could tell by the urgency in her friend's tone that something bad had happened.

She reached the arm of her throne in time to see Apollo and Artemis arrive on either side of Hecate. The three of them stood in the middle of the court. In Hecate's arms was some kind of creature. As Demeter studied the thing more closely, she was shocked to realize it was a child. It was two-toned and misshapen, with wild, frightened eyes—one black and the other white. Demeter shuddered. As she stood by her throne, she was anxious to learn how Hecate had come to possess such a thing.

Since the Greeks and Trojans had recently taken a break from the war to bury and mourn their dead, all of the great Olympians, except for Poseidon and Hades, were present.

Zeus stood up from his throne with a look of disgust on his face. "What's this?"

Artemis was the first of the newly arrived to speak. "Persephone's child."

"What?" Demeter cried, unable to contain her horror. Then she covered her mouth when the child glared at her.

"How can this be?" Athena asked. "Did something cause…" Athena didn't finish her question.

As Demeter glanced around the room, she noticed that every god there gazed at the child with a look of revulsion. Even Zeus's face was pale.

"Perhaps Hecate should take Melinoe into another room while we determine the best way to help her," Apollo suggested.

So, her name was Melinoe.

Zeus nodded his agreement. Hecate crossed the room with the child. Demeter avoided the eyes of both as they passed her throne where she stood, clutching the arm of her chair for support.

"Do we know what caused the child to be deformed?" Hera asked once Hecate and Melinoe had left the room.

Apollo took another step forward. "I had a vision."

Zeus's face turned red. "And what did you see?"

Apollo raked a hand through his light brown hair. "Hades."

Gasps filled the room. Demeter lost her breath.

Apollo continued, "I saw the lord of darkness lie beside his sleeping wife, thrust his hand into her side, and attempt to destroy the innocent babe."

Demeter fell to her knees. Two of Aphrodites's Graces rushed to her side to help her to her seat, where she sat, trembling.

"Hades was with *me*," Hermes said. "We went to stop Achilles. You saw the dishonor he did to Hector. Hades and I helped Priam get his son's body back."

"How do we know Hades didn't do this evil deed as soon as he returned home?" Ares asked him. "Or before he left with you?"

"But why would he?" Hermes asked.

"That's what I want to know," Aphrodite said. "Why would he do such a thing?"

"Who knows what motivates the lord of darkness?" Zeus said. "Maybe he was tired of his wife being pregnant. She gave birth only four months ago. Perhaps he was motivated by selfish desires."

Demeter clutched her stomach, feeling ill.

"Maybe the child doesn't belong to Hades," Hera said. "If Hades caught Persephone having an affair, he had a motive to destroy the child."

Blood rushed to Demeter's face. "How dare you accuse my daughter?"

"I'm not accusing her," Hera said. "I'm merely speculating about why Hades might commit this crime."

"Let's bring him here and ask him!" Demeter cried as her heart pumped furiously. "I will not allow my daughter's reputation to be tarnished by speculation."

"How clear was this vision?" Hephaestus asked Apollo.

"Crystal clear," Apollo admitted. "I had it years ago. I tried to warn Persephone, but she didn't want to listen. I had the same vision again two days ago."

"Apollo never lies," Zeus said.

Artemis added, "When the child was born, she said someone had reached inside and tried to kill her."

"How frightful!" Aphrodite cried.

"We can't let Hades get away with this," Ares said.

"Poor Persephone!" Hestia said as she covered her face with her hands and wept.

Demeter was grateful for her sister's tears but still in shock. She couldn't believe this was all happening. It felt like bad dream.

Zeus turned to Hermes. "Will you summon Poseidon and Hades, and bring them both here? We shall have a vote to determine the innocence or guilt of my brother."

Hermes disappeared.

"Can you help the child?" Artemis asked her twin. "Or is her deformity permanent?"

"I'll examine her more carefully after the hearing, but I don't think there's much I can do."

"Maybe she needs more time inside the womb," Hestia offered. "Maybe she wasn't finished developing yet."

"Can she be returned?" Athena asked Apollo. "Is that possible?"

"That method worked for our father when Semele died before she could give birth to Dionysus," Apollo said.

"Please don't remind us," Hera murmured.

"But the transference from the womb to our father's thigh was immediate," Apollo said, in spite of Hera's comment. "I'm afraid it may be too late for Melinoe to gestate further."

The idea of putting the monstrous child back into her daughter made Demeter feel faint again. But before another word could be said about it, Hecate rushed into the room, empty handed.

"Melinoe is gone!" Hecate cried. "She tricked me into putting her down, and then she flew away before I could stop her!"

"Go look for her," Zeus told Hecate. "I'll have Hermes disintegrate and help in the search as well."

Hecate gave Demeter a forlorn glance before she flew away.

As much as Demeter wanted the poor, misfortunate child found, she was even more concerned that the girl might want to do harm to her mother. More than ever, Demeter wished Persephone was at her side, so she could guard her from all evil—especially from the lord of darkness.

C H A P T E R   F I F T Y - F O U R

Hermes Comes for Hades

As Persephone lay there in her bed praying to Apollo with Hades kneeling beside her, stroking her hair, her other five children suddenly returned unexpectedly from the war, and the first thing they did was come looking for her.

She'd hoped to spare them from the sight of her bloody sheets, but they burst into her room without knocking, just as Meg was warning them that they shouldn't, because it wasn't good manners.

"Oh, no!" Alecto cried, clinging to her cat, when she saw the blood.

Tizzie leapt forward, with her dog at her heels. "Mother, what's happened?"

"Is that blood?" Zao flew up and hovered over her.

Meg came up behind them. "Father, is she sick?"

"Your mother had another baby." Hades climbed to his feet. "Another girl. But the child isn't well, and Apollo took her to Mount Olympus."

"Is she going to be okay?" Zao asked.

"Of course, she is," Gelos said. "She's a goddess. Duh."

"What's her name?" Tizzie asked.

"Melinoe," Persephone said.

"There's something you all need to know," Hades started. "She was born with some…deformities."

"You mean she isn't beautiful?" Alecto clung to her cat.

"Don't be rude," Meg warned.

"She's beautiful in her own way," Persephone said.

"We have to learn to find the beauty within," Hades added gently. "Now why don't you all go and check on Cerberus and the horses and let me help your mother change her bedcovers?"

"When will we get to see Melinoe?" Alecto asked as she flew to the door.

"Soon, I hope," Persephone said.

"Does she know her purpose?" Zao asked.

"Not yet," Hades replied. "Now scoot."

Before the children had left the room, Hermes appeared in the doorway. "Zeus has asked me to summon you to Mount Olympus, Lord Hades."

Persephone tried to sit up in the bed but only managed to prop herself on her elbows. "Is Melinoe okay? Was Apollo able to help her?"

Hermes hung his head. "I'm afraid she's flown away."

"What?" Hades bellowed. "How could Apollo let her out of his sight?"

"She was in Hecate's custody," Hermes explained. "The child tricked her and took off. Hecate and I are both out searching for her now. I promise you we'll find her."

"If Melinoe has run away, why am I wanted on Mount Olympus?" Hades asked. "I need to join the search."

When Hermes didn't reply, Persephone realized he was speaking to her husband telepathically. She turned and studied her husband's face to find it deathly pale.

"What is it?" she asked him.

Hades met her eyes. *Apollo has accused me of attempting to murder our child before she was born.*

Persephone's heart felt as though it had stopped beating. The air left her body, and her throat closed up. Since she couldn't speak, she allowed the despair to take over, and she pressed her face into her pillow and wept.

"Father?" Alecto asked. "Please tell us what's wrong."

"Stay here and take care of your mother," he said. "I'll be home as soon as I can."

CHAPTER FIFTY-FIVE

Hades Is Judged and Sentenced

Hades stood in the middle of the court on Mount Olympus facing his accuser, Apollo.

"The old prophet, Tiresias, told me of this same vision after Persephone and I were first married," Hades said.

"He saw the same evil deed?" Aphrodite asked.

Hades turned to her. "Yes. But knowing I would never do such a thing, I went to see Cassandra—Priam's daughter."

"And what did she say?" Apollo asked.

Hades folded his arms at his chest. "She had the same vision as you."

"Three prophets have all seen the same thing," Zeus said. "And you expect us to believe you're innocent?"

Hades regretted sharing the information. The rage and despair mixed together in his throat, but he pushed through it to say, "I did everything in my power to avoid my wife each time she was pregnant, just to be safe. I wasn't even home when my wife was molested."

"He was with me," Hermes said. "As I told you before. We were helping Priam."

Hades nodded. "That's right. I returned home to Persephone's screams. Hecate was close behind me."

"Hecate isn't here to speak on your behalf," Zeus said. "But if she was close *behind* you, that means there was some time, however short, when you were alone with Persephone, when you might have committed the crime."

"That's not how it happened," Hades insisted.

"Or, he could have hurt his child before he left for Troy," Ares pointed out.

"But I didn't," Hades said.

"Does he speak the truth?" Athena asked Apollo.

Apollo hesitated. "I sense some self-doubt in his words. I don't think he knows himself whether he is innocent or guilty."

Hades threw his arms in the air.

"Is this a fair assessment, Hades?" Poseidon asked. "Are you unsure of your innocence?"

"Of course, it is," Ares said. "Three different prophets have told him the same thing."

"Maybe he committed the crime in his sleep," Hephaestus offered. "That was the plea made by my mother after she threw me from Mount Olympus."

Hera stiffened. "He might have been drunk. It's happened before, hasn't it, Poseidon?"

"Indeed," Poseidon said.

"Oh, dear gods, this is impossible!" Hades shouted. "It seems there's nothing I can say to convince you of my innocence. You will believe what you want to believe."

"Surely you must understand how this looks from our point of view," Athena said. "We have the word of three prophets, and one of them is the god of truth. How can we not doubt you?"

"Especially when you abducted your wife in the first place!" Demeter accused.

"But…" Hades started to object, but then remembered his promise to his wife.

"Maybe we should question Persephone," Hermes suggested. "Let her speak on her husband's behalf."

"No," Zeus and Hades said together.

The last thing Hades wanted was to put her through this miserable ordeal.

"She's still healing from her wound," Hades said. "She needs rest, not interrogation."

"For once, we agree," Zeus said. "Enough talk. Let's put this to the vote. I want each of you to recall the deformities of the child as you cast your vote. How many of you believe Hades to be guilty of molesting his daughter while she was still forming in the womb?"

Hades held his breath and looked around the room. Apollo, Zeus, and Hera raised their hands immediately, followed by Ares and Demeter. Poseidon and Hephaestus then raised theirs as well. Athena and Artemis followed. Just as Hades thought Aphrodite might withhold her vote, she burst into tears and lifted her hand as well. Only Hestia and Hermes had believed him.

"The vote is ten to two," Zeus declared. "The court finds Hades guilty."

The room spun a few times. Hades stumbled but caught his balance and his breath. If he had ever thought the other gods had little love for him, it had been nothing compared to what he felt now. All but Hermes and Hestia looked at him with utter hate and disgust. They believed him capable of the vilest act he could imagine. To bring harm to one's own child was the lowest of the low. And that's what they thought of him.

He fully expected them to strip him of his kingdom. Perhaps he would even be thrown into his own pit in the depths of Tartarus. He stood before them on weakened knees, barely able to breathe. But he held his head high, in spite of the dizziness, because he knew he was innocent and undeserving of their judgment.

"Now to determine your punishment," Zeus said.

Apollo said, "As you must all be aware, a god does not possess immortality until it is born. This evil deed was meant to kill a god before it could be born. We have to take this seriously if we're to protect the future progeny of our race."

"This is not the time to send him back to work among pigs," Poseidon said. "We need something graver and more serious."

"The punishment should fit the crime," Athena agreed.

Demeter glared at Hades. "Sentence him to the Titan pit in Tartarus and return my daughter and her children to Mount Olympus."

"No," Hestia said. "Kronos is bound to swallow him again."

Aphrodite put a hand to her mouth. "The Titan pit is too severe. Hera has done terrible things to Zeus's children, and no one here would imagine sentencing *her* to that pit."

Hera blanched. "I never tried to kill a god before it was born."

"Take away his kingdom," Ares suggested.

"That's too harsh," Hermes objected. "Besides, who else among you wants it?"

"Why not you?" Artemis asked him.

Hermes shook his head. "It belongs to Lord Hades."

Hades was grateful for Hermes and Hestia's support. He would never forget it.

"The surest way to punish Hades is to punish his children," Hera said.

Hades stumbled as the room began to spin again. "Not my children."

"Melinoe has suffered enough," Apollo pointed out.

"I meant the others," Hera said. "Throw them into Tartarus."

"No," Athena said. "They've been useful and dedicated to their duties."

"Hera is right," Zeus said. "Punishing his children is the worst thing we can do to Hades. But Athena is also right. They've been useful and dedicated. So this is what I propose."

Hades held his breath.

"The Kindly Ones will henceforth be known as the Furies," Zeus continued. "Instead of blessings on the wounded and dying, they will spread fear to murderers and thieves. They will serve as the avengers of injustice. Blood will pour from their eyes. Their hair will turn into snakes. Even their familiars will become fearsome. I'll turn the parakeet into a falcon with a deadly beak. It will pluck out the eyes of the murderers and thieves. And the dog will become a fierce wolf. Its howls will drive men mad. And the cat will become a deadly snake that will squeeze the breath from a man."

"Please don't do this," Hades said, falling to his knees. "They're innocent. They've helped on both sides of the war all these years."

But Zeus did not listen to him. "The boy you call Gelos will no longer bring laughter and merriment to those who are bored or melancholy. Instead, he will henceforth be known as Hypnos, and his presence will put people to sleep. Hermes will no longer serve in the Dreamworld."

Hades imagined his clever son with his witty remarks. He was born to bring cheer, not sleep. "This isn't fair," Hades objected again.

But Zeus continued. "And the boy you call Zao will henceforth be known as Thanatos—not Life, but Death. He will no longer protect life. He will be the end of it. He will relieve Hermes of his duty as Death."

Hades leapt to his feet. "But he's still a child! You can't give that responsibility to someone so young. Give it to me, instead. Make *me* Death and turn my kingdom over to my wife."

"No!" Demeter cried. "Persephone is the goddess of spring. She's everything light and beautiful!"

"Then make Hecate the queen of the Underworld," Hades begged.

"She's a Titaness," Hera objected. "We can't trust that much power to someone who was once our enemy."

"*You* will remain the lord of darkness," Zeus said to Hades. "And *you* will oversee your children's new duties. Now that Hermes has been liberated of them, there should be no reason why any other Olympian should ever have to set foot in your realm again. We will live separate lives from you—though, for Demeter's sake, Persephone will continue to return here for half of every year."

"He's our brother," Hestia said. "He should still have a vote at this council."

"I agree," Poseidon said. "Hades must remain a member of this court."

"I'm surprised to hear you speak on our brother's behalf," Zeus said to Poseidon.

Poseidon looked around at the other gods. "I cannot support a precedent that might lead to any of us being stripped of our right to vote in this council. If we take it away from Hades, we'll begin a descent down a slippery slope that could eventually lead to one among us becoming a supreme and tyrannical ruler—our oppressor. Would any of you risk that?"

Hades couldn't care less about being a member of the court. His heart was aching for his children and his wife.

"I hate to admit it," Athena said, "but Poseidon's words are wise."

"Hear, hear," Artemis agreed.

"And another thing," Athena said. "It would be wise to remove the memories of Hades's children, so they can better adjust to their new roles. Without their memories of a happier time, they won't be sad for the rest of their days, because they won't know that their lives have ever been anything different."

"Remove their memories?" Hades repeated. The thought of them forgetting all the many times they shared meals and stories together— the pig races and frog races and wrestling with Cerberus. "Is that really necessary?"

"Do you want your children to feel deprived of the happy lives they once had?" Artemis asked.

"They'll be healthier without them," Apollo agreed.

"If anyone objects to the punishment laid out, let him say so now," Zeus said.

"I object!" Hades cried.

"I object!" Hermes and Hestia also shouted.

"All in favor, say *aye*," Zeus said.

"Aye."

"Aye."

"Aye."

Hades fell once more to his knees as all save Hestia and Hermes sentenced his children to their new and terrible roles.

He was a god of justice, but there was no justice for him.

<u>CHAPTER FIFTY-SIX:</u>

Selene

When she finally felt well enough to get out of bed, Persephone changed from her bloody gown into fresh robes and went looking for Melinoe. She flew aimlessly, desperately, and in a heightened sense of panic in the pre-dawn night, until Selene, the moon goddess, called out to her.

"Come here!" Selene cried. "I have your daughter!"

The moon goddess was riding in her silver chariot toward the east, dipping down past the Aegean Sea toward the mountains beyond Troy. Her long, silver hair fanned out behind her, as did her long, white, luminous robe. Her robe formed a crescent at the collar, tied at her throat. Her chariot was pulled by two silver horses with manes as long and iridescent as hers.

Beside her in the chariot sat Melinoe, clinging to the edge of the silver car with white knuckles. Persephone caught up to them and joined them in the chariot, putting her arms around her lost girl, just as Selene drove into the mountains and parked inside a cave.

Lying on a mattress stuffed with feathers at the back of the cave near a fountain was the man Persephone knew must be Endymion, a shepherd and astronomer who was loved so much by Selene that she placed him in an eternal sleep. Each day, she brought her chariot here, and she lay beside her love, until Nyx awakened her for her nightly ride.

"Thank you for rescuing my daughter," Persephone said. "I've been worried sick."

"Asteria brought her to me," Selene replied. "She asked me to wait here with her for Hecate."

Melinoe allowed her mother to hold her in her arms, but she didn't speak. She was shivering with fear and wore a blank look on her face.

"It's okay, darling," Persephone said, holding her close. "I won't let anything bad happen to you."

"You already have," Melinoe said. "I've just seen my reflection in the sheen of this chariot. Who did this to me?"

Persephone smoothed her daughter's hair—both the white on one side and the black on the other. "I don't know, my sweet daughter. I was asleep when it happened. Will you forgive me?"

Melinoe's two-toned face crumpled like parchment, and her mouth turned down in a frown, her lips quivering.

"Listen to me," Selene said to both of them. "Hecate is on her way with Hephaestus and Thetis to talk to you both about how Melinoe's misshapen form might be cured. They should be here any moment."

While they waited, Persephone rocked her child in her arms and smoothed away the tears trailing down her cheeks—both the white and the black. As she did so, she sang the song her mother used to sing to her when she was a child:

Sweet little cherub, don't you cry.
Sleep will be coming, and soon you'll fly
Up to the stars and into the night.
A kiss for Selene and all is bright.

As Persephone sang, the day wore on, and soon Melinoe fell asleep in her arms. Eventually, Selene climbed from her chariot to lie beside Endymion, and she, too, fell asleep. Her luminous robes and hair continued to illuminate the cave, even while she fell into a sound sleep. Not knowing what else to do, Persephone continued to sing.

While she sang, she gazed at her daughter's sleeping face and discovered that when she wasn't frowning, with her brows bent in anger, Melinoe possessed a certain kind of handsomeness. It wasn't beauty, per se, but it wasn't ugliness either. Persephone wondered if the girl smiled, if that would make all the difference.

She stopped singing when she sensed a godly presence outside the cave. In another moment, Hecate flew to her side, followed by Thetis and Hephaestus.

"Look how lovely she looks when she sleeps," Hecate said of Melinoe, which further reinforced Persephone's own conclusions.

"Do you have any news about my husband?" Persephone asked.

Hecate frowned. "Yes, but first, let Hephaestus and Thetis tell you what they came to say."

Although Persephone was eager to hear what the other two gods had to say, she wondered why Hecate put off her answer about Hades.

Thetis climbed into the chariot and sat beside Persephone. "When Hephaestus was born, he, too, suffered from deformities. He was weak and lame and had a hunchback."

"I wish my mother would have rocked me in her arms as you're doing now with your child," Hephaestus said. "But as I'm sure you've heard—hasn't everyone heard my story?—Hera threw me down from Mount Olympus. She couldn't love a malformed child."

Persephone *had* heard the story, and she'd always felt sorry for Hephaestus. Hera could be gracious and loving at times, but she could be just as cold-hearted and cruel.

"He landed in the sea, near me," Thetis said. "So I pulled him from the water onto my Hippocamp, and we rode together to a grotto, where I raised him with love."

Hecate leaned close to the silver car and brushed a strand of hair from Melinoe's sleeping face. "That's the point I wanted to make by bringing them here. Look at Hephaestus now, how beautiful he is. He may still have a slight limp when he walks, but there are no other signs of his birth defects. His hunchback is gone, and he's certainly no weakling."

Hephaestus laughed. "Stop now before I blush. The point is, Thetis deserves all the credit. She loved me and helped me to love myself."

"That really is the key to helping your daughter," Thetis said. "If you can teach her to love herself and to have a positive disposition, her inner beauty will shine through. Then over the years, her physical features will begin to mirror the beautiful person she is inside."

"I know I could have told you this without bringing these two with me," Hecate said. "But I thought hearing it from them would be more powerful. I hated seeing you so distressed, my dear. I wanted to offer you hope."

Persephone smiled at her good friend, realizing she loved her like a sister. "Thank you for this. You succeeded in your mission. I'll give my daughter nothing but love and teach her how to love herself."

Suddenly, Thetis stood up with a grief-stricken face and wailed.

Melinoe awakened from her slumber as Persephone asked, "Thetis?"

Even Selene sat up beside Endymion to learn what had happened.

"My son! My dear Achilles!" the sea nymph cried. "He's praying to me to say goodbye. He's been struck in the heel by an arrow from Paris! I must go to him!"

Thetis disappeared, leaving the rest of them frowning and sorry that war was a necessary part of life.

"We knew it wouldn't be long," Selene said. "Achilles was told that once he killed Hector, he would soon die, too."

Knowing didn't make it any easier, Persephone thought.

"He was the greatest warrior on the Greek side," Hephaestus said. "I'd like to look at him one last time."

"I would, too," Hecate said.

Persephone carried Melinoe and followed Hecate and Hephaestus from the mountains to the sky above Troy and watched as Thetis flew down to her son, where he lay amid other warriors still fighting outside the walls of the city. Before Achilles drew his last breath, Thetis had the chance to tell him she loved him. At that moment, Persephone was thankful that she had no mortal children, because the thought of saying goodbye to them forever seemed unbearable. This thought made her realize why her mother had been against her marriage to Hades. Demeter must have seen it as a kind of death. As hard as it was for Persephone to leave her husband for six months out of the year, she was glad she'd made that arrangement. As she held Melinoe close to her breast, she hoped with all her heart that her children would likewise honor her with their presence throughout their lives.

Her thoughts were interrupted by the sudden appearance of Zao flying swiftly down toward the battlefield. She wondered if she'd have the chance to see him protecting the life of a child caught in the crossfire. She scanned the ground below, however, and could spot no child. Then she gasped when Zao flew directly to the body of Achilles and took away the warrior's soul.

"What's this?" Persephone asked. "What's my son doing down there?"

Hecate and Hephaestus exchanged hard looks before Hecate said, "Let's go back to Selene's cave, so I can tell you what's happened."

Persephone shook her head. "Tell me now. Please. What's going on?"

C H A P T E R   F I F T Y - S E V E N

The Fearsome Underworld

Six weeks after Hades had been sentenced by the court, he sat alone in the main room of his palace, hardened and bitter. It wasn't because his first five children had suffered from their transformation. Athena had been right. Erasing their memories had made it possible for them to be somewhat happy in their new roles—the Kindly Ones especially. The Furies, as they were now called, seemed to take pleasure in hunting down murderers and thieves and punishing them first on earth before finding them again in Tartarus to continue the work.

Hypnos, or Hip, as his sisters called him for short, used his creative mind to find pleasure in the Dreamworld. Unlike Hermes, who'd depended solely on the figments to people the dreams of his sleepers, Hip enjoyed participating in them. At a young age, he'd already found his favorite form of entertainment: flirting with girls in their dreams. He hadn't lost his sense of humor. Gelos was still very much a part of Hip's personality.

Of the five, only Thanatos seemed less happy than he'd been before his transformation. As Zao, he'd taken great pride in protecting the lives of children caught in the crossfires of battle. The same stamina that had driven him to save his newly born brother's life had driven him as Zao. As Thanatos, or Than, as his sisters called him, he was dedicated and serious, but not particularly happy.

When Hermes was Death, he'd had other duties to divert and satisfy him, but Than hadn't had the chance to develop those other interests.

So day in and day out, the only thing he ever did, aside from an occasional meal and sleep, was escort the souls of the dead to the Underworld.

And Thanatos had seemed a natural from the moment he'd taken over, in spite of the fact that Hercules had tied him up on his very first day as Death to steal Cerberus. It had been the last of the labors for Hercules, and his soul was now here, in the Underworld, at peace, while his bow and arrows were being used by the Greeks in their final stand against the Trojans. Without Achilles, the fate of the Greeks was dim.

Nevertheless, Than, like his brother and sisters, didn't seem to be entirely miserable, as Hades had feared when the council had agreed on his punishment. The disposition of his children wasn't the cause of his grief.

It was the toll the transformations had taken on his sweet, beloved Persephone.

Even though she said she believed in his innocence, Hades could sense her doubts. He sensed it when he went to their bed at night, and she turned away from him. She spent more time with Hecate these days than with him. At least she had her friend.

As heartbreaking as it was for Hades to sense Persephone's lack of faith in him, her grief over losing what her children once were was devastating to him. Like him, she missed hearing the stories of how their children blessed the wounded and dying, or brought laughter to the melancholy, or saved the lives of innocent children. If their children told stories to them at all these days, it was about the look in the face of a murderer just before Meg's falcon plucked out his eye.

But Persephone's greatest pain came from her inability to teach Melinoe to love herself. Because the memories of their youngest child weren't erased, she was aware of the transformation in her brothers and sisters. Even though she knew it wasn't her fault, she still blamed herself. Melinoe never said as much, but she didn't need to. Persephone and Hades had agreed that Melinoe considered her birth the cause of her parents' unhappiness. They could read it in their daughter's face: she wished she had died before she was born.

Hades had tried to appeal to the court to erase Melinoe's memories, too, but all of the gods were too busy in the final days of the war. They considered the matter of Hades behind them, and they'd moved on to what were, to them, more important matters.

As often as Hades and Persephone tried to be tender with Melinoe, she resisted them. Within three weeks of being born, she flew away, and this time, she managed to avoid being found.

Hades wondered how things might have turned out had he been more proactive with the information he'd been given by the prophets. Maybe if he'd told Persephone what he'd heard, and maybe if he'd been open about it with the other gods, they might have worked together to solve the riddle. The only thing that made any sense to him at all, now that he'd had time to give it more thought, was that some demon must have disguised himself as Hades. But who would do such a thing? And why?

As he sat ruminating, more miserable than he'd ever been, his thoughts were interrupted by the sudden appearance of Thanatos.

"You won't believe what's happening," the boy said. "You should come with me, Father. You need to tell me what to do."

"What is it?" Hades asked as he climbed to his feet.

"Troy is in flames, and, well, you need to see this for yourself."

CHAPTER FIFTY-EIGHT

Troy Burns

Hades followed his son through the chasm and up into the dark sky. The stars spread out over the land like a glittering veil, but even their shimmering light was eclipsed by the solid wall of fire that reached into the sky from within the walls of Troy.

As they flew toward the burning city, Hades noticed Athena and Hera hovering above it with satisfied smiles on their faces. They'd wanted Troy destroyed, and now their desires had been realized. Had they no remorse for the innocent who were also killed in the goddesses' haste to teach Paris a lesson?

The Greek fleets had already begun to sail away. How had they managed to get away so quickly?

Hades turned to Thanatos. "The Greeks are already at sea."

"That's only half of them."

"Only half?"

"The others tricked the Trojans with a monument to Athena—a giant wooden horse bearing the Palladium."

"The Palladium? The Greeks stole it from Troy?"

Thanatos nodded. "Weeks ago. And then last night they left behind a man who pretended to escape his execution."

"Why?"

"The man told the Trojan leaders that the Greeks hoped they would desecrate the monument and incur the wrath of Athena. Instead, they brought it into the city to beautify and honor it."

"Then why is Athena smiling down on their destruction?" Hades asked.

"She was in on the trick," Than said. "Hiding inside the monument was the rest of the Greek army."

Hades sighed. "I see."

"Cassandra tried to warn her father, but…"

"He didn't believe her."

"No."

Hades turned to Thanatos. "I imagine this will be a busy night for you. Is this what you wanted me to see?'

"There's more. Brace yourself."

Hades couldn't imagine what could be worse than the sight of hundreds of people trapped inside a wall of flames, burning to their deaths.

"This way," Thanatos said.

Hades followed him into the fire.

Hades saw Cassandra and her mother Hecuba, along with a few other women, being led by Greek warriors away from the burning city. He wasn't sure how much better off they were than those who were dead, however, since they would be treated as spoils of war. But hadn't Cassandra predicted her death? And hadn't she said something bizarre about her mother, Hecuba, turning into a dog and serving him in the Underworld?

As they neared the interior of the walls, Hades saw Thanatos disintegrated into the dozens as he escorted soul after soul from their bodies toward the Underworld. But wait a minute. What was this?

Hovering among the dead and dying was his youngest daughter, Melinoe. She stood with a silver whip in her hand, and before Thanatos could reach some of the dying, she coaxed the souls from their bodies and gathered them to herself.

"What is Melinoe doing with the dead?" Hades asked in disbelief.

"She's taking the souls and leading them away from here," Than said. "She's already led at least another dozen away from the city."

"For what purpose?"

"I don't know."

Hades flew over to his daughter. "Melinoe? What are you doing here? Why are you taking these souls? You're interfering with your brother's duties!"

"I know I'm a disappointment to you, Father!" she said with a sarcastic cackle. "But leave me be! Someone more powerful than you has taken me under his wing, and I want to please him."

"But I'm your father. Don't you want to please *me*?"

"It's too late for that. Even I know that. There's nothing I can ever do to please you. So leave me be and let me find happiness where I can."

"But what you're doing is the most atrocious thing anyone could do!" he shouted. "This is worse than murder! Don't you understand? You're robbing all these people of their eternal rest."

"Who needs eternal rest?"

"Not just that, but also their judgment, their chance to atone for their wrongs, their purification. What you're doing here…you're sabotaging my entire kingdom!"

She opened her mouth wide and laughed as she flew away with her entourage of lost ghosts.

Hades tried to stop her. He prayed to Hecate for help. But even she could not get the souls to turn away from Melinoe.

After hours of chasing her around the dark skies, Hades and Hecate returned home to discuss a strategy for stopping Melinoe.

Persephone came into the main chamber, asking what was wrong.

Hades wished he could protect her from the knowledge of their daughter's betrayal, but withholding information from her in the past had only made things worse, so he told her the truth.

Since that day, his sweet Persephone hadn't been the same, and neither had he.

<u>EPILOGUE</u>

Change

In the wake of the Trojan War, Cassandra's predictions came true. Cassandra was killed, along with Agamemnon, by his wife, Clytemnestra, who'd never forgiven him for sacrificing their daughter, Iphigenia (the mortals weren't aware of Artemis's switch). Persephone waited for the old king in Tartarus and ordered the Furies to let her handle his punishment.

Cassandra's prediction about Hecuba also came to pass. Wanting to protect the queen from Odysseus, who planned to use her as his lover, Artemis transformed her into a Doberman Pinscher, made her immortal, and gave her to Hecate. From that moment on, Cubie, as they came to call her, remained loyal to Hecate and helped her in her duties as a guide for those who needed help finding their way.

But because Odysseus had been cruel to Hecuba, they did not help the Greek warrior in his efforts to get home, which were continually thwarted by Poseidon after the warrior blinded Poseidon's son, Polyphemus, in the wake of the Trojan War.

Over the years, the Olympians kept their distance from the Underworld gods. Hades and Persephone became more and more used to their misery. There were even moments when Hades experienced something like pleasure—though he wouldn't call it happiness. Those days seemed far behind him until...

Centuries later, while Hades was making his rounds throughout his realm and ensuring that all was running smoothly and up to his standards, he stood near the chasm, where the Dreamworld and Underworld intersected, and witnessed something out of the ordinary. The soul of a living teenage girl was talking to both of his sons. The soul seemed ignorant of the fact that she was among gods, but her irreverence didn't offend the twins. They seemed smitten with her.

Then she did something no living soul had ever done before. She flew to Charon's raft and boarded it, wrapped her transparent arms around Thanatos's neck, and kissed him.

Although Than pushed the soul away and ordered Hip to take her back to the world of dreams, Hades could clearly see that Than had been altered.

Could this be an answer to his prayer? Hades had been praying to the Fates, day after day, month after month, decade after decade. What had been his request?

Bring me change. Anything is better than this.

Hades had a strange feeling that things were, indeed, about to change.

Author's Note

Those of you who are knowledgeable about Greek mythology might be wondering about a few of my choices, so I want to explain them here. Also, please note that this prequel can be enjoyed before or after the other nine books in *The Underworld Saga*.

First, my decision to make Thanatos and Hypnos the sons of Hades and Persephone contradicts most ancient versions, in which the twins are the sons of Nyx. I chose to put them in the house of Hades because I wanted to focus on the Underworld gods, to defend Hades against his conflation with the Satan of Christianity made by so many modern texts (such as in Disney's animated film *Hercules*). But when I first conceived *The Underworld Saga*, I envisioned a contemporary romance, and for this, I wanted an unmarried god. So, I chose Thanatos. And since I needed him to be a younger god, I made him and his brother the sons of Hades.

I found an Orphic Hymn in which the Furies (usually depicted as the children of Nyx) are the daughters of Persephone, and I thought it would be fun to make them the older sisters of the twin boys.

Second, although I use Greek names for most of the gods, I chose to use the more popular Roman names Cupid (instead of Eros) and Hercules (instead of Heracles). I regret these decisions now. I thought the names would be more recognizable for a thirteen-year-old reader (my target audience), but I should have given those readers more credit and stuck with the Greek names.

Third, in this prequel, I took liberties with the timeline in ancient Greek mythology. Although Hercules/Heracles completed his labors and Pelops was served by Tantalus to the gods long before the Trojan War, I was forced to place those events in the early days of the Trojan

War for two reasons. One reason is because I moved the existence of Thanatos to a later period, and I'd already referred to him being bound by Hercules in *Thanatos*. The second is because I wanted the Persephone myth to correspond with the war, so I could use the drama of the war to heighten the drama in the Underworld family. Since Demeter's preoccupation with her daughter's abduction is what causes her to eat Pelops in the ancient myths, it seemed fitting to include that detail in Demeter's story here.

I also want to explain my elaboration on Demeter's story with Demophoon. Although the ancient stories tell of her visit to his family and of her attempt to make him immortal, the part about him dying and Metaneira's trade was all my invention. I wanted to justify Demeter's contempt for Hades and to emphasize the themes of maternal love and sacrifice.

The twist I gave the Persephone myth in this prequel was my own invention and part of my plan to elevate attitudes toward Hades and the Underworld gods. Hades is depicted in the ancient stories as abducting Persephone after receiving permission from Zeus, but back then, attitudes about women as property were prevalent, and this action wasn't perceived in the same way as it is today. If I was going to succeed in my efforts to make the Underworld gods leaders in the Athena Alliance and the reformation of the male-dominated pantheon, then I needed Hades to be a more progressive male deity. This desire to elevate Hades was also behind the origin stories of the Furies, Hypnos, and Thanatos. Again, this was purely my invention, though the origin story about Melinoe is very close to the way it's depicted in the ancient stories. In those earlier stories, however, Hades is never charged or sentenced for abusing her in the womb.

I hope you enjoyed my version of this beloved story. If you did, please consider leaving a review. Reviews help readers to find my books, which helps me.

Please enjoy an excerpt from the first book in *The Underworld Saga, Thanatos.*

Just in case you've already read Thanatos, I've also an excerpt from the first book in a series that shares the world of *The Underworld Saga.* The book is called *Vampire Addiction: The Vampires of Athens, Book One.*

CHAPTER ONE:

The Drowning

Therese Mills peeled the white gloves off her sweaty hands as soon as she and her parents were in the car. Now that her mother's thing was over, she could finally get home and out of this blue dress. It was like being in a straitjacket.

Anything for Mom, of course.

What the…

A man glared at her through her backseat window. She jumped up, sat back, blinked. The man vanished, but when she blinked again, she could still see the eerie face behind her lids: the scruffy black beard and dark, haunting eyes.

"Thanks again for making tonight so special," her mother, apparently not seeing the man, said from the passenger seat as her father started the engine. "You two being there meant a lot to me."

"Did you see that man?" Therese peered through her window for the face.

"What?" Her mother also looked. "What man?"

"What man, Therese?" her father asked.

"Never mind."

Therese did not find it unusual that her mother hadn't noticed the man. Although her mother was a brilliant scientist, she wasn't the most observant person.

Just last spring after all the snow had finally melted around their house in the Colorado mountains, and Therese and her mother had been able to enjoy their wooden deck with the melted lake spread out in front of them and the forest rising up the mountains behind them, Therese had spotted the wild horse and foal she had seen just before winter. They both had reddish brown coats with a white stripe between their eyes, the foal nestled beside its mother's legs, staring intently at Therese without moving. The animals stood beneath one of two magnificent elm trees ten feet from their back door—the tree her mother said had gotten the Dutch elm disease. Therese relaxed with her mother at the wooden table on the deck, each of them with a mug of coffee in the bright Sunday morning. Her mother had the paper but wasn't reading it. She had that look on her face when she was thinking of a scientific formula or method that she planned to try in her lab. Therese stared again at the horse and didn't move. She whispered, "Mom."

Her mother hadn't heard.

"Mom, the wild horses," she whispered again.

Therese looked from the beautiful creatures to her mother, who sat staring in space, transfixed, like a person hypnotized.

"Mom, are you deaf?" she blurted out, and then she heard the horses flee back up the mountain into the tall pines. She caught a glimpse of the foal's reddish-brown rump, and that was that.

As Therese strapped on her seatbelt, she also considered the possibility that she had only imagined the man in the window. She was, after all, prone to use her imagination and fully capable of making daydreams as real as reality, as she had, just now, with her memory of the horses.

Her phone vibrated. A text from Jen read, "Heat sheets r n call me when u get home." Awesome, she thought. Therese was anxious to see who would share her heat in tomorrow's championship meet. She hoped she would be swimming breaststroke in the top heat against Lacey Holzmann from Pagosa Springs. She wanted to beat her this time.

She searched outside her window for the scruffy face but saw only a line of headlights as others, like they, exited the parking lot of the concert hall. Maybe she had only imagined the man. It was getting dark. The mountains across campus were barely visible as dusk turned into night.

"We're both so proud of you, Honey," Therese's dad said from behind the wheel.

Therese probably got her imaginative talent from her father, who was a successful crime fiction writer. As soon as his first book made the New York Times bestsellers list, he moved his family out into their big log cabin in the San Juan Mountains.

Therese saw her father eyeing her in the rearview mirror. "Aren't we, sweetie pie?"

She wondered at her father's need to praise her mother all the time. Didn't her mother already know she was brilliant and that her husband and daughter looked up to her? "Absolutely. You're awesome, Mom."

Therese's phone vibrated again. A text from Paul read, "Wat r u waring?"

She cringed and murmured, "Oooh. How gross." She couldn't believe he had got her number. He had been stalking her around campus just before school let out for the summer.

Before she had a chance to delete the text, Therese heard the rear window behind her head explode. "What the…" Glass shards pricked at her neck and bare shoulders. The car swerved left and right. She looked back to see the window behind her busted. The line of headlights had dispersed into chaos, horns blasting, people shouting.

"What the hell was that?" her father yelled. "Oh my God! Linda! Linda!"

"Dad, what's wrong? Is Mom…"

Another explosion rang out, and something zipped just past Therese's head.

"Therese? Are you okay? Get down!"

"What's happening? What's going on?" Therese cowered in the back seat as a third explosion sounded, this time near the windshield. Therese could barely breathe. She gasped for air, her heart about to explode.

"Stay down! Someone's shooting at us!" her father shouted.

The car swerved, slowed, and turned. The smell of burned rubber permeated the air. Therese's head whipped back as her father gunned the accelerator. Her fingers trembled so wildly that she was barely able to punch the correct numbers on her phone. She messed up twice and had to start over. Finally she pressed them in slow motion: 911. It seemed an eternity before a woman answered on the other end.

"Nine-one-one, is this an emergency?"

"Someone's shooting at us! You've got to help us. We're leaving Fort Lewis College. Dad, where are we?"

"Heading toward Huck Finn Pond."

"Huck Finn Pond!" Therese screamed into the phone as the car swerved, her seatbelt digging into her hip. Then she noticed the blood dripping down the back of her mother's neck and onto her mother's silk scarf. "Oh, my God! Mom? Mom, are you okay?"

"She'll be okay, Therese!" her father shouted.

"Oh my God! I think my mom's been shot! You've got to do something! You've got to help us!"

A crushing sound shot through the car, and Therese felt herself jolted hard to the right. She hit her head on the window and dropped the cell phone. When she bent over and tried to pick it up, the back end of the car lurched upward like a seesaw, and her head hit the back of her mother's seat in front of her. She sat up and saw they were sailing through the air over the lake. The front end of the car hit the water, causing her head to flop forward and back. She heard the air hissing through the airbags as they inflated in the front end. She was so stunned, she couldn't speak. She watched in silent shock as water crept into the front end of the car, up to her father's neck, the untied bowtie of his tuxedo floating around him. The front airbags pressed against her father's cheek, her mother's face. Water spilled over the front seat and onto the floorboard in back where she sat elevated higher than her parents.

She unfastened her seatbelt and leaned over and looked down at her mother in horror. A bullet had put a hole in the back of her neck, and blood rushed from it. Her head lay against the airbag turned to one side, toward Therese's father. Her eyes were open, and she was gasping for air, but blood was pouring from her mouth and choking her.

"Mom! Oh my God! Mom!" Therese's teeth chattered uncontrollably as her mother strained to look at her. She reached down and caressed her mother's hair. "Mom! Oh my God!"

She realized her father had been shouting her name for several seconds. "Listen to me, Therese! Therese! Try to open your window. Therese! Try to get out of the car!"

His voice sounded like it did when he was cheering her on from the deck of the pool at her swim meets. "Keep going, Therese! You're looking good! Kick! Pull!"

Except now it was tinged with desperation.

"I'm not leaving without you and Mom! I'm scared! Dad, please! Can't you get out?" Her teeth continued to chatter.

The water level rose to his mouth. He shook his head. "I'm stuck!" He shouted through the water. His eyes widened as the water crept to his nose. He was drowning right in front of her.

"Dad! Dad!"

In a state of frenzy, he turned from side to side, only the top of his head visible.

Therese watched in silent shock.

She looked at her mother. Her mother's eyes met hers briefly, then closed as the water washed over all but her red hair. Unlike her father, her mother didn't move, but simply relinquished herself to the water. Her hair danced like seaweed, like long veins of blood. Therese became aware of the coldness of the water that had been sucking her down. Its cold fingers crept up to her shoulders. Her white gloves floated beside her, pointing at her. *You! Do something!*

She took a deep breath and went underwater toward her father. She couldn't see in the dark, so she pushed against the airbag and felt around for the harness. The belt was undone, but the steering shaft was crushed across her father's lap. She pulled with all her might on the steering wheel. It didn't move. She tried to puncture the airbag but without luck. Then she yanked on her father's lifeless arm. She couldn't lift him from the seat.

Another memory shot through her mind: She was pulling her father's arm, coaxing him from his recliner. "Come see the deer," she was saying. She was small—maybe six. "Come on, Dad. Come see." He had laughed and made a comment about her chipmunk cheeks and dimples, that he'd do anything to see those dimples. She pulled at his arm and he laughed and climbed out of his chair to follow her outside.

But now she could not get her father to follow her.

She felt her mother's hand and flinched. She found it again. It was as cold as the water and as limp as a dead fish. She hugged her mother, held on to her for dear life till her brain hurt and she needed air.

Therese popped back up near the top of the car for air, but there was none. She hitched her body up and hit her head on the roof of the car. She then noticed a bright light shine on her through her backseat window. She thought she saw someone swimming toward her. She heard another crash and a surge of water, but she needed air! Panic overtook her like a wild beast, and she opened her eyes as far as they would open, writhed her body against every molecule in reach, and strained her mouth wide open. Her lungs filled with burning water, the cold water burning her like fire. She gagged on the water, gagged, kicked, went wild with fear, and then stopped and gave in to the darkness.

CHAPTER TWO

Thanatos

Humans didn't realize how lucky they were, Than thought as he took the woman's hand. At least, if they were mostly good, they could live a brief life with some kinds of freedoms and then spend eternity in a dreamlike trance, unaware of the monotony around them.

"Just this way," he said to the woman and the man as they floundered above the abyss, disoriented, like all of them were at this stage of the journey.

"What about Therese?" the woman asked. "Where's Therese?"

Than sighed. He couldn't imagine the pain they almost always showed on their faces. He couldn't imagine it because he had never felt it. At least it was temporary. The Lethe, the river of forgetfulness that flowed from the Acheron, would soon ease that pain, so long as these two souls were destined to the Fields of Elysium. The judges would soon decide.

"It's not too much further," Than murmured. "Come along."

"But what about our daughter?" the man asked.

The three of them now hovered up to the muddy bank where Charon waited on his raft. Than brought them down and allowed some of the water to wash up against their feet. It would help fog their memory until they reached the Lethe.

"Oh, that's cold," the woman said softly. "But it feels nice."

"Very nice," the man agreed.

Than gave a curt nod. "Time to board."

Charon nodded back as he dug his slender pole into the mud to hold the raft steady. He rarely spoke, with his nearly bald head, long, white mustache, and pale, cracked skin, and seemed more a cog in the wheel than any of them, churning on and on, back and forth, up the river and down, in an endless cycle. Than supposed Charon's existence was still worse than his own. At least Than got to travel the world. Charon saw the same sights day in and day out. His life never varied.

Than put a hand on the shoulder of each of the passengers, knowing it would comfort them. Yes, he thought again, humans were lucky. A brief, exciting life trumped a dull eternity. As his father always said, nothing ever changed. A few details might, but the big picture always remained the same. Than realized that none of the gods was really all that different from Sisyphus who, each day, must face his rock.

But what if things could change? Than wondered, not for the first time. He sighed and once again shook his head and waited as the raft approached the gate.

CHAPTER THREE

Sleep

Therese opened her eyes and found herself standing on a cool, muddy bank. Fog curled around her, and through it she could see water in front of her, and it flowed in a narrow gorge between two ominous granite mountains. "Mom! Dad!" Her screams were stifled by the thick fog. "Mom! Dad!" She looked around the empty bank. Her bare feet sunk into the itchy mud. Where were her shoes? Her white gloves were back on her hands, her gown perfectly dry, and her hair back up in its fat clip. Tall blades of grass as high as her knees grew in tufts along the shore. Mosquitoes swarmed over one area of the water. Three large boulders leaned in a cluster on the left side of the shore against the base of a steep, massive wall of rock. How did she get here?

She waded into the icy lake. The cold water crept up her thighs. She couldn't see Huck Finn Bridge. Nothing looked familiar, but she had to find her parents. Isn't this where they went under in the car? She dove into the freezing water.

Long, snakelike tendrils of hydrilla weeds grabbed and scratched at her ankles. She flinched, kicking her legs all about.

"She's moving," a familiar voice above her said.

"Therese?"

She resurfaced. "Who said that?" Her voice was only a whisper, though she tried to speak loudly. It was hard for her to move her mouth. "Who, who said that?"

When no answer came, she dove back into the icy lake. "Mom! Dad!" Why was she looking for them? Her memory went fuzzy. "Mom? Dad?" She could talk underwater as though she were talking through air. She could breathe without water entering her mouth. How strange, she thought to herself. She felt as though she had turned into some kind of mer-creature. The lake transformed into a beautiful world of colorful coral, tropical fish, and sunken treasure chests.

She swam back to the muddy shore. "I must be dreaming." She walked over to the three boulders and sat on one of them. "Or I'm dead." She pulled off the wet gloves and tossed them on the ground.

Therese jumped into the air and swam a breaststroke through the fog, like she always did to test if she was dreaming. She went up above the curling, iridescent moisture where she could see the twinkling stars. Therese turned somersaults, forward and backward, dolphin-kicked a loop-de-loop, and then floated on her back. "Yep. I'm either dreaming or I'm dead."

She made the fog disappear, so she could see all around her. She reached up and touched a sparkling star, turned it into a diamond ring, and put it on her finger. Then she plucked her flute out of the air and played a Handel sonata. The flute felt comfortable in her hands, the cool, shiny metal beneath her fingers. The tones flowed smoothly as she blew, moving from one fingering to the next with perfect fluidity.

"I've never seen anyone like you," a voice came beside her.

Therese stopped playing. She hadn't willed him, as she had willed other guys to appear in dreams past, but she was glad he was there floating in the night sky alongside her. His thick golden hair covered his ears and fell on his forehead almost into his eyes. His eyes were blue, his skin fair, and his lips moist and peach. They parted into a smile.

"Are you checking me out?" he asked.

Therese blushed. "This is my dream, isn't it? Or am I dead?"

"You're not dead."

"So I'm dreaming, then. I can do whatever I want." She tossed the flute and willed her parents to appear, and they did.

"Mom! Dad!" She flew across the sky and into their arms. They were still in their formal wear. Her mother's neck, face, and scarf were perfectly clean, and she smelled like Haiku, her favorite fragrance. Her father smelled like musk, like the deodorant he always wore. Unlike Therese, her parents wore their shoes. Therese decided she should have her new shoes back, so she willed them to appear on her feet.

"Fascinating," the boy said. He wore a white, opened shirt, and his tight abs gleamed in the moonlight. White loose pants covered his legs, and he wore brown sandals on his feet.

Therese willed his shirt off, and the shirt disappeared.

The boy laughed. "You have so much control. Very few people are lucid dreamers, and I've never known anyone like you."

Therese turned to her parents. "I thought you were dead."

"Silly girl. Of course not," her mother scolded. "Give me a kiss."

She kissed her mother's cheek. It felt warm and soft and fully alive.

"Who's your friend?" her father asked.

Now that Therese had been comforted by her parents, she could let them go for a while. "I'll be home later. 'Kay?"

"Not too late," her father said.

Therese willed him to take it back.

"Whenever you get home is fine," he said.

Her parents vanished, causing a vague sense of panic to quell her excitement over the boy, but she pushed the panic down, reminding herself this was just a dream. She turned to the sexy guy, still shirtless, beside her. "So what's your name?"

"I have many. Most people call me Hip, short for Hypnos."

Okay, that's strange. Whatever. "Hip. I'm Therese."

"Are we going to make out now, or what?" He took her in his arms. "Is this a projection, or your real image?"

Therese had willed many sexy guys to appear in her dreams and have romances with her, but even there, she had kissed and made out with them on her own terms, and in the awake, real world, kissing was still a faraway anticipation. The eager look in the boy's face made her wary.

She pushed him back. "Why are you in such a hurry?" She looked over her body. She decided to make her boobs bigger. She smiled down at the soft, round flesh protruding from the top of her blue formal gown. Nice cleavage, she thought. "How's that?"

He threw his head back and guffawed. Then he shook his head, regaining his composure, and said, "I liked them better before."

"You've got to be kidding." She blushed and deflated herself. "It's my dream, not yours, but okay."

"No kidding. And I like your dimples. You've got a cute round face and full lips. I wouldn't mind kissing them."

Another voice sounded above her. "Therese?"

"Who is that? Who keeps calling me?"

A vague inkling of a car in a lake threatened to impose itself into memory, but Therese turned back to the boy and took in his beauty, forgetting all else.

Hip said, "They're trying to wake you up. But I'm not ready for you to go yet. You're such a nice diversion."

"How old are you?" She turned and floated on her back and looked down her body at him where he hovered near her shoes.

"Ancient."

"You look eighteen. I'm seventeen. I'll be a junior this year."

Down below, she noticed a raft floating across what she now saw was a river. There were four people on it, but she couldn't make out who they were. She swam the breaststroke through the air toward the water to get a better view. Her teeth felt loose. They started to crumble. She willed her teeth back into her mouth and licked them to be sure they were set correctly. Satisfied, she smiled.

Hip was fast behind her. "You're so incredible. People usually wake up when their teeth fall out."

She saw an old man standing on the raft dragging a long paddle through the water. Alongside him stood two familiar people and one other she didn't know. "It's my mom and dad. Hey, wait up." She flew above them, but they didn't seem to notice her.

The old man and the other passenger, whom she could now see was another guy, as cute as Hip, looked up at her. He looked sad and serious, like the silent moody type. His eyes were blue, and his hair was nearly black. He's so awesomely beautiful, she thought. He wore loose white pants and an opened white shirt like Hip had worn earlier, and, as with Hip, she willed the shirt to disappear. The boy looked startled, but her parents didn't react. They stood expressionless on the raft.

Hip laughed at the other boy's bewilderment. "That's my brother, Thanatos. Everyone calls him Than. I'm pretty sure that's a first for him."

"He looks a lot like you."

"We're twins, but not identical. I got the sense of humor, the easy-going disposition, and the charm with all the ladies. He got, well, not a whole lot, actually. I suppose he's trustworthy. My father says dependable and responsible, but those are pretty boring qualities, if you ask me. I sometimes feel sorry for him."

"What's he doing with my parents?"

"He's taking them to the Underworld, where all the dead go."

"My parents aren't dead." Again, the vague inkling threatened to return to memory, but Therese shook her head. She willed herself back home in her own cozy bed with her dog, Clifford, curled beside her. Hip was not with her.

"Time to wake up," she said to Clifford.

The brown and white fox terrier licked her cheek.

Therese tossed back her comforter and climbed out of the bed, the warm, wooden floor familiar beneath her feet. She dropped some hamster food into Puffy's hamster cage and turned on the lamp over her Russian tortoise's tank.

"Good morning, Jewels," Therese said.

The tortoise winked at her.

Therese headed downstairs. Clifford bounded behind her, as usual. Her parents were in the kitchen sitting at the granite bar drinking coffee and reading the paper, as on any Saturday morning.

They were still in their pajamas, but she was in her blue formal gown.

She replaced the gown with a nightshirt. Poof: There, better.

"Good morning," she said to her parents.

She went through the screened front porch and out into what she was expecting to be the sunny morning on their wooden deck in the mountains but was instead the night sky over the foggy river. Hip greeted her.

"Nice outfit."

"So this really is just a dream," she said. "None of it's real."

"What makes a dream any less real?" he challenged.

"Hip, let her go!" the boy from below on the raft warned. "They need to revive her or she's going to die!"

"Therese?" a voice came from somewhere above.

Than flew up and pulled Therese away from Hip. "Let her go, brother. You're endangering her life."

Therese felt weak and she tried to wriggle free but nearly fell from the air.

Than held her up. "You shouldn't be here," he whispered, close to her ear. He sent a shiver down her spine, but his breath was sweet.

She didn't like the direction this dream was going. In the dreams in which she was about to die, she usually bolted into the air and changed the events into something happy. Although she couldn't find the strength to jump up and twirl around, she did manage to throw her arms around the good-looking boy holding onto her. She could make the dream into a new romance. "My dream," she managed to say as she clung to him. She put her lips against his lips. "You're…so…lovely."

"Whoa, brother," Hip said. "Today's full of all kinds of firsts for you, man."

Than seemed shocked. He looked at her like she was an alien. "You can't do this," he said, but he didn't push her away. His eyes closed, he sighed, and, almost reluctantly, it seemed, he put his strong arms around Therese, who felt weaker. She could feel his mouth near her forehead. A sound came from his throat, something like a groan.

She liked being in his arms. "You're…so…lovely," she murmured, growing weaker and weaker.

"Take her back." Than seemed to be fighting an inner battle. "I'm to take her parents, but not her. It's not her time."

Therese willed herself up. "My parents? Where are you taking them?"

Than looked into her questioning eyes. He looked as though he wanted to kiss her. She wanted to kiss him, too. His face moved closer. She nearly lost her breath. But her parents! She flew from his arms and down to the raft.

"Charon, don't board her!" Than growled, fast on her heels. "She's not to go across."

"Mom! Dad!"

Her parents didn't seem to hear her.

"This is my dream, dammit. Look at me!"

Her parents turned toward her. "Therese?"

Than gave Therese a look of astonishment. "How did you do that?"

Therese flew down to her parents.

Strong arms went around her and pulled her away from the raft. The brothers were on either side of her. She was fighting a futile battle. The brothers were much too strong for her to break free from them.

Than smiled. "You're right. She's a powerful soul. I've never known someone to follow loved ones down this far."

"You're forgetting Orpheus and Hercules," Hip pointed out.

"But they were demigods." Than's hands tightened their grip on Therese. Hip started to say something, but Than interrupted, "And Odysseus was sent down, so he doesn't count, either." Hip opened his mouth, but as before, Than was too quick with his retort, "And Aeneas had a guide and a golden bough, unlike this girl who came all on her own with no bribes."

Hip finally got his say, "I told you this girl was powerful. You're making my case, brother." He pulled Therese closer to him. "I want to keep her."

Therese wondered if they could possibly be talking about her. Powerful? She was anything but, as her inability to break free from them proved.

Than frowned. "If you try, she'll die, and then what fascinates you about her will be lost."

"Therese?" the voice from above called.

"Let her go!" Than implored.

Hip moved his lips to Therese's ear. "Seek me out in your dreams. I want to find you again. Look for me. Call for me."

To purchase your copy of *Thanatos*, please visit my website at www.evapohler.com.

Below is an excerpt from *Vampire Addiction*.

CHAPTER ONE

The Boy on the Bus

I hadn't realized you packed *that* coat," Gertie's mother complained as Gertie and her parents were leaving their room at the Hotel Excelsior in Venice. "It's not one of your best."

It was a gray puffer coat that tied at the waist and had a soft flannel lining.

"Then it's a good thing you won't have to look at it," Gertie muttered.

Her father glared at her but didn't comment. Instead, he went ahead of her through the lobby to the front desk to check out.

On the way to the ferry, in the back of the limo, Gertie sat across from her parents and said, "It's still not too late to change your minds."

"We're not having this discussion again," her father said. "End of story."

"Don't worry, Gertrude. You'll have the time of your life."

Somehow, Gertie doubted that.

"I know *I* did," her mother added. "I'm jealous of you, actually."

Gertie frowned. "You're welcome to go in my place."

Her mother leaned forward and patted Gertie's knee. "Everyone's frightened of trying new things."

She flinched, unused to being touched. "I'm not," she lied. "I just like my own bed."

"It will be there for you when you get back," her father said. "You're seventeen, now. It's time for you to venture away from the nest."

"Happy Birthday to me," she muttered beneath her breath.

Gertie tried to ignore the fact that they were more excited for her to go than she was. She'd never heard of two people more eager to become empty-nesters than her parents. And it wasn't like she was the last in a long line of siblings. She was an only child—an independent one at that. Why couldn't she stay in her room and be left alone?

She wasn't surprised when they didn't get out of the limo and walk her to the ferry. Instead, they had their driver do it. They had offered plenty of excuses—it was too windy out for her mother's asthma and too sunny for her fair skin. Plus, her father had a heart condition. And so on and so forth.

Once she was onboard and inside her cabin, she sat on the bed and cried. She hated her parents for making her do this. They had told her to enjoy the scenic boat ride along the Adriatic Sea, but she was determined to spend it all indoors. She rummaged through her bag, found her e-reader, and read until she fell asleep.

It was dark the next day when she got off the ferry in Patras to board the bus to Athens. So much for seeing the sights.

The wind blew strands of her blond hair into her mouth, her eyes, and the sweaty crease of her neck. It wasn't cold—was actually quite warm—but she was glad to have her coat as she pulled her bags behind her.

Gertie expected more people to be riding the bus, but there were only three: an older couple sitting together in the front seat and a boy her age near the back. He was cute and was looking at her with interest. She sat two seats in front of him, without returning his gaze.

"People like you don't usually ride the bus at night," he said after a few minutes. His Greek accent was thick and sexy.

She glanced back at him. "People like me?"

"Young and wealthy."

"Well, if you want to rob me, go for it."

He laughed. "I don't want to rob you."

"The bus driver seems to think so," she said. "He keeps looking at us in his mirror."

"He's bored and has nothing else to do."

She didn't reply but pulled out her phone and logged on to Goodreads.

"You must be pretty hot," he said after a while.

"I beg your pardon?" She felt a blush coming on.

"In that coat. It's eighty degrees."

"Yeah. I didn't have room in my luggage." She spoke without turning back to face him, while scrolling through Goodreads on her phone. She wanted to update her status on where she was in her book.

"Where are you going?" he asked.

"Athens."

"I guessed that much. Are you going to visit relatives?"

"Nope."

"Then you must be one of those visiting students," he said, moving to the seat behind hers.

He smelled like soap.

"Yep. You nailed it."

"I did what?"

"I'm sorry. That's just an expression." She glanced back at him. His face was so close, that she could see the big round pupils in his dark brown eyes. His dark curly hair fell around his face, nearly touching his shoulders, which were bare except for the one-inch strap of his blue cotton tank. The muscles in his arms were solid and well defined. If he weren't so cute, she might be uncomfortable.

When she looked into his eyes, she found it difficult to pull away. He was mesmerizing.

Her phone vibrated, stirring her from her stupor. It was a text from her mother, asking if she had landed yet in Patras.

"On bus to Athens," she texted back.

When the boy said nothing more, she rummaged through her bag for her e-reader and returned to the world of her book.

Not thirty minutes had passed when she felt the boy lean on the back of her seat and ask, "What are you reading?"

"*Interview with the Vampire*, by Anne Rice."

He gasped.

She spun around to face him. "Have you read it?"

"No, no. Is it good?"

"So far, yes. I'm loving it." Then she added, "I've always been fascinated by vampire stories."

The corners of his mouth quirked. "Is that so?"

"What's so funny?" She narrowed her eyes. "I don't believe in them or anything; I'm just interested in the mythology."

"I see."

She didn't like that he was laughing at her, so she turned around in her seat to face the front and continued reading. It was difficult for her to get back into the novel after that. She kept seeing the boy's face in place of the words.

Only a few minutes had passed, however, when the boy leaned forward and asked, "So what interests you? About the vampires?"

"A lot of things." She glanced back at him. "Their superpowers, for one: invisibility, flight, mind control…"

"Don't forget x-ray vision," he said, giving her a once over.

"Yeah. Right." She laughed. "You're thinking of Superman."

He laughed, too. "What else?"

She turned in her seat and rested her back against the bus window so she could face him. "I guess the idea of conquering death is interesting to me."

"Are you afraid of death?"

"No. Not really. But I suppose I'm curious about it."

"In what way?" He leaned closer.

"Well, don't you wonder if there's life after death? Do we go to heaven? Or do we go to sleep? Or do we just stop existing? Not that it matters. I just wonder, that's all."

"If it doesn't matter, then why do you wonder about it?"

"It *matters*. I just meant we're going to die regardless of what happens." She twisted the belt of her coat. "Like my grandma. She just died. And so I wonder if she can still hear me and stuff, you know?"

He sat back in his seat and studied her, like he was assessing her.

She blushed. "What?"

He shook his head. "So what else about vampire *mythology* do you find interesting?"

"I don't know." She twisted the belt in the opposite direction. "The combination of power and powerlessness, I guess. It makes them trag-ic."

"Powerlessness?"

"They can't help what they are. They don't usually choose to become vampires."

"But they prey on humans, yes?" he asked.

"In the story I'm reading right now, a vampire is trying to live on the blood of animals, but it's very difficult for him."

"Thee moy." The boy cringed. "I can imagine."

"I once read that vampires are a reflection of us. We created the my-thology to represent ourselves."

He leaned forward again, his arm almost touching her. "Explain."

She bit her lip, searching for the right words. She must have been thinking hard, for she drew blood. The boy leaned in, and for a mo-ment, she thought he would kiss her.

The bus hit a bump, and she fell back against the window, hitting her head. The boy eased back in his seat. She rubbed her head and turned to face the front.

"You okay?" he asked from behind.

She nodded without looking at him.

"So, tell me," he said, leaning on the back of the seat. "How are vampires a reflection of humans?"

"Deep down inside, we're all monsters."

"You really think so?"

She nodded. "And yet we have so little control."

"Power and no power."

She glanced back and gave him a subtle smile. "Exactly."

He said nothing in reply, so she turned to her book. After several minutes, she was finally able to get back into the story. A few times, she wondered about the boy behind her, but she didn't see any reason to try to talk to him. She would be leaving this country in one year, to never return, so what was the use of making friends?

She could hear her mother's voice in the back of her head reminding her that she had no friends at home, either, but it wasn't Gertie's fault that everyone at her private school in New York was fake.

At some point, she must have fallen asleep. When she opened her eyes, she saw the boy leaning over the back of the seat looking down at her with a mouth full of fangs and blood.

She cringed and opened her eyes—for real this time. She glanced back at the boy, but he was gone.

CHAPTER TWO

The Host Family

When she arrived at the station in Athens, she found a boy holding up a sign with her name written on it: Gertrude Morgan. She almost didn't see the sign, because the boy holding it was so beautiful. He was flanked by another boy about his age—eighteen or nineteen, but shorter—and a girl, either the same age or younger.

The girl had studs in her nose and cheek and had spikey, short hair. All three wore summer shorts, flip flops, and t-shirts with graphics of what appeared to be bands. Gertie realized the outer two were related, both having the same brown hair and brown eyes and petite build. They looked nothing like the boy in the middle, who towered over them and was breathtaking, like a Greek god.

"Gertie?" the girl asked as Gertie came to a halt in front of them.

"That's right."

She was astonished when the girl nearly plowed her down with an embrace. "I'm Nikita! It's so great to finally meet you!"

Nikita was the name of one of the members of her host family. She and Gertie had been texting and emailing the past two weeks about the trip—what to bring and what to expect. Surely this girl wasn't one and the same.

"You're Nikita?"

The girl frowned. "This is Hector, our friend. And that's Klaus, my brother. I'm pretty sure I told you all about him. He's been dying to meet you."

"Okay, Nikita," Klaus said. "You don't have to make me sound so eager."

"It's nice to meet you," Gertie said, still a little shocked. They didn't look like the private school kids back home.

"Our parents and little sister are waiting in the car," Nikita said. "Can you boys help her with her bags?"

The two boys took her rolling suitcases—one apiece—and Nikita took one of her shoulder bags, and then they followed the boys through the station to the sidewalk outside. Gertie found herself studying the lines on the back of the taller boy named Hector.

When they reached the car, Gertie had another shock. It was a two-door coupe meant for four passengers, but there were already three inside.

They weren't inside long. Just as Nikita had done, the man, woman, and child, all thin and petite and dark-haired like their other family members, climbed out and hugged her. The mother even kissed her on her cheek.

"We're so glad to have you join our family," the mother said, cupping Gertie's face in her hands. "Look at you, Gertoula! You're so beautiful, koreetsi mou!"

"It's Gertie," Gertie said.

"Of course, Gertoula! I mean Gertie."

"Mamá puts oula and itsa and aki on the end of everyone's name. Even Babá's!" Nikita explained. "She calls him Babáki mou!"

"Yes, Nikitsa, koreetsi mou!" her mother said, and turning to Gertie, said, "So you call me Mamá, too. Yes?"

"And I'm Babá," the father said affectionately. Then he picked up his little girl, who seemed seven or eight years old, and said, "And this is Phoebe."

"Mamá calls her Phoeboula, so don't get confused," Klaus said.

"Hello," Gertie said to the girl.

The girl smiled but said nothing. Then Gertie remembered what Nikita had said in her text about the fire three years ago. Their baby brother had died. Phoebe hadn't spoken since.

Babá and the boys put her luggage in the trunk of the coupe before piling into the car. Phoebe sat in the front seat, without a seatbelt, and Nikita climbed on her brother's lap.

"Should I call a cab?" Gertie asked.

"No, no!" Babá said, holding the door open for her. "There's room for you."

Hector climbed out. "Take my place. I need to head home anyway. I'll take a cab or the bus."

"No, Hector. I promised you baklava," Mamá insisted.

"I'll come by for some tomorrow," Hector said. He waved goodbye and then raised his hand for a cab.

Gertie climbed in beside Klaus. Nikita shifted from her brother's lap and squeezed between them. No one wore their seatbelts. Gertie wasn't even sure the old coupe had them.

The car smelled like onions, mold, and sweat, but Gertie resisted pinching her nose as they drove through the streets of Athens from the bus station. Mamá and Babá spoke animatedly about their country, the American school, the ruins, and many other topics during the thirty-minute ride. When they pulled up in front of a dilapidated apartment building, Gertie thought they were playing a joke on her.

It wasn't a joke.

Babá and Klaus dragged the heavy suitcases up the three flights of steps to the apartment. Apparently, there were no elevators. When Mamá opened the door and flipped on the light, at least a dozen roaches scrambled for cover.

"Get them!" Babá called.

Nikita dropped Gertie's bag and rushed in behind her brother, stomping like winemakers in a vat of grapes. Phoebe joined them, enthusiastically, like it was a game.

"Good! Well done!" Babá said as they scooped up the dead bugs with their bare hands and threw them in the garbage can across the room.

Gertie was afraid to step inside.

"Come in! Come in!" Mamá said. "It's not much, but it's very comfortable. No? Let me take your coat. You won't need that here but maybe a few days out of the year."

Gertie kept her coat. "That's all right. Thank you."

The furniture was shabby, but tidy. The kitchen across the room was neat but very outdated. The lighting was poor, which Gertie thought was probably good.

"I'll show you where to put your things," Nikita said. "Let's go."

"And then come back here for my baklava, so Gertoula has a proper welcome," Mamá said.

As they turned down a narrow hall, Nikita said, "That's my brother's room, and my parents have a room down the hall. There's the bathroom, and here is my room, where you'll be staying."

Gertie's face paled. A family of five shared a three-bedroom apartment? The living area and kitchen were tiny, so Gertie had hoped there were bedrooms to escape to. How did everyone fit?

"You can have Phoebe's bed. She'll sleep on a cot with Mamá and Babá while you're here."

"I don't want to be any trouble," Gertie managed to say.

"You must be joking!" Nikita said. "We're all so happy to have you. It's all Mamá and Babá have been talking about. It's been the American girl this and the American girl that for two weeks!"

"I don't understand why they are so happy to have me," Gertie said.

Nikita shrugged. "They are very proud of our country and relish the opportunity to show it off to a young, impressionable American. In other words, they have plans for you every day between now and the start of school. Tomorrow, we go to Crete, Babá's favorite island."

Gertie took in a deep breath. A tiny apartment filled with people and daily activities galore. She wondered when and how she would have time to be alone to read and relax.

She wanted to call her parents and tell them she was sick.

"I'm not feeling well," she said to Nikita. "Can I go straight to bed?"

Nikita's eyes widened. "Oh, no. You just arrived! Mamá and Babá and Klaus and Phoebe—they will all be so disappointed. They've been anxious. I'm sure Mamá has some medicine to make you feel better. Come with me."

Gertie hesitated, so Nikita waited for her in the doorway as Gertie looked around the small bedroom, with its plain white walls and short metal beds. Two scratched-up wooden chests of drawers took up all the wall space between the beds, and there was no on-suite bath—just a small closet without a door, stuffed to the gills with clothes and books.

Gertie stepped closer to the books. "You like to read?"

"Oh, yes. Klaus and I both read voraciously. This is only a small part of our collection. We have many more books downstairs in the basement."

"There's a basement?" Gertie wondered if that might be her getaway.

"It's not very pleasant, but yes. I'll show you tomorrow. Right now, Mamá wants us to eat her dessert."

CHAPTER THREE

The Basement

Gertie had hoped to sleep in, but the walls were thin and the rooms too close to keep the apartment quiet much later than nine o'clock, so she crawled out of bed and asked to use the shower. Because the shower in the main bathroom didn't work, Gertie was forced to use the one in Mamá and Babá's room. Nikita warned her, however, that the toilet in that bathroom was broken, so she should use the one in the hall. So between the two bathrooms there was only one working shower and one working toilet, but plenty of roaches.

"When do we leave for Crete?" Gertie asked Nikita once she had finished dressing and had put on her shoes.

"Not until tonight." Nikita plopped on the rickety bed across from Gertie's. "Want some breakfast?"

"No, thank you. Why tonight?"

"Well, mainly because Babá works all day, but also because it's better to take the ferry while you're sleeping, so you don't waste time."

Great, Gertie thought. Another long ferry ride. She wondered how many people would be sharing her cabin.

"Babá wants us to lunch at his café," Nikita said.

"He owns a café?"

"No, no. He's the cook. He wants to show off his culinary skills. So what do you want to do until then? Hector offered to drive us wherever we want to go. Maybe you want to see the Parthenon?"

"Maybe." She wouldn't mind seeing more of Hector. "But what I'd really like to see is the basement. Before we go sightseeing, will you show me the rest of your books?"

Nikita frowned. "I don't know."

"Please? You were okay with it last night."

Nikita stood up and crossed to the door. "Okay, but don't touch anything."

Gertie followed her out.

When Klaus heard where they were going, he wanted to come too. Mamá begged Gertie to eat something, but Gertie said her stomach was upset.

"Don't touch anything that doesn't belong to you down there," Mamá said to her children as the three teens waved goodbye.

The stairs to the basement were not well-lit, so Gertie held tightly to the railing as her eyes adjusted to the darkness. Once they had made it all the way down, Klaus pulled a chain above his head, and a single bulb illuminated the cavernous room. It was a fairly massive basement, with the dimensions of the building broken up into many nooks and crannies, and entire rooms closed off with heavy wooden doors.

"Our books are over here," Nikita said.

Gertie followed Nikita through a maze of boxes and crates toward a wooden bookshelf against the back wall. Along the way, Gertie noticed two chests in the middle of the room resembling antique coffins. One was as large as a man, and the other half its size.

"Are those what I think they are?" Gertie asked. Heavy chains and padlocks wrapped around the middle of both coffins.

"Of course," Nikita said. "But they don't have dead bodies in them." She laughed—nervously, it seemed to Gertie. "Just a bunch of old stuff."

"How old are these?" Gertie touched the top of the one nearest her.

"No!" Klaus grabbed her hand. "Don't touch that."

Gertie lifted her brows with surprise. "Why not?"

Klaus was still holding Gertie's hand. He dropped it, blushed, and averted his eyes.

"There really are bodies in them, aren't there?" Gertie said without inflection.

"Yes," Klaus said. "So, leave them alone."

Nikita narrowed her eyes at her brother. "He's joking."

"Why are they kept down here?" Gertie asked. "Instead of a cemetery?"

Klaus turned to Nikita. "We should tell her."

"Shut *up*, Klaus!" Nikita gave him a threatening glare.

"Tell me what?"

"She's going to find out sooner or later," Klaus insisted.

"We are *not* having this conversation. It will gross her out." Nikita turned to Gertie. "Just ignore him. He wants to frighten you with old stories about the dead, but they are *just* ghost stories."

"I love ghost stories," Gertie said, brightening. "I'm especially fond of vampires."

Nikita clapped a hand to her forehead and closed her eyes. "Can we just look at the books and leave?"

Gertie moved closer to the bookshelf and read the titles along the spines. Many of the books were in Greek, but at least a third of them were in English. Of the English books, most were children's classics, such as *The Secret Garden, Charlotte's Web, Huckleberry Finn, Little Women, Island of the Blue Dolphins,* and *Treasure Island*—all of which Gertie had already read. They also had the Harry Potter books, all Rick Riordan books, most of Tolkien's works, and—of all things—all ten books of Anne Rice's *The Vampire Chronicles.*

"Have you read these?" Gertie asked.

"We've read everything down here," Klaus replied.

"I'm on the first one." Gertie plucked the dusty paperback from its place on the shelf and cracked it open. "I have it on my e-reader."

"You're welcome to borrow anything you see," Klaus said.

"Any *book* you see," Nikita qualified. "Most of this stuff down here doesn't belong to us."

"So which one of you is the vampire lover?" Gertie asked, as she returned the book to its shelf.

Before the siblings could answer, a loud noise, like the sound of a thud, startled all three of them.

And it came from the smaller of the two coffins.

All three looked first at the coffin, and then at each other with shocked and terrified eyes. No one breathed for a full five seconds.

Then Klaus said, "Let's get out of here."

The teens scrambled up the basement stairs.

In the doorway, Gertie said, "The light."

"Leave it," Klaus said. "Let's go."

EVA POHLER

Eva Pohler is a *USA Today* bestselling author of over thirty novels in multiple genres, including mysteries, thrillers, and young adult paranormal romance based on Greek mythology. Her books have been described as "addictive" and "sure to thrill"—*Kirkus Reviews*.

To learn more about Eva and her books, and to sign up to hear about new releases, and sales, please visit her website at www.evapohler.com.